Corruption

Corruption

Alexander Verbeek-van den Toren

Space Wizard Science Fantasy
Raleigh, NC
www.spacewizardsciencefantasy.com

Publisher's Note: This is a work of fiction. Names, characters, places, and incidents are a product of the author's imagination. Locales and public names are sometimes used for atmospheric purposes. Any resemblance to actual people, living or dead, or to businesses, companies, events, institutions, or locales is completely coincidental.

Cover art by Moorbooks
Editing by Heather Tracy
Book Layout © 2015 BookDesignTemplates.com

Corruption/ Alexander Verbeek-van den Toren.— 1st ed.
ISBN 978-1-960247-51-3

For Derk Anne, my husband, who has helped in the
creation of this book in more ways than either of us will
ever be aware.

CONTENTS

Chapter One — 7
Chapter Two — 15
Chapter Three — 25
Chapter Four — 37
Chapter Five — 48
Chapter Six — 53
Chapter Seven — 57
Chapter Eight — 65
Chapter Nine — 71
Chapter Ten — 82
Chapter Eleven — 88
Chapter Twelve — 93
Chapter Thirteen — 103
Chapter Fourteen — 112
Chapter Fifteen — 117
Chapter Sixteen — 123
Chapter Seventeen — 131
Chapter Eighteen — 137
Chapter Nineteen — 150
Chapter Twenty — 157
Chapter Twenty-One — 166
Chapter Twenty-Two — 172
Chapter Twenty-Three — 178
Chapter Twenty-Four — 188
Chapter Twenty-Five — 198
Chapter Twenty-Six — 206

Chapter One

Revan could no longer form a gate with his magic. In his mind he once again visualized his destination and made the accompanying gesture with his hand, but nothing happened. It didn't work when he closed his eyes either. He swallowed, his mind racing towards hundreds of explanations for why he couldn't do something he'd done so many times before, but none of them made sense. He had been working on his gates ever since coming to Samillan College, so Revan started sweating when he tried and *again* failed.

"Revan?" Mr. Havelna asked.

Revan looked over his shoulder to the other students in the line who were waiting for him, only making him more nervous. Mr. Havelna, the teacher, looked at him, eyebrows raised. "It doesn't work, sir," Revan stuttered. He tried again, made the same gesture with his hand, but once again there was no gate, as if he couldn't access the magic anymore. "I can't do it..." Revan said, baffled, and he hated how close to tears he sounded.

"Hmm," Mr. Havelna responded. He frowned at Revan, disappointed. Revan was eighteen, but that look made him feel five years old. "We'll talk about this later, Revan. Gaveh, it's your turn."

Revan sighed and went to the back of the line. One after another all the other students had to make a gate—it was obligatory after every magic class, practice made perfect. Magic was simply the ability to make a gate, but it was also the only way to cross great distances. A gate meant you were able to see and hear everything on the other side. Students at Samillan College had a normal education, like everyone else, but with extra classes to become full-fledged magicians. With the extra training, they could make gates. That was the only way people could get from one island to another, and once they graduated from the college they would all serve the people travelling among the different islands. Once he was back in line, Revan looked at Gaveh, his Koden, who tried it a couple times, but without result. The slightly tanned boy cursed and looked at Mr. Havelna. "I can't do it either."

"That is strange," Mr. Havelna said. "Arana?"

Gaveh joined the back of the line, and it was Arana's turn, the other best pupil, apart from Revan. She made the gesture a couple times, then shook her head as well.

"Back of the line," Mr. Havelna said.

Revan allowed himself a quick glance at Arana while she was looking away, as he'd done more often than he'd ever admit last year, since she joined the college. He admired her beautiful long hair and brown eyes. Then Arana looked back at him, and he quickly turned away.

"I don't get what changed," Gaveh whispered, right behind Revan. "I did what I normally did. Where was the gate?"

"I don't know," Revan said. It gave him a weird feeling in his stomach. Wilan, the next student, also couldn't make a gate, which only made the feeling in Revan's stomach worse. Something bad was going on; if the four of them couldn't make a gate, it couldn't have been them. Something was wrong with magic—but that was impossible. Magic never stopped. The Flow controlled all magic and if the magic stopped, that meant the Flow had abandoned them—right? If Revan couldn't make a gate at all he wouldn't be able to go home, the only place he could be himself. The thought of not being able to visit home made him swallow hard. Revan hoped nobody heard.

Making gates was very complicated, which was why they had to practice a lot at the college, as it involved clearly imagining the destination and using the magic the right way—but his class was in the highest grade of the school, so four people in a row failing to do it was wrong in many ways.

The line moved as all students tried and failed to make a gate. Revan realized he was holding on to his skill crystal again—he felt the cool crystal's round shape through his shirt. Revan quickly put his hand behind his back, hoping nobody had seen the movement. He looked over his shoulder again, first to Gaveh, but he happened to look the other way.

His eyes went back to Arana. She was looking right at him, raising her eyebrows and nodding towards Mr. Havelna, as if asking, *Do you have any idea what's going on?* Revan shook his head, mesmerized.

Someone knocked on the door, all of a sudden, then Mrs. Garedna, the History teacher, entered. "Gather in the eating hall!" she said. "Principal's orders!"

Mr. Havelna immediately took charge. "Everyone line up to go to the eating hall!"

That meant they'd have to take the elevator. The eating hall was twenty floors down. On the way there, Revan saw that all rooms were being emptied. Absolutely *everyone* was summoned.

That feeling in Revan's stomach only got worse. Whatever was going on, this wasn't just anything, and he wouldn't be able to go home any time soon.

"Arana's right behind me, shall we switch places?" Gaveh whispered in Revan's ear.

"I'm not exactly thinking about her right now," Revan whispered back.

"Just a suggestion," Gaveh responded. He touched Revan's butt very lightly, in a way others might think happened by accident. But Revan knew better. Gaveh liked using sex as a distraction. Gaveh and Revan were each other's Koden—a kind of "pre-relationship"—someone to have sex with if you weren't in a relationship yet, provided you didn't have sex with anyone else. Kodens also always shared a bedroom. If Gaveh wanted that distraction he could go to Revan, if they were both in the mood. But Revan wasn't.

It was completely quiet when they were all in the elevator. The mood was grim, and nobody dared to say anything. Revan looked out the side of the glass elevator absent-mindedly, to the lava sea coming closer as the elevator descended. He tried to reassure himself by hoping it'd all go back to normal soon. There was probably a very rational explanation to all of this, and he was just panicking.

The elevator doors opened again. Revan left the elevator but stopped in surprise at the entrance to the eating hall—all places to sit were already taken by students from different classes, from the pupils who had just gotten to the college up to pupils from his year. The *entire* college had been summoned to the eating hall. They made the room a mixture of red and black: red for the color of the students' non-mandatory uniforms, and black for the color of the walls. A few students didn't wear their uniforms, and their clothing was informed by their lit-up crystal. Practical, simple clothing for the people with a lit-up skill crystal, and wealthy-looking clothing that was hard to miss for those students that had a lit-up central crystal. Up above were windows to let the light through, but they were up so high it was impossible to look through them. There wasn't much to see through them anyway except for lava. The hall was a mixture of students from all the different ages—from twelve, the earliest age admitted at the college, to Revan's peers at eighteen. A couple students were sitting on the tables, which was normally not allowed—but the room wasn't even close to large enough for everyone, so they had no choice. Usually, all the ages were in the hall at different times. Almost everyone was quiet, except for murmuring here and there. The mood was cold and unpleasant. The black walls of the eating hall made it even more grim. Revan's stomach turned and he started sweating. All of this was wrong.

Somebody took Revan's hand. Revan looked up, startled, and saw it was Gaveh. "What?" he asked.

Gaveh swallowed. He didn't look at Revan. "I'm scared," he said softly—nobody else could hear.

Revan sighed and squeezed Gaveh's hand. They almost looked like a couple to outsiders, Revan mused—but, as close as they were, Revan liked someone else. Gaveh was clearly as scared as he was, and the feeling lessened once he held Gaveh's hand. Mr. Havelna brought them to a small empty spot near a wall—there was no better option. Several elevators kept dropping off classes, and the eating hall kept getting fuller.

"Did the Flow abandon us?" Arana asked softly. Revan was standing close to her too, not entirely by accident, as he'd done quite a few times over the past year as well. He didn't say anything, and neither did the other pupils who had heard. What were they supposed to say to that? The Flow couldn't leave you; the Flow knew about everything and everyone—right?

It took about twenty minutes to gather the whole school. A couple people sat against the windows, and a couple late classes sat down on the floor. All teachers were at the big table. Mrs. Dahena, the principal, finally appeared and the murmuring died down as soon as she took her spot. She didn't have to raise her hand to get the room to quiet; the office of principal came with a certain amount of respect. If the principal spoke, you weren't expected to talk.

"All of you must have noticed," she began, "that it's impossible to make a gate right now." She was silent for a moment. "I'll be honest with you all. I can't make it work either. Magic seems to suddenly have stopped, and I don't know why."

The room was still very quiet. Revan swallowed. The principal was one of the best magicians and if *she* couldn't use her magic anymore, who could?

"I asked around, as fast as I could, to see who could still access the magic, and the answers worried me. Nobody, not in this college nor on this island, can. This doesn't make sense. Magic always works, and I don't understand what happened—but we're going to investigate how this is possible."

Interestingly enough, Mrs. Dahena avoided the word *Flow*, very clearly sidestepping any religious connotations or fears that the Flow had abandoned everyone. "I don't know if it's only on our island. As the only way to travel between islands is through gates, I don't know how the other islands are doing. And I understand this is a horrible thing that startles all of you, and you're all so scared you can't go home anymore. But you don't have to be scared you are going to starve; we have enough food supplies to last a while, and the farmers we have here are going to try their hardest to make it work. We don't know how long this problem will last, but you can stay here if it continues during the weekend. You don't have to panic. Things will indubitably work out, and I'll let you know as soon as I know more. In the meantime, all classes that require magic are temporarily cancelled. If you want to talk about this, you can talk to the assigned teachers. If this problem persists tomorrow morning, I'll have more information at breakfast. For those whose parents live on this island, I assure you I'll be here on the weekend, if they have questions. And if any of you have any questions about the religious ramifications, you know where to find our Religion teachers."

Mrs. Dahena nodded, her speech was over. The hall filled with an explosion of students speaking, and Revan listened half-heartedly. At least the speech was clear. Mrs. Dahena had no idea why this happened and if she didn't know, who did?

Revan touched his skill crystal again and then, almost involuntarily, he touched his calm crystal as well. Once he realized he'd done that, he quickly went through his remaining three crystals so it wouldn't stand out.

Everyone was born with five crystals. One at the center of their chest, one between their chest and right shoulder, one on the bottom right of the stomach, one between the chest and the left shoulder and one at the bottom left of the stomach.

One of those crystals would always light up. With Revan it was the crystal close to his right shoulder, the skill crystal. At least, the rest of the world thought so, and Revan did his very best to maintain that illusion. Strictly speaking it wasn't untrue—but it didn't tell the whole truth.

Everyone with a lit-up skill crystal—the crystal between the right shoulder and chest—went to Samillan College, or a similar college, to learn magic. Everyone with a lit-up skill crystal dressed in practical clothing. Revan wore his uniform as much as possible so that he would stand out even less, but when he didn't wear it, he still made very sure his clothing style fit perfectly with all the other people with a lit-up skill crystal. Gaveh also usually wore his uniform, though he didn't wear it as much as Revan and would sometimes come to classes in his own clothes.

Everyone with a lit-up crystal had their own role and dressed accordingly—like how people with a lit-up central crystal were considered the leaders and could usually do what they wanted. Most teachers had a lit-up central crystal. If you had a lit-up central crystal you had the honor of adding "-na" to your name, and you had to dress in clothes that were usually gold- or silver-colored to reflect how wealthy you were. If you didn't follow the role your crystal assigned to you—like, for example, going to art school when your skill crystal had been lit up—you got some raised eyebrows, some conservative people didn't like you, but in general you were fine. The rules were clear on all of the crystals—not just skill and central, but also the art, calm and force crystals.

Most people had one lit-up crystal. *Most* people, but Revan wasn't among them. Revan's calm crystal was also lit up, and nobody in the whole college knew. Not even Gaveh— Revan wore his shirt when they were having sex. Revan was Othercrystalled, and while Othercrystalled weren't killed upon discovery like during the first days of Samillan College, they were still hated and loathed. Where not following the role of your crystal would get you some raised eyebrows in some circles, pretty much everyone agreed that Othercrystalled were lazy, as it supposedly took them so much energy to keep multiple crystals lit that they couldn't do anything else. The world was a dangerous place if you didn't play by the rules, and Revan's existence did just that. Thankfully the uniform had a shirt that was bound at the hem, which was how Revan had been managing to keep it a secret so far—and he was very careful to avoid the calm hues people with a lit-up calm crystal wore when he was out of uniform.

The only people who knew were Revan's parents and his little sister Fenna, and being allowed to visit them on the weekends made keeping such a big secret possible for Revan. Going home had always felt like a breath of fresh air, and the safety of his home made keeping his secret here possible.

Now he lost that safety, and Revan didn't know how sane he would be without it.

Chapter Two

Revan slumped into his bedroom, feeling more exhausted than ever. The moment he closed the door behind him, he crashed down on the bed, moaning softly. The rest of the school day had been very difficult. Normally the idea of not having to learn anything would've been great news, but with all that talk about magic disappearing, and nobody able to make any gates, most of the lessons were spent talking about the event. Most of Revan's classmates were spiraling, and the teachers were trying their best to avoid them sinking into despair, saying that whatever was happening, it would surely be fixed soon.

Wilan, a friend of Revan's, had asked multiple teachers whether the Flow had abandoned them. Pretty much all of them had the same answer; the Flow was not only magic, the Flow was everything and everyone. If the Flow had abandoned them, life all around them would disappear. But all teachers sounded unsure. This was uncharted territory; nobody knew what was happening exactly. Magic wasn't supposed to go away on a whim. And all students, Revan included, were worried that they wouldn't be able to make it home for the weekend.

Well, *almost* all students. Gaveh entered the room behind Revan, looking chipper despite the circumstances. Revan saw how he was smiling, even if he tried to suppress it for Revan's sake. "I'm glad someone's happy, at least," Revan said to him.

"Sorry," Gaveh replied, allowing his smile to be visible. "I'm genuinely sorry for you, you know. I know you were looking forward to the weekend." He sat down on the bed, next to Revan, leaving the bedroom door open as they usually did when they didn't mind being interrupted.

Revan shrugged. "You could always have chosen to come with me instead."

"Yes, my parents would've loved hearing that," Gaveh said, rolling his eyes. "'My ungrateful son,'" Gaveh began, stretching out his o's and a's in an exaggerated Maran accent, "'for whom I do so much just leaves me behind because his parents aren't fun enough!'" He sighed. "I hadn't been looking forward to that conversation. Now at least I can say, 'I'm sorry, but I literally couldn't come to you.'"

"At least you can see a silver lining," Revan sighed.

"I'm mostly relieved that I can skip the standard questions this weekend. I don't want to hear my mom asking me again, 'Gaveh, when are you going to propose to Revan?'"

From thirteen to sixteen, students were given extensive sex education on how to have sex safely and with consent, and once you turned sixteen, you were expected to pick a Koden—if the other person agreed—together you slept in one room, in one bed. You were expected to have sex with that person, and nobody else, under certain conditions; you were only allowed to have sex in your bedroom, you were expected to stay at least relatively quiet during it, and if there was a risk of pregnancy you were expected to wear protection. Every year a couple students got caught having sex at different places, or having sex very loudly, and they were always handed an appropriate punishment, like temporarily breaking up the Kodenship. Some people were good friends with their Kodens, as Revan and Gaveh were, and sometimes it even blossomed into a full-blown relationship. However, this wasn't obligatory—it was fine to just have sex with your Koden and prefer other people's company. You could always decide to break your Kodenship, but then you were expected to get another Koden after a medical inspection; the only circumstance where you weren't expected to have a Koden, at Revan's age, was when you were already in a relationship. At that point you were expected to break your ongoing Kodenship and sleep with the person you had decided to partner with; at no point was it allowed to have sex with multiple people. Which meant that, should Revan ever get the guts to ask Arana to be in a relationship with him, he'd have to break his Kodenhood with Gaveh. Not something he was looking forward to, but it'd be okay with both Revan and Gaveh in the end.

Everything about Kodenhood was very weird to the Maran culture, which Revan didn't quite understand. It boiled down to, if you were fifteen you were expected to propose to someone—but it was never expected of you that you actually married. Revan thought it was confusing, and Gaveh wasn't able to explain it very well. It came down to, if you had sex with someone you at least made an attempt to marry that person.

"Anyway," Revan sighed. "We have some time off. What do you want to do?" Revan didn't need to say sex was out of the question. Gaveh could already see on his face how tired he was.

"I don't know. Do you need me to be here?"

"Not necessarily," Revan replied.

"Then I might go to the library to do some..."

"Oh hey, guys," a third voice said, and Wilan appeared in the doorway. "Mind joining us for a game of Island Hopping? We've got two people, and we're looking for two more."

Revan looked at Gaveh, who shrugged, saying with his eyes, *It's up to you and I understand if you want to be alone.*

Revan decided he didn't want to sit with his sadness and anger. "Yeah sure," he responded.

* * *

Island Hopping was a card game that students were encouraged to play in their downtime, as the game involved magicians trying to hop from island to island in as few jumps as possible—according to teachers, it helped with strategic thinking, a skill every magician was supposed to have if they were to accurately transport other people. Right now, though, it just served to remind Revan what he was no longer able to do.

Back when they'd just joined the college, Revan, Gaveh, Wilan and Javik played the game regularly, and they hung out frequently together. They grew apart as they got older and had to pick Kodens, and so they hadn't played together a lot lately, but now was the best time to pick it back up.

All four of them sat on Wilan and Javik's bed. Wilan put down his final two cards and smiled. "Back home," he said. "In only five jumps. Anyone who can best that?" The question sounded rhetorical, and Wilan was proven right when Revan, Gaveh and Javik all shook their heads. Wilan usually won this game.

Normally he wouldn't shut up about it, but today he just sighed as he took the cards back from the others.

"Won't be making it home in any kind of jump," Javik said what Revan was thinking. He put his hand on Wilan's arm. Wilan wrapped his arm around Javik and pulled him in closer; he didn't say anything, he just kissed Javik's brow. Stuff like, "I'm sure everything will work out in time," had been said all day long, and they were all tired of hearing platitudes—particularly since those didn't take away any of their worries.

Wilan and Javik started two years ago as Kodens but were now boyfriends as they realized there were more feelings at play. A relationship upgrade like that happened frequently enough that it wasn't seen as weird, but most Kodenships remained just that, and people moved on to form a stable marriage with a long-term partner once they'd turned old enough. It was evident in the way Wilan kept his arm around Javik, and Javik put his head on Wilan's shoulder; Revan and Gaveh would never sit that way.

Javik broke the embrace by reaching for the cards and dealing them out. He asked, "Do you guys think Samillan came back?"

Hearing that name made Revan's insides twist. He swallowed, suppressing the feeling. "I don't think he can."

"I'm just saying," Javik said, "Samillan was just an embodiment of the Flow, that's what made him such a heroic figure. And able to manipulate it. If the Flow has changed, then that means Samillan has come back, right?"

"Maybe someone else manipulated it," Revan said, which earned him a funny look from both Wilan and Javik.

"The Flow, that's part of everything?" Wilan said. "Pretty much everyone agrees you evaporate the moment you come in contact with it. Only the Flow can change itself."

"Not everyone thinks Samillan was a part of it," Gaveh said softly. "Some people say he was just a very powerful man."

"Then how do you explain..." Wilan said, gesturing around himself, "*everything*?" It sounded like a retort. Gaveh opened his mouth and closed it again. Revan decided not to say anything. "Samillan was a hero, and part of the Flow. Even a very powerful man wouldn't be able to do what he did."

"Who's starting?" Revan asked when Wilan was done talking. "I'll start." He immediately put down a card, shutting down any further conversation.

Samillan was the man responsible for the last time the Flow was manipulated. Before Samillan manipulated the Flow, the world had apparently been filled with grass and water, stories told of "animals" populating the world, and magic could be used for multiple things and not just making gates, like nowadays. But Samillan changed all that. It was his final act; stories told of eleven works he'd undergone, travelling the world, trying to find justice and peace. Some of those works were breaking up fights, killing monsters, and saving a heathen people from disaster. Everyone universally agreed that Samillan was a hero, including Revan.

His second-to-last act was writing a couple books dictating how people should live. They were the only books that survived his manipulation of the Flow. One of those books dictated how the world should treat Othercrystalled people; with death, because they weren't useful for anything else. After all, it took them a lot of energy to keep more than one crystal alit, and all that spent energy made them lazy and made it impossible for them to get anything useful done.

Samillan's teachings were still followed, though they had become a lot milder. At first people were forced to walk around topless all the time, and they would be executed if their crystals changed. Nowadays that was no longer the case. Back then, seeing someone's genitals or breasts was absolute taboo unless you were in a close relationship with them, but showing your crystals was fine with everyone. Now genitals or breasts weren't even nearly as important as crystals, though you were still expected to keep both hidden. And Othercrystalled people were just kicked out of school and left to fend for themselves instead of being brutally murdered, if they were discovered. Or Othercrystalled people were told to hide themselves at all costs—to the point where Revan wasn't even able to muster up the courage to tell his Koden and best friend.

"There must be some rational explanation for all of this," Wilan said as he played his first card. "Magic doesn't just stop. Nobody could manipulate the Flow. Maybe it needs to cleanse some corruption for some reason." He shrugged. "But I'm still worried."

"Yeah, I'm worried too," Gaveh said. Javik and Revan nodded in affirmation.

"Well, then," Wilan said with a smile, "at least we're with friends. We're all in this together."

Just when Wilan had finished his sentence, someone knocked at the door. "Hello?"

"Yes?" Javik asked. "Come in?"

The door opened and Mr. Khandar appeared. "Everything all right here?" He smiled. Mr. Khandar was a religion teacher, and therefore also a priest; he wore the typical robes that were expected for priests to wear.

"Yes, we're all right," Wilan said.

"Great," Mr. Khandar said. "I've been doing the rounds, seeing if anyone needed any help or had any questions. About the Flow, or about magic." As the priest-teacher, Mr. Khandar was one of the few teachers without a lit-up central crystal, having a lit-up calm crystal instead. This meant that he was usually sent out for the odd jobs that none of the other teachers wanted. This was probably one of those. "So, any questions?"

"Actually, we've had a bit of an argument," Wilan said. "About Samillan. Whether he was just a human being who was powerful, or the embodiment of the Flow." Wilan shot Gaveh a look that made clear that he expected to be fully vindicated by Mr. Khandar.

Mr. Khandar furrowed his brow. "This seems like an...interesting time to discuss the role of the prime disciple of the Flow, but..."

"We were worried somebody else had manipulated the Flow," Gaveh said. It sounded like a confession. "And from there, we talked about Samillan. As he was the last person to have done it."

"Ah, and you're Maran." Mr. Khandar still smiled patiently, something he usually did when dealing with students. His confusion seemed resolved. "Over here, we believe that Samillan was part of the Flow all along, and him changing the Flow—for whatever reason, that we as mere mortals simply cannot comprehend—was the Flow taking back what belonged to it. Though there are islands whose beliefs are different"—Mr. Khandar nodded to Gaveh—"and we respect those beliefs deeply, this is the faith that Samillan College espouses."

"Thank you," Wilan said, shooting Gaveh another look that radiated "I told you so." Revan felt more and more uncomfortable every second the conversation lasted.

"Any other questions?"

Revan wanted to send Mr. Khandar away but Javik barged in with, "I hope the college will stay unified." It wasn't a question, but it was clear Javik was worried.

Mr. Khandar smiled. "Why would you worry otherwise?"

"Well," Javik said, "in times of crisis sometimes the teachers of the college go against one another."

"You're fairly knowledgeable on the history of our college, Javik."

Javik shrugged. "I'm just saying, I read about when principal Erchina was...let go of her position early. The college hasn't been very unified in the past. I'm just hoping that there won't be much conflict." Revan caught some hesitation in Javik's first sentence that he couldn't place. "I've always been interested in history and this kind of stuff."

"Well," Mr. Khandar said, "I can't see into the future, but I'm certain our teachers aren't planning on fighting any time soon. You shouldn't have to worry. Anything else?"

It remained quiet in the room as all four boys shook their heads.

"All right, then I will continue on my rounds. But if you have any questions or need someone to talk to, I'm free for confessions or emotional support. The Flow wouldn't want you to walk around with your thoughts all imprisoned in your mind, after all." Mr. Khandar smiled again. "Good luck with your game, children."

He disappeared again, closing the door, and before the discussion could carry on, Revan said, "Let's play another game, yeah?"

* * *

"That was fun," Gaveh said once they'd said goodbye to Wilan and Javik and were back in their room. Revan sat down on the bed; Gaveh stood, leaning against the door.

"Yeah," Revan replied without really feeling it. They'd played one more round of Island Hopping before Revan had said he wanted to spend some time in his room before dinner. Gaveh had decided to follow him. "Just like old times. We should've done this more often."

"Maybe," Gaveh said. "But we grew apart."

"Uh-huh," Revan said, and then fell quiet.

"You okay?"

"Yeah," Revan said, shrugging. "Just wasn't feeling it anymore with Javik and Wilan."

"Not up for socializing," Gaveh assumed.

"Uh-huh," Revan said, and wanted to leave it there. The whole discussion around Samillan had opened up more inside himself than he wanted to admit even to Gaveh. That discussion once again pointed out to Revan that he wasn't quite as safe here as he would be at home. Lots of people who didn't know who or what he was, and this time he had to walk around with his crystals carefully hidden all the time. "Hope we'll be able to get home soon."

"As does everyone," Gaveh said.

"Almost everyone," Revan said, winking at Gaveh.

Gaveh chuckled. "Yeah ok. I'm just hoping everything will get fixed soon enough."

"You and me both," Revan said.

"Until then, I'm here for you," Gaveh said, sitting down next to Revan and putting his hand on Revan's. "For sex, but also, you know, support."

"Thanks," Revan said, and he looked at Gaveh thinking, *I could tell Gaveh. I'd have one more ally in my corner.*

Revan could tell him that he was Othercrystalled, that this was the reason why he'd felt so uncomfortable earlier. Gaveh saying he thought Samillan was "just a heroic guy" felt like a defense of Othercrystalled, somehow, because it meant Gaveh wasn't taking Samillan's words as gospel. Revan could just take off his shirt—it was bound by a small rope at the hem so that nobody could look under, as was customary with all shirts—and take the tape off his crystal to see how Gaveh would respond. His very best friend wouldn't react like everyone else, would he?

But Revan also knew what would happen. Last week an Othercrystalled had been kicked out of college. Not because they'd misbehaved, although the school quickly made up an excuse about a fight having escalated. But that Othercrystalled—Gabon was their name—had three lit-up crystals and it had recently gone public, and the principal couldn't have that.

Revan valued the college and his friends too much. He didn't want to lose either. So, Revan sighed, standing up, taking his hand from Gaveh's as his courage evaporated.

Nobody will know, Revan told himself, *it's too dangerous. Nobody.* Revan hated coming to that conclusion, it forced him to realize that he would be alone.

It made him want to be alone for a bit, away from Gaveh. So he said, "I think I'm heading to the eating hall early. See you there?"

Gaveh looked at him quizzically. "Yeah, ok," he said. "See you there."

Chapter Three

Revan got to the eating hall early to be alone, knowing few people would be downstairs. It wasn't dinner time yet, so there would be one or two pupils, but he would be able to sit with his thoughts. However, once there, he saw Arana sitting at her usual spot.

He looked at her, she looked back at him, and Revan had to suppress the urge to look away. He raised his hand, suddenly feeling very clumsy. "Hey."

Arana waved back, smiling at him. "Hey."

Revan walked up to her, deciding he should have no reason to feel nervous, this was just his usual seat, and they'd been in this configuration many times over the last year—but that was always with other people, and now they were basically alone. "Hoping for an early dinner?"

"No, you?"

"No," Revan said, and he laughed without joy. He sat down across from Arana. The food wouldn't be served for an hour, so all they could do was wait. "I guess I was just tired of being stuck in my room. You?"

"Something like that," Arana said, sighing. "I'm tired of the forlorn mood everywhere. At the same time, I get it. But at least I can still get home. I live on the same island. I couldn't even use magic to get home if magic had still been here." Magic was easier to use between islands than across them. To perform magic to cross a very great distance was hard—just as much as crossing too small a distance. Only the best magicians could do it at a non-standard distance. "But you live on another island."

"True," Revan said, and then asked, "How do you know?"

"You told me," Arana said and smiled. "I remember a lot."

"Oh," Revan said. "So do I," he added, making what he was about to say a little less creepy. "Was your sister home when it happened?"

"Unfortunately not," Arana said. "My dad came here to check on me yesterday evening. He told me everything."

"I'm sorry to hear that," Revan said. "Hope this'll all work out soon."

"Yeah, that'd be great," Arana said.

Revan did remember a lot about Arana—it was how he dealt with his crush. Everything Arana told him about her, Revan made sure to remember. He'd been attracted to her from day one of them meeting, and that attraction didn't lessen as he got to know her better. At the same time, thanks to his feelings, he'd always been a little scared, opting instead to keep her at a distance and just talk about school stuff.

Arana had joined Samillan College a year ago, having moved to this island from Imbido Island, a couple jumps away. Her old college had been too far away, so she'd moved here. She'd been the smartest person in her class; she'd been so smart she'd skipped a grade and so she was one year younger than Revan. Revan, meanwhile, had gotten the highest grades in his own class before she'd joined. Two very smart teenagers in the same class could've meant they'd become bitter rivals—but Revan fell head-over-heels for her, and made sure to make her feel as comfortable as possible. He'd wanted her to stay; not only because he liked her, but also because he was happy someone else was getting the best grades. He'd stand out less. During their conversations, Revan found out Arana's older sister was still working on Imbido Island as a construction worker, and would commute up and down every day. She was probably still stuck there now that the magic wasn't working.

"Actually," Arana said, jolting Revan out of his thoughts, "can I be honest with you?"

Revan licked his lips and swallowed away a lump in his throat. "Yeah?"

She looked around to see if there were any listeners, and then leant forward conspiratorially and whispered, "Don't tell the others, okay?" It was just loud enough that Revan could hear. He also leant forward. "My Koden is kind of down as he can't go home." Revan knew Arana's Koden, Havelt, vaguely. He seemed like a nice guy, but Revan hadn't talked to him too much.

"Makes sense," Revan said.

"Yeah, well," Arana said. "Havelt's been muttering for days that he's had enough of school, that he can't wait to be done, et cetera, et cetera." Arana shrugged. "And he just keeps talking, but instead, er…" She sighed. "I had kind of hoped to fulfill my…desire tonight, but then the magic stopped, and now he's no longer in the mood." She laughed awkwardly. "I completely get that this is not a very good reason to be bummed about the magic stopping, but, you know. The desire stays, so I guess I have to take matters into my own hands."

"Ah," Revan said. "Havelt sounds a little tiring, honestly. I don't know him that well."

"Yeah, he's not necessarily a nice guy," Arana said.

"Really?" Revan frowned. "You can always switch Kodens, you know." Switching Kodens was allowed, if there was no match, but it didn't happen too often. Both parties were then tested to make sure there were no diseases. If they both came out clean, the switch was approved and not a problem. The same process happened if one of the parties wanted to become a couple with somebody else. Gaveh knew Revan was interested in Arana and was very supportive; if Revan and Arana were to hook up, Gaveh and Havelt would both have to end their Kodenships.

Briefly, Revan allowed his mind to go over the idea of him and Arana becoming Kodens, but he very quickly discarded that idea. With all the feelings at play, that would result in either a relationship or a heartbreak, and either way, the Kodenship wouldn't last very long.

"Nah, too much hassle, and he's got his moments." Arana smiled. Once again, she looked around to make sure nobody was looking at her, then pointed at her crotch and kept her hands a fair amount away from each other.

It took a couple seconds before Revan realized what she meant. It made him blush. "Ah," he said.

"So, that's really why," Arana said. "I couldn't stand to be around my moping Koden for a bit. Hi."

"Hi," Revan chuckled. "Hope I'm better company."

Arana nodded. "Hey, come to think of it, you got any plans this weekend, now that you're not going home?"

"...No?" Revan asked, hesitating.

Arana shrugged. "If you're looking to get out of the college for a bit, my house has a spare bed that's big enough for two. If you want to, you can stay at my house. You'll at least be away from the college. Bring Gaveh, I'm sure that'll be fun."

Revan needed to take a couple seconds to process those words. *Arana* invited *him* to *her* place? Revan realized his jaw had dropped, so he forced himself to shut it. Just before things got awkward, he managed to say, "Sounds like a plan. I've got to run that by Gaveh, of course." Thankfully it sounded quite normal. He was going to Arana's home. Arana *had invited him.* Maybe Arana could visit his home as well some day...Revan sighed. The thought of his home brought him back to hard reality. "Maybe tomorrow I can join you, after I've talked to Gaveh?" Today after dinner would probably also have been fine with Gaveh, but Revan decided it was too late to change skyscrapers.

"Sounds great," Arana said, then Gaveh came in. Revan waved at him, and Gaveh waved back, his eyes briefly darting between Arana and him. Revan could see what he was thinking. "Fancy coming to my place for the weekend, Gaveh? Revan can come too." She smiled at Revan. "Now you don't have to discuss it with him anymore."

Gaveh hesitated briefly, so briefly that Arana probably didn't even notice. Then his expression changed into something that was best described as admiration. "Yeah, that sounds lovely," Gaveh said.

"Tomorrow," Revan quickly added. "I'm not eager to start packing today." He yawned a little. He really wasn't in the mood to stay in a strange place immediately.

Gaveh turned to Arana and said, "Yeah, sure, let's make it happen. What's your address?"

* * *

A little later dinner was served, and Revan and Gaveh ate and didn't talk much, but in between bites, Gaveh whispered to him, "I think you need a distraction."

Revan didn't need to ask what Gaveh meant. "Why?"

"Because Arana offered you to stay with her, and instead of jumping at the opportunity you're sticking around here for one more day. You're really not well."

"I'm not in the mood," Revan replied. "But thanks for the offer."

"Okay," Gaveh said. He smiled, leaving the next bite on his plate and said, still at low volume, "But tomorrow, we'll be going to Arana's. Isn't that exciting?"

Revan laughed despite himself. "Yeah," he admitted, feeling mildly embarrassed at the same time. Gaveh was playing wingman, and that was very kind of him—but it felt weird too, because he was advocating for his own Kodenship to end and that wasn't something Revan was ready for. Sure, once people were between twenty to twenty-five, they were expected to either break their Kodenships and settle down with someone else, or turn their Kodenships into full-blown relationships, but Revan was only eighteen. Part of Revan regretted telling Gaveh he had a crush on Arana. But not telling Gaveh had never been an option. After all, they were best friends and told each other everything.

Well, *almost* everything.

* * *

The uppermost floors of the skyscraper didn't belong to Samillan College. Only the students of the highest years were allowed to go there by day because they were older and considered more trustworthy, but nobody was allowed to leave the college at night. In the past Revan had gone to the highest floor with Mr. Havelna to look at the other islands. Revan had missed his home so much, and the highest floor had the clearest view of the other skyscrapers, one of which was Revan's own. Now Revan, just before going to sleep, took the elevator to the highest floor he was still allowed to go to.

He was able to find his way thanks to the lights on the walls, which were always lit up in the evening to prevent students from getting lost. He went to a window and found, in the distance, the skyscraper where his parents lived: Alstran Island. He managed to find the right skyscraper too; he recognized its shape, thanks to a couple lights that were on over there as well.

He didn't know which window was the right one. He just hoped Fenna, his sister, was at her window looking back at him and missing him. Revan was supposed to take her to Samillan College this weekend, as she would go there herself once she was old enough. And even though he was eighteen, he still yearned for his mother to ask him, "So what did you learn today, and how was your week?" Or the proud look his father got whenever Revan talked about school, as Revan's father had attended Samillan College himself. Revan could walk around without tape and without a shirt that was tied at the hem. Revan looked at the hallway and briefly wondered if he should go back to the elevator, disregard the rules, and just go to the highest possible floor so that he would be able to see everything, because then he'd feel better. But no. Revan stayed where he was.

The chance that there'd be a teacher on the highest floor catching him in the act was as good as zero. Revan could go up there if he wanted to. But disregarding the rules on your own was dangerous, it made you stick out like a sore thumb, it made people ask questions. It was better to not stand out and not draw attention, so people wouldn't ask any difficult questions about him and his crystals. It didn't matter how desperately he wanted to break the rules, being caught and possibly exposed wasn't worth it. Revan had become an expert at being a Goody Two-shoes, because those remained unseen, and Revan couldn't afford to be too visible. So, he suppressed all the desires he wasn't supposed to have, no matter how hard that was, as he'd been doing all his life.

Hopefully everything would work out quickly.

* * *

The next day at breakfast, Revan nursed a mild headache. He hadn't slept well. Just as he finished, Mrs. Dahena appeared again—she radiated so much authority that the room slowly fell quiet. Only the ones in a higher year were eating; the younger students had already eaten and had already heard the speech. The room was emptier than normal because it was the weekend and some of Revan's peers had gone home. Like Arana, who had dropped by just before breakfast and told him her address. Once the room was actually quiet, the principal began to speak. "Students! I'm here to bring the news about what happened last night. First of all, I want to emphasize that there's no need to panic—but so far, you've all kept your cool in these trying times, and for that I am grateful. I want to reaffirm, for the time being, we have enough food. Your meals might become less diverse, depending on how long it will take before the magic returns, so it might mean you'll all have bread three times a day. But we can keep that going for a while."

Revan looked at his oatmeal. *I'd better enjoy you as best I can, then. It might be the last time.*

"Unfortunately, it's still unclear why the magic stopped working," she added, "but I'm staying optimistic. The magic disappeared all of a sudden, and it could reappear just as quickly. It's important we stick together and keep supporting one another. We don't know what's going on, but we'll get out of it together." The principal looked over the crowd before carrying on. "I have scientists and theologists who are studying the magic disappearing. I have people going through the library, looking for possible solutions. I have the best means at my disposal, and I guarantee all of you, we will find a solution together. After the weekend, normal classes will continue, except for the ones requiring magic. For those lessons, we'll consider an alternative, and you'll hear more about that after the weekend. Thank you all for your attention."

After the speech was over, the silence was deafening. Revan focused on his oatmeal, but after a few bites he was no longer hungry. The worried feeling wouldn't go away—he wasn't going to be home any time soon, he feared, and Mrs. Dahena hadn't given any new information either. From the corner of his eye, he looked at Gaveh and considered his decision. He decided to go for it. "I want a distraction."

Gaveh had just taken a bite of his oatmeal, but he quickly swallowed and grinned. "No problem."

"See you in the bedroom?"

Gaveh shook his head. "I might know a better spot, if you're into that."

Revan was.

* * *

After breakfast Gaveh said, "Trust me," and guided them to the elevator. Revan's heart pounded like they were already doing it. It wasn't the first time Gaveh had a weird plan, and his plans never disappointed. They usually went against the rules. In the past Revan had protested, but Gaveh had always said, "If you're caught, you can blame me." Breaking the rules was terrifying all alone. But together, with Gaveh—whom he trusted implicitly—offering to take the full blame...well, it became a lot more tempting and valid. So, Revan had joined him on multiple occasions.

One possible option suddenly went through Revan's mind. "You don't want to go at Arana's place to..." he began.

Gaveh laughed. "No, of course not." And they got into the elevator with a couple other pupils. Everyone pressed the buttons for their floor, so nobody noticed what Gaveh pressed—the button to the highest floor. All Revan's blood seemed to flow to his head. "You want to..." he whispered, just loud enough for Gaveh to hear. His jaw dropped. "But..." he started softly.

Gaveh took his hand and squeezed it. "Trust me." And he raised one corner of his mouth in half a grin.

Oh Flow, he's so sexy when he does that. Gaveh knew that was Revan's weakness. Revan didn't say anything else. It felt like everyone in the elevator was looking at him and they all knew of their plan. But as the elevator went up it got increasingly empty. Nobody noticed Revan and Gaveh. A couple others joined them; a couple farmers from the vegetational floors of the skyscraper entered the elevator and left a couple floors later. But none of them were looking at Revan or his best friend. Of course not, they were allowed to go to the highest floor, it was daytime.

Ten floors away from the highest floor they were finally alone, and Revan finally dared to open his mouth. "Gaveh, we *can't*."

"Of course we can," Gaveh said, still grinning.

"But we'll get caught, we'll have to talk to the principal, and..."

Gaveh teetered his head a little. "What's on the highest floor?"

"A couple wealthy people's apartments."

Gaveh nodded. "Exactly. They got the highest floor because they wanted the best views. Now, I happen to know there's a sort of alleyway between two apartments. It has a very good view, and nobody comes there. Normally there's security wandering around, but I *also* happen to know that the guards have a leave of absence to be with their families. After all, this is a time of crisis." Gaveh grinned.

"But..." Revan protested, "*everyone* can go to the highest floor." Including students when it was daytime, which it was.

"And who's going to go there right now? Everyone's worried, is in their bedrooms, or with their parents, or talking to teachers."

"Or they're homesick and going to the highest floor to see their homes." They had arrived; the elevator doors opened.

Gaveh got out first and made a wide gesture with his arms. "Indeed, and as you can see it's super crowded right now." The hallway where they arrived was entirely empty—the walls were the typical black of the skyscrapers, and their footsteps echoed in the silence.

Revan swallowed. "But..."

"We'll be absolutely safe," Gaveh said soothingly. "Everyone's home, being worried. Trust me."

Revan swallowed. "Okay."

Gaveh smiled and took Revan's hand. "Follow me." Gaveh led him through a couple hallways, looking around as he did. Revan followed him, still very tense, but he admitted to himself he was also aroused, and that arousal got worse with every step. Finally, they entered a sort of room with a big window looking over a lava sea with barely any islands. The only island Revan saw was one in the distance that appeared to have no skyscrapers; it seemed to be completely empty. Briefly, Revan's mind wandered—why was there an island basically empty? All islands were filled with skyscrapers; space was a scarce resource if everyone lived on an island.

"Trust me," Gaveh said. "It's safe here." It snapped Revan's attention back to his Koden. Nothing else was in the room, just them and the two hallways leading to it. There was no door. Gaveh squeezed Revan's hand. He turned around and his lips floated over Revan's. "Or have you lost your appetite?" It was as if he'd guessed how turned on Revan was.

Samillan be cursed, Revan thought, *Gaveh knows me too well*. Revan pressed his lips to Gaveh's. Gaveh moaned softly in the kiss and started to undress him.

* * *

Afterwards, both of them panted. Revan was leaning against the wall, his heart still feeling like he'd run a very long distance. "Yes..." he sighed, only wearing his shirt. "That was an okay distraction." They had done it against the window. The cold glass had been a nice contrast to the warmth Gaveh gave him. Gaveh was lying on the floor, also tired, and beautifully naked. Revan saw the skill crystal glow, between Gaveh's stomach and right shoulder.

Gaveh grinned ear to ear. "Happy to hear." Their clothes were spread across the room. "If you want, I'm up for round two."

Revan laughed. "No need, but thanks." He rubbed his temples. Yes, now he was able to put what had happened that day behind him. He started gathering his clothes. Gaveh didn't get up, so Revan threw him his clothing.

Of course Revan had kept his shirt on the whole time, it was still bound at the hem. The first time they'd had sex Gaveh had asked why Revan did that and Revan had replied, "In my family you only show your crystals to someone if you're married to them." Gaveh had understood and left it there. There were cultures where this was really the case; Revan not being a part of them was something Gaveh didn't need to know. But the relaxed mood immediately disappeared once Revan heard something in the distance. He hoped he was wrong. He lifted a finger to warn Gaveh. But Gaveh heard it as well. Footsteps. Gaveh cursed. He had just put on his pants. "Can we leave safely?"

The footsteps seemed to come from the hallway on the right. Revan nodded.

Both boys gathered the rest of their clothes. "It doesn't make sense," Gaveh grumbled in the meanwhile. "*Nobody* comes here right now, why would they..." Gaveh sprinted away once they'd gathered everything and Revan followed him. But just before he left, he saw a bit of the cloak of the person interrupting them. Revan recognized it immediately and quietly gasped.

He snuck to the left hallway, as fast as he could. "It's the principal," he whispered.

Gaveh cursed. "We're caught."

The two boys snuck through the hallway, barely clothed, and Revan expected to hear his name at any time. But nobody said anything. Revan allowed himself one look over his shoulder, and there he saw the principal—but with her back to them, making Revan stand still in surprise. She hadn't come for them, thank the Flow. Gaveh didn't seem to catch on. But there was something in her posture that drew Revan's attention. She wasn't standing firmly, like with her speech—her shoulders were slumped, she looked tired, and she shook her head.

It was quiet for a couple seconds. Then something in the room glowed in a way Revan immediately recognized. The glow of a magic gate. The gate itself was probably just out of Revan's view. Revan's jaw dropped, but before he could say anything the principal walked towards the light, where a wall was supposed to be. The light of the gate disappeared. Revan could only draw one conclusion.

"Revan?" Gaveh said, suddenly standing next to him, pulling his sleeve. Apparently, he'd noticed Revan hadn't followed. This shook Revan out of his daze. Perhaps he could go home, perhaps the Flow had been restored and they got the magic back, so Revan visualized a random destination and tried to make a gate—but no, the magic still didn't work.

So, what had the principal just done?

Chapter Four

"Are you sure you saw it right?" Gaveh said. They were back in the room they had just snuck out of. Revan looked around, expecting the principal to show up from nowhere. They were still barely clothed; Gaveh hadn't put on his shirt yet and apart from his shirt Revan was only wearing underwear, but their earlier mood had completely disappeared.

"Absolutely," Revan insisted. "Every time you make a gate, the edges give off a little bit of light. That's the light I saw."

"But you didn't see the gate yourself," Gaveh said, eyebrows raised.

Revan gestured around him. "Then there was no gate. So where did our principal run off to? Did she just disappear into the Flow?"

Gaveh raised his hands soothingly. "I'm not saying I don't believe you, but she might have walked away."

"Did you hear footsteps then?"

Gaveh sighed. "No."

"She was right there," Revan continued, "the gate appeared, and she walked through. She summoned the gate, there's no doubt about it. She used magic and didn't tell anyone."

"Maybe someone else summoned that gate?" Gaveh asked. "Maybe on the other islands they still have the ability to summon gates, and she somehow managed to contact somebody else?"

"Then why wouldn't she tell the school about it?" Revan replied.

"Because she's still figuring it out, and wants to get out the right message first?"

"She can use magic, and we can't," Revan said. "That makes no sense, right? Maybe she has something to do with it."

Gaveh hesitated for a moment before replying, "It's possible. I'm just saying, don't draw conclusions too quickly."

"So, you do believe she used magic?"

Gaveh hesitated once again, licking his lips while pondering. Then he replied, "It looks like it. But there are a lot of explanations possible." He shrugged. "Anyway, let's go, before she returns and we'll have another problem. I think my distraction failed."

Revan shrugged. "Maybe, but I was having fun." He smiled despite himself. "Although it was way too dangerous."

"That's what made it fun," Gaveh replied and the sexy grin briefly returned, then quickly disappeared. "Are we going to Arana's soon?"

"Sounds like a plan," Revan said. "But first...is it okay if I do some things at the college? I'll join you this afternoon."

"Sure," Gaveh said, and they walked to the elevator, but Revan stayed tense. The distraction had indeed failed.

* * *

The "some things" Revan was supposed to do at the college meant telling someone else about what he had just seen, but Gaveh didn't need to know that. Revan felt others had to know, in case something bad happened, and he wanted to tell it to someone he trusted and who might be able to do more than he could himself. Gaveh and he had gone back to the college together, and Gaveh quickly packed his bag and went to Arana's. Revan had waited until Gaveh disappeared, then took the elevator to the teachers' floor. Once he'd gotten there, he found the right room and knocked on the door, hoping the teacher would be there.

The door opened and Mr. Havelna's balding head appeared. "Hm? Oh, Revan, hi."

"Hello, sir," Revan said. "Am I disturbing you?"

"Not really," Mr. Havelna said, "but you do know this is my private room."

"I know," Revan said, "and I'm sorry, but I have to discuss something with you. I wouldn't do it unless it were an emergency. Plus, I've been here before."

"Hm," the teacher said, and opened the door. He wore a shirt, the color of gold, and dark pants instead of the red uniform most teachers wore. It was weird seeing him in such regular clothing, though his shirt was still silver-colored, as it was supposed to be. Mr. Havelna sat down on a chair in the corner of the room. "Come in then. Been a while since you were last here."

"Yeah," Revan said. In the first years he'd been to the college he'd been scared of the switch; he had never been so far away from home. Mr. Havelna, who wasn't just a teacher in magic but also the school's counsellor, had offered to talk to him once a week to see how he was doing. As there wasn't a good room, the counseling sessions happened in Mr. Havelna's private room. Those conversations had helped Revan through his fears, though he didn't know Revan had a second lit-up crystal either.

Mr. Havelna's private room was just big enough. He didn't like grandeur, so his room was *just* a little bigger than that of two normal students, though he did sleep in it by himself. It contained an old red metal desk situated against the window, and a chair in the same color behind it. Right next to that was a bookshelf filled with books. In the corner stood a small sofa, on which Mr. Havelna sat down, just like back when Revan had had his conversations with him. Mr. Havelna's bed was against the other wall. "What's going on?" he asked.

Revan had decided he'd be as direct as possible, even though he was terrified to speak. "I watched the principal use magic," he managed to say.

Mr. Havelna fell quiet for a moment. "What?"

"I'm very sure," Revan said. "But I saw it at a weird place. The uppermost floor."

"Oh?" Mr. Havelna asked. Revan was sure his face got redder with every second, even though he tried so hard to relax. "What were you doing there?"

Revan shrugged, trying to seem at ease. "I missed home. I wanted to see my home skyscraper through the window." He just hoped it would sound convincing enough. He cursed himself silently. Why had he trusted Gaveh again? He was such an idiot.

"Hm hm," Mr. Havelna replied, and Revan was certain his lie had been seen through. "You are sure it was magic?"

"Very," Revan said. "Gaveh said there were many reasons why she could have used magic, but...I thought it was weird."

"Your Koden was there," Mr. Havelna said and the edge in his voice was now also there in his gaze, looking at Revan. Revan felt like he was dying. The teacher said nothing for a while and watched him before saying calmly, "That she would be able to access magic is suspect for sure, but your Koden is right. We shouldn't draw too many conclusions too quickly. What do you want me to do with this information?"

Revan shrugged. "I don't know," he admitted honestly. "I'm just...worried, I guess, and I wanted to know if you knew already."

"Hm," Mr. Havelna said. His gaze softened. He shook his head and smiled. "I didn't. Thanks for letting me know, Revan."

"You're welcome," Revan said.

"And Revan?" Mr. Havelna said, and his gaze turned back to steel. "Next time you miss your home skyscraper you can do so without your Koden. Am I making myself clear?" Revan nodded nervously. "You can go." Mr. Havelna nodded. Revan left, his face beet red.

* * *

As usual, there were few people outside the skyscraper. Revan was usually outside once or twice a week, at most. Most people lived inside the skyscrapers as they contained everything anyway, and few people went outside often. If they travelled between islands, they'd do so through gates anyhow. Outside wasn't a very comfortable place to be. Even now, Revan felt the heat coming off the lava. Revan looked up to the skyscraper he'd just come out of. As usual, he could barely see the top because it was so high. The skyscraper was made of the same material all skyscrapers were made of; that material could become any shade of white, black or gray at will, and as a result all skyscrapers were usually one of those colors. Both his own skyscraper and Arana's skyscraper were black.

When Samillan had finished with the Flow, everyone on the planet found themselves on one of those islands with enough material to build the skyscrapers as high as they could. The material was said to be "smart": once one brick was put on top of another with the intent of building, the bricks would attach themselves firmly. It made all the skyscrapers look the same, though they weren't all equally as high and the shapes were a little different. That material could also double as soil for plants to grow on, which is how most people got fed. That was how so many skyscrapers were built—space was scarce if you could only live on an island.

Revan missed home, but Arana's skyscraper was the next best thing for the next few nights. Revan met a few people on the way, finding Arana's skyscraper based on her directions. The elevator took him to the right floor, and when Revan rang the doorbell, Arana opened the door.

"Revan," she said. "So happy you're here!" and she hugged him.

Revan knew he was supposed to reciprocate the hug, but instead he froze. Arana had her arms around him. Revan had never been this close to her before and her scent filled his nostrils. She had never been this touchy and his whole body panicked. Finally, he managed to pull himself together and reciprocate the hug, but he didn't know for how long he'd been flummoxed. Over Arana's shoulder, Revan looked into her house; apparently it was usual in this skyscraper to have the front door facing a window, because that was what Revan saw. On either wall was a couch; two grown-ups, presumably Arana's parents, were sitting on one couch, Gaveh was on the other. Gaveh winked at him, seeming proud.

Eventually Arana let go of him again. "How are you?"

"I'm fine," Revan managed to say. "All things considered. You?" Thankfully he sounded normal. He was calmer again.

Arana sighed. "My sister didn't come home, as I feared."

"Oh no, I'm so sorry to hear that," Revan said.

"Yeah, ah well…" Arana said. "You know what it feels like, with your sister."

"True," Revan sighed.

"Good to meet you, Revan," came from Arana's parents. Revan immediately hoped he was making a good impression.

And he could see her home from the inside. The walls were painted white, with two paintings on them, probably of the family. This skyscraper was built slightly differently from Revan's, the windows slightly thinner and smaller, but the material was the same. The walls were filled with bookshelves and books—this was a family that read a lot, more than Revan's. Revan's heart beat wildly as he walked into the home and introduced himself to Arana's parents.

* * *

"It'll surely be over soon," Arana's mother sighed. "There must be a very good explanation for all of this." She had said it repeatedly throughout the whole dinner. They were eating white rice with thruv-sauce. "I'm not worried, my children will manage, both of them." But she didn't convince anyone, as she sat close to her daughter, regularly touched her husband, and often looked out the window.

It somehow helped Revan, knowing he wasn't the only one who worried. Arana's mother was clothed like someone whose art crystal lit up; bright colors, as expected from most artists. Arana's father clearly had a lit-up central crystal as he wore clothes that had a subtle tint of gold.

"These are weird times," Arana's father said after the fifth time his wife had expressed concern. They had all finished dinner. "And I have no idea how this all happened. But our daughter is a strong woman, she'll manage."

"Yes, I know," Arana's mother said. "Really, I do."

"Of course. But let's change the subject," Arana's father said. "Revan, Gaveh, I assume that, like Arana, you're training to become magicians? Arana told me you're one of the best scoring pupils, Revan."

"That's true," Revan laughed awkwardly—he didn't know how to deal with this kind of compliment. "That's what we're going to the college for."

"Transporting people is a noble job," Arana's father said. "Hope you'll be able to do that again soon. I do hope you're not studying all day, though."

"No," Revan said. "Right now, I'm not even studying all that much. Just can't get myself to do it."

"I understand," Arana's father said. "So what do you do when you're not studying? You seem to be the reading type."

"Every now and then," Revan said, "if I have time."

"And you, Gaveh?"

Gaveh shrugged. "Not really. Reading isn't my thing."

"Revan, have you read Samillan's theories?"

"Of course," Revan said, "we get taught them at school. Samillan's written a lot of books, reading a couple of them is mandatory."

Arana's father smiled. "Good. My favorite book of his is still *The Right Roads*. Did you read that?"

Revan suppressed a sigh. He nodded and smiled and tried very hard not to show what he felt. "So his first work. I understand. I'm more into the *Dance of Balance*, it's more philosophical."

"A philosopher," Arana's father said, and he nodded a couple times, suddenly lost in thought. "I like that you're well-read, Revan. But what don't you like about *The Right Roads*?"

"It's his first work," Revan said quickly. "His writing was still rough; the rhetorics aren't as high in quality." He wanted to change the subject as soon as possible, before someone would really see how he felt.

"You're not wrong," Arana's father said, "but that roughness makes it a better read, I think. It has some marvelous truths." He smiled. "But you seem like a good kid."

"Thanks," Revan laughed awkwardly. "So is Gaveh." He had been in the spotlight for long enough.

* * *

Revan only allowed himself to feel the grief and fury that related to the conversation with Arana's father in the evening. It shouldn't get to him after this many years, but it unfortunately still did.

Samillan had written multiple books before manipulating the Flow, all books that still influenced current society and were obligatory for everyone at Samillan College. The books talked about how people should behave, and how society should be. *The Right Roads* was his first and most influential book, and Revan had unfortunately memorized the passage that was the reason for his anger now.

> *Pity the Othercrystalled. They have multiple crystals lit up, which takes far more energy than other people. It confuses their thought process, and as a result they can't do anything productive. They will return, every single time, but it is the duty of normal people to eliminate them as quickly as possible. It is sad, but it's important that the Flow-worshippers continue to do good. So take them out of their misery. Othercrystalled are lazy and you can never count on them to do anything useful.*

The Right Roads had become incredibly influential—after Samillan had manipulated the Flow and the planet suddenly was bathed in lava, with a couple islands here and there—all books from before the Flow had disappeared, except some of Samillan's work. All other books of his, among which was the *Dance of Balance*, were more philosophical and moralistic, but that first book was one big rant against the Othercrystalled. Nowadays most people were much milder than the book prescribed, and *The Right Roads* had faded into the background—but Arana's father still following it meant he hated Othercrystalled. Revan was in the home of someone who thought he shouldn't exist.

It was still on Revan's mind when they were heading to bed, and Gaveh interrupted his thought process. "You okay?" He stood on one side of their two-person bed, already holding the sheets, about to get underneath.

"Hm?" Revan said, still getting into his pajamas.

"You've been very quiet since talking to Arana's dad." Gaveh smiled invitingly. "What happened?"

"Nothing," Revan said quickly, shaking his head. "I've just been sad about not going home. Arana's home, why can't I be?"

"Ah," Gaveh said. He got into bed, already ready to sleep, and Revan continued to undress but left his shirt on, as usual. Revan thought that was the end of the conversation, but then Gaveh said, "How long have we known each other, Revan?" His face was still visible above the blankets.

The question took Revan aback for a bit. "Couple years?"

"Five, I think," Gaveh sighed. "Or something like that. I think I know you a little because of that."

"You know me inside and out," Revan tried to joke. Where was this conversation going?

Gaveh let out a short chuckle, but his voice was serious when he said, "Sometimes I feel like you're not letting me in."

An uncomfortable silence dawned over them. What was Revan supposed to say to that? It was true, but how could he avoid Gaveh's suspicion as quickly as possible? It couldn't have been more than a few seconds, but to Revan it felt like an eternity that gave him away when he said, "That's not true. I've just been worried."

"I'm sure that's it," Gaveh said, his voice level. It was impossible to tell whether he saw through that excuse. "I guess I'm just not feeling your worry as much."

"You don't really hate your parents *this* much," Revan said, glad the subject had changed. "You don't get along with them. That's different. Surely at this point you're worried too."

"A little," Gaveh admitted matter-of-factly. "I guess I'm still not as concerned, though. Magic left, magic can come back. I guess I'm more worried about you than about the world. You can tell me anything, you know?"

"I know," Revan said. And after a while he added, "You really think Samillan is 'just a heroic guy'?"

It was Gaveh's turn to be taken aback. Revan heard it in his voice when he said, "Well, I guess it's just where I'm from. We don't worship Samillan like you guys do."

"Nice," Revan said, and then wondered if he should tell Gaveh, once again.

But then, as if it was a sign, the tape over his calm crystal started to let go. That wasn't a problem, as Revan always carried a spare. He sighed, annoyed, and said to Gaveh, "I'll see you in a moment, I have to go to the bathroom." He hadn't put on his pajama pants yet, and barring his shirt he was naked, but that wasn't really a problem, he wouldn't run into anyone on the short trip to the bathroom. And if he did, well, at least his crystals wouldn't show.

"Okay," Gaveh said and rolled over, no longer looking at Revan, allowing him to take a small roll of tape out of the pocket of his regular pants. Revan left the bedroom, heading for the common bathroom at the end of the hallway.

Once inside, Revan untied his shirt and took it off, then took off the tape of his calm crystal and looked at himself in the mirror, completely naked. The light of two crystals—one green, one red—filled the room, shining against the light that was on. He was naked. Not for the first time, Revan hoped his calm crystal would stop lighting up. He had just grabbed the roll of tape when the door opened.

"And that's why I'm called Arana, just a cultural reason, has nothing to do with central crystals," Arana shouted, apparently to Gaveh. She hadn't seen him yet.

Blindly panicking, Revan grabbed his shirt. He thought he'd locked the door, right? It didn't matter. "Oh, sorry!" Arana said, shocked, and Revan hoped for a second that she hadn't seen it as he put on his shirt. But then she said, "Wait...*two*?!"

Chapter Five

It would be pointless to try and keep it a secret. Revan had his shirt partially on, but his calm crystal still shone underneath. Arana looked at it shamelessly, her jaw dropped. She was about to turn back around when she said, "But..." and turned back to Revan. "But..." she stuttered, and she pointed, and she wanted to turn around again—clearly both embarrassed and curious. Revan wasn't, he was just deeply ashamed and his face got even hotter. "But..." Arana said, and she pointed at Revan's crystal. She didn't care that Revan hadn't put on pants or underwear. "You're a..." She rubbed her temples, her mouth still open, still looking for words. "I have a...I invited someone who...You're an Else."

The seconds of silence that followed lasted forever. Revan wanted to ask for privacy, anything to get things back to how they were before, but he couldn't afford to. Arana *knew*. All she had to do was to go to her father and Revan would be kicked out of the house. If Arana wanted to ruin his life further, she could go to the principal and pass on what she had seen. Such an annoying "Else" would never be welcome. Arana had *all* the power. All Revan could do was stare at the ground.

"Does Gaveh know?" Arana finally asked.

"No," Revan stuttered, his face still hot and red—when would that stop? He wanted to say more but the words were stuck in his throat.

Arana still stared at Revan's second crystal and it made Revan feel extremely uncomfortable. "But you are...lazy. People like you are lazy. And on top of that...you go against the Flow." Of course she'd say that. Her father was still a follower of *The Right Roads*. After hundreds of years, things weren't as bad as they used to be, but this was still a problem. He'd heard this more often—his parents had begged him to keep quiet about his crystals at all times.

"And yet, we exist," Revan said, for want of a better phrase. Once again, it was quiet for a few seconds. Only then did Revan dare to look up.

Arana's disgust shone off her face. "But...but..." she tried to say, but that was all she could gather.

Finally, Revan said, "Arana..." if only to break that excruciating silence.

Arana shook her head and stormed out of the bathroom. Revan cursed and put on his shirt as quickly as he could. He had no time to tie the hem or to reattach the tape, or to put on his pants. He sprinted out of the bathroom. "Arana!" he called after her, as softly as he still could, with his left arm over his calm crystal, hoping nobody else would notice. "Arana!" he called again.

Arana was in the hallway when she turned around again. "I can't keep this a secret," she said, her eyes filled with tears that Revan didn't understand.

"You can," Revan said. "Please."

Arana shook her head. "You...you...you're so pious and hardworking and smart...and then you are...you're *lying*. Someone like you..."

"That hasn't changed, I'm still the same guy," Revan begged. "Please. I'll do anything if you don't tell anyone."

Arana looked at him for more excruciating seconds. Then a door opened, and Revan pushed even harder against his calm crystal with his left arm. "What's wrong?" Gaveh. "I heard shouting."

Revan couldn't beg more than he already had, and at this point he was just expecting the words, "Revan is an Else." Arana blinked a couple times. "Nothing," she finally said.

Revan was unable to suppress a relieved sigh. Arana looked at him as if she was surprised she'd made that decision. In his mind, Revan thanked the Flow. He'd hear later what Arana would ask of him. He turned back around to the bathroom. He didn't care to explain himself to Gaveh. He slammed the door shut behind him, locked it, checked twice to see if it was really locked, then he burst into tears. Arana had total control over him.

In his frustration he beat against his calm crystal a couple times, vaguely hoping punching it would cause it to stop glowing. Of course it didn't, the hard flat structure of the crystal just bruised his hand, and it still hurt much less than what Arana had done to him. Crystals didn't suddenly stop shining, no matter how hard you tried—and neither did they fall off to leave a crystal-shaped hole in your skin. The crystal was part of him, no matter how much he despised it. While cursing, Revan taped over his crystal again and left the bathroom fully clothed.

Gaveh was still at the door when Revan was back. "Could you tell me why you were talking with Arana while basically naked?" he asked stunned.

Oh, right, Revan hadn't worn his pants. "No," he bluntly said. He walked past Gaveh and fell down on the bed, biting his lip to stop himself from crying.

* * *

He didn't sleep very well that night. Every time he was almost asleep the thought went through his mind, *Arana's going to tell everyone.* He knew for sure, all of a sudden, that once he walked out of the spare bedroom, Arana's father would ambush him and beat him up, or worse. But that thought didn't last long, because then he wondered why Arana's father hadn't stormed into the spare bedroom yet and he didn't have a satisfying answer. But the worries remained. Every time Revan's exhaustion seemed to finally catch up to him, the thoughts went through his mind again.

Arana had been full of disgust when she saw him. That expression was burned on Revan's retinas; he would never forget it. The girl he'd found so beautiful, that he'd fallen for the moment he saw her for the first time as she had both beauty and brains, turned out to be a crystallist, and that hurt so much Arana might as well have stabbed him with a knife.

The first and last person he'd told on purpose was his sister Fenna. His parents already knew, of course, Revan's crystals had never changed since his birth. And Fenna had reacted with surprise, she'd had lots of questions, she'd been very uncertain about it, but she'd finally accepted him and had promised she wouldn't tell anyone else. Fenna wouldn't. For an eleven-year-old, she was surprisingly reliable and mature.

Revan missed her so much. He would've loved to go back home and to be surrounded again by people who loved him for who he was, people who accepted him. Instead, he was awake, sharing a bed with his Koden who had no idea of his second crystal. Revan was so jealous of Gaveh, because he had been down and out within seconds.

All he could think of was that Arana had called him lazy and devilish, just like what *The Right Roads* had said. She'd essentially quoted Samillan. And then she had used that slur—*Else* was a word Revan had read about in textbooks, particularly the more recent ones lambasting people like him. It was never used positively.

And yet, despite all those thoughts plaguing him, Revan had somehow fallen asleep, because at one point he suddenly opened his eyes and the sun was up. Revan stretched himself and looked next to him. Gaveh was still out cold, but sounds came from the hallway that had apparently awoken Revan. He sighed. He gave himself a couple minutes to wake up and took a couple deep breaths. Did it make sense to stay here in bed? No, Revan had to get out, or Arana's father would kick him out. Of the bed and their house. Revan got out of bed, put on his clothes, triple-checked whether his shirt was bound at the hem and the tape was still sticking, then headed for the living room on the other end of the hallway. Arana's father was sitting there, his back to Revan. Arana looked up precisely when Revan opened the door; her eyes drilled into his, but then she looked away again. Arana's father turned around and looked at Revan too. For one second Revan was terrified the man would shout at him, but then Arana's father smiled. "Revan, did you sleep well?"

"Yeah," he lied with a smile. "Just a minor headache. No idea where it came from."

"I made you a great breakfast. Gaveh's still asleep? Let him. Come join us, Revan." Scared of a trap, Revan took a couple steps in his direction, but then gathered his nerves and joined them at the table. Arana's father had made porridge, but also a couple filled thruvs and some bread. "I didn't know what you guys would like," Arana's father said, "so I thought I'd give you a choice."

Revan took a bowl of porridge. "Delicious, thank you. I'll stick with this for now." He wasn't hungry yet.

"It's a good thing at least one of us can cook," Arana's father said teasingly. "Did Arana tell you what once happened when she…"

"Dad," Arana said angrily. She looked at Revan with the same anger in her eyes, after which she stood up and walked away without saying another word.

"What are you doing, honey? These are your guests, you…"

"You said to join you at the table until Revan or Gaveh would come," Arana shouted from the hallway. "I did just that."

It was quiet for a while; a silence Revan was grateful for. Arana hadn't told her father. "I don't know what's up with my daughter today," Arana's father said, shaking his head, then he turned to Revan. "Anyway, I just wanted to follow up on our discussion yesterday. What did you like so much about the *Dance of Balance*, Revan?"

Revan swallowed his porridge and thought carefully on how to reply. He wasn't fond of discussing anything about Samillan—but Arana's father challenging him to a discussion he'd rather not be in was so much better than the alternative.

Chapter Six

"I'm getting more and more curious about what you discussed with Arana last weekend," Gaveh said in the elevator as they were heading to the eating hall. They were back at Samillan College; Arana's parents had offered to have them stay the first school day as well, but both Revan and Gaveh had politely declined. The rest of the weekend had been awkward. Arana avoided Revan and every time one of her parents asked what was wrong, she was evasive.

"Yeah, well..." Revan sighed. He still hadn't thought up a good excuse.

"Was your member that traumatic?" Gaveh whispered, and he winked. Revan laughed without feeling any joy, then he shook his head. He was briefly worried Gaveh would keep asking, but Flow be thanked the elevator doors opened and they walked straight into the eating hall.

The first thing Revan noticed was that Mrs. Dahena wasn't at the big table. Mr. Havelna was in her spot; he seemed to wait until everyone was there. Without talking any more—it was very quiet in the eating hall—they both sat with the other people from their year. Revan sat down next to Wilan. "*What's wrong?*" he whispered, but Wilan's expression said that he didn't know either.

Apparently, they were just in time, because just after they'd sat down Mr. Havelna said, "The principal is missing."

It was as if a bomb had gone off. The silence was immediately gone. Everyone started talking and yelling—and Mr. Havelna raising his hand trying to calm the hall didn't work at all. The noise didn't die down.

"Quiet, all of you!" Mrs. Garedna shouted without any effect—she was barely audible over the sounds.

"The Flow has actually left us!" one student shouted.

"The Flow didn't leave us!" That was Mr. Khandar—his loud voice drowned out the noise, and suddenly everyone was silent. "I understand you all are terrified, but that isn't necessary! We don't know where Mrs. Dahena is, but we'll find her! There's no point in worrying. We have enough supplies, so please focus on your tasks as a student. We will deal with the missing principal!"

Suddenly the whole hall was quiet, not only because of Mr. Khandar's words, but from the shock of it all—if the others felt the same thing Revan was feeling. Mr. Khandar didn't have a lit-up central crystal, he didn't dress like one either. The fact that he took charge of making the hall quiet was bizarre and that made it effective. Even if the other teachers gave him cold looks.

Mr. Khandar sat down again, clearly embarrassed. He'd gone against the natural order of things, surpassing the other teachers whose job it was to speak to the assembly like this.

"I understand you all have a lot of questions," Mrs. Garedna, who was Mrs. Dahena's wife, said again, now that everyone could hear her. She indeed had a very good reason to panic, but wasn't, at least visibly. "I understand this is a scary situation, for all of you, and you're all worried. But Mr. Khandar is right." Mrs. Garedna shot Mr. Khandar a look that made clear that this wasn't what she'd intended, and Mr. Khandar shot back an apologetic look. "We don't know where our principal is, but she'll return. What I can tell you in the meanwhile is that we're looking through the archives, finding an explanation for the magic disappearing. Some of us have already found something. It's entirely possible we'll find out why this all happened, we just need a little more time. I would like to ask you to remain calm. I understand that's difficult, and that you would love to shout and demand answers. I would love to do the same thing. But I would like to remind you what Mrs. Dahena said. Don't panic, it doesn't help anyone. If you want to talk to someone, go to one of the counsellors. Please stay calm. I'm worried as well and I have the best reason to of all of us, but I'm not panicking, and I would recommend you all follow my example."

Mrs. Garedna sat back down and the usual murmuring filled the hall—though it was a little louder than Revan was used to. Revan looked around and saw some panic still on the other faces, panic he felt as well. "She's missing," Gaveh said softly. Revan turned to him. "We saw her up there, and now she's missing. What happened?"

Revan looked around but thankfully nobody seemed to hear what Gaveh had said. "I have no idea," Revan replied.

* * *

Once the murmuring had died down, an awkward silence settled in the hall. Everyone had questions and nobody had any answers. From the corner of his eye, Revan saw Wilan pray to the Flow. He understood that decision. Wilan and Javik did the same; they held each other's hands while praying.

Revan's first lesson today was a magic lesson, and since magic lessons were on hold, Revan was free for the first hour. Thankfully, because he felt like withdrawing to his bedroom to pray out loud. He was already on his way when someone stopped him—Mr. Havelna.

"Revan?" he said softly, and he walked a bit further out of the hallway, gesturing for Revan to come with him. Once they were at a spot that was a bit more secluded the man said, "Thanks for coming to me just before the weekend."

"Do you know more now?"

Mr. Havelna shook his head. "But I'll spare you the details. I discussed what you saw with the other teachers, and we had plans to confront her once she came back. But she didn't, and..." He sighed.

The teacher didn't have to say it, because Revan had the same suspicions, and it caused his stomach to churn. "She's responsible, somehow." Though the idea of Mrs. Dahena somehow manipulating the Flow was ridiculous, her disappearance was a weird coincidence.

"We'll have to arm ourselves if we want to weather this crisis. If she doesn't come back, we'll have to figure it out by ourselves."

"Thanks," Revan said. He was about to walk away when the teacher stopped him by touching his shoulder.

"Can I tell you something in confidence, Revan?"

"...Of course?"

"My coworkers mean well, but they're all old. Fossils, you can call them, for sure." He chuckled. "And I think it's important we let the students weigh in as well. You all are younger and more flexible. It's important we weigh in all perspectives to get out of this mess." Revan frowned, tense. "You're one of the best scoring students at this school. Your perspective is extremely important. I want to found a kind of committee of the best pupils at this school, so that you can all weigh in. Led by me, of course, but I want to hear what you have to offer. Is that okay?"

Revan hesitated. "Er..."

"I think you would be a great help."

Ah, what harm could it do. "Sure. Can Gaveh join?"

The teacher shook his head. "Gaveh's an average scorer, and I really want the best pupils there. I understand he's your Koden and you wish him all the best, but let him do his own thing."

"Okay," Revan said.

"The first meeting is tomorrow, directly after class, in my classroom. I have to go ask a few others. You'll hear from me." And Mr. Havelna was gone.

Revan realized he was relieved. He was eager to contribute, and this was one way to do that. It was a pity Gaveh couldn't help, but he'd understand—right? After all, Mr. Havelna had invited him, and Revan couldn't say no to him.

Plus, if he said no, he would stick out like a sore thumb.

Chapter Seven

Arana was on the committee too, which wasn't a surprise—both Arana and Revan were high scoring students, so of course Mr. Havelna approached her too. Arana looked away the moment she saw him and shook her head. She'd successfully ignored him the past few days—Revan had kept expecting Arana to blackmail him, but that hadn't happened yet. Would it soon?

A big, oval table was in the center of the classroom. Mr. Havelna was at its head, Arana sat next to him. "Revan, welcome," he said. "Take a seat."

There were a couple spots free. Revan recognized everyone at the table, but he didn't know all their names; he'd mostly seen their faces in other classes. The majority had a lit-up skill crystal, which was visible from the practical, simple clothing that they wore. There were also a couple people at the table wearing the wealthy-looking clothes expected from those with a lit-up central crystal. Surprisingly, one or two students wore the calm hues that were expected of people with lit-up calm crystals, a couple wore very well-designed beautiful clothes that said their art crystals were lit-up, and a couple wore clothes with low v-necks, clothing that accentuated their muscles very clearly, as was expected of people with lit-up force crystals.

The people with lit-up crystals that weren't skill or central crystals weren't Othercrystalled, but they also didn't stick to the role society assigned to them—they weren't expected to transport people, they were expected to fulfill the roles that belonged to their lit-up crystals. If a crystal lit up, a certain role in society was expected of you and if you did something else you were looked down on. It wasn't like you were Othercrystalled, you weren't hated, but life was made suitably more difficult—nonetheless, Revan was happy to see them, as they made him feel a bit less alone.

Once everyone had arrived, the teacher started with, "Good that everyone's here. We could introduce ourselves, but I think we all know who everyone else is. The college is pretty big, but you're all in one of the last grades. Am I correct?"

Most people murmured something in agreement.

"Great. So I'll just get right to the point, in complete honesty. We're not doing well. Mrs. Garedna said we might have found a clue at breakfast, right?" Mrs. Dahena hadn't been found yet, so Mrs. Garedna had more or less repeated the same speech this morning. Once again, people murmured in agreement. "That's a lie to make sure everyone stays calm. We don't know anything, and we haven't been able to find anything." A stunned silence followed as Mr. Havelna paused to make his point.

"You all understand this is the reason why I summoned you. Among the teachers, there's a lot of discussion on why this is all happening, and everyone has different reasons, from religious ones to a natural disaster, but at the end of every talk we haven't progressed in the slightest. That's why I created this committee. And I'll stay completely honest; my fellow teachers have no idea this is happening, because most of them feel you're not fully grown and therefore shouldn't be responsible for the solutions. They say to leave it to the experts. I wanted to go past that discussion, because this is just as hard for you as it is for us." Mr. Havelna swallowed uncomfortably. "Because our supplies are, unfortunately, dwindling. We're fairly certain the farming floors on the skyscrapers on this island aren't enough to feed everyone."

A stunned silence filled the room as everyone gathered their thoughts. This was bad news. Every skyscraper had a couple floors where soil grew, from where plants could be grown to supply as many people as possible with plants and fruits. But there was a lot of import and export between islands through gates—allowing some islands to focus more on food, and others, like the island Revan was on, to focus more on other services—like Samillan College, where all the necessary food items would come in through the portals anyway. Or at least, that was *supposed* to happen. Nobody had counted on the magic disappearing all of a sudden.

Mr. Havelna resumed his story. "We're still running the numbers on how much we still have in stock, but estimates are that we've got enough to last us just a bit over a week. After that, we don't know. Which is why it's urgent we come up with a solution."

"Flow be damned," one of the students said.

"And choices will have to be made," a dark girl said. Hdar, Revan knew; she had been one of the other students who had regularly had conversations with Mr. Havelna.

Mr. Havelna sighed. "Unfortunately, there's more. Our principal has gone missing, and...I suspect she's behind all of this." Once again, a stunned silence filled the room; Mr. Havelna explained that a student had told him she'd been using magic recently, after the portals had stopped working. Mr. Havelna left out that Revan was that student, for which Revan was grateful. Mr. Havelna ended with, "We don't know why she did what she did. But you're the smartest people of the college and young too. I hope you can all figure out a solution. I just want you all to know what we're fighting against. Obviously, what I told you has to stay between these walls."

Another stunned silence. All the students were looking around, as was Revan, hoping one of the others would be the first one to talk. Mr. Havelna was asking a lot of them. "Everyone's lives are at stake, quick, figure out a solution" was quite the assignment.

"Can I speak freely?" someone said in a trembling voice, and Revan recognized them as Strayi.

"Go ahead," Mr. Havelna said.

"Is it possible that, well..." They swallowed. "Someone found the Flow and manipulated it?"

A tremble went through the rest of the committee. Anyone else but Samillan having found the Flow wouldn't make any sense, and before the magic had disappeared, this wouldn't even be uttered. But circumstances had changed, and the look in Strayi's eyes told Revan they knew this wasn't even the most controversial part of their statement. They left that out.

But Mr. Havelna stated it out loud anyway. "And that person might be our own principal." A few more people shuddered. To state that it was the *principal*... "It's okay," Mr. Havelna quickly added, "right now we have to face the facts, and they are clear. One, our magic no longer works. Two, our principal is missing. Right now, we need to not be scared, and state what we're thinking." Mr. Havelna's words made Revan feel a little more comfortable, but he still felt queasy and plenty of people around him seemed to be feeling the same. Of course this was possible, and everyone had probably already thought it as such. But only Samillan could manipulate the Flow, that was the position Samillan College had taken, and to even suggest someone could find the Flow was a controversial statement at best, in easier times, and would probably land you a lecture on religious dogma if you were unlucky and a teacher overheard you.

"Why would she do that?" Hdar asked, breaking the tension a little bit. "She's the principal of the biggest college that teaches people magic. Making it disappear will only make her job harder."

"We don't know," Mr. Havelna said, looking tired. "We don't have any answers. Because you're right, Hdar, it doesn't make any sense. Maybe someone else has manipulated the Flow, as loath as I am to say it. Maybe the Flow changed itself and our former principal has something to do with it. We don't know. But we can't ask her, as she's gone missing."

"So, our primary goal is to find the Flow and fix things," Hdar said, pondering.

"The library," Arana said, her gaze fixed on Revan, even though he hadn't said anything yet. Revan immediately felt like hiding. "If we can find the location of the Flow anywhere, it'll have to be there, right?"

That, too, was quite the assignment. The library was huge—hundreds of bookshelves, impossible to archive. The library's floor was as tall as ten normal floors. It contained some books from just after Samillan manipulated the Flow, hundreds of years ago, but those were hard to find. As long as the college had existed, multiple people had been trying to apply a system to the library, but they all died before they had fully applied their systems.

"And if you've found the location of the Flow," Mr. Havelna said, "how do you want to get there, without magic?"

"No idea," Arana said. "The Flow has its own will, right? It can be manipulated, but it's so strong it's almost impossible to do that. Maybe we should draw the Flow's attention. We have to do *something*, and if there's a clue anywhere, it *has* to be in the library."

"Some of the teachers have already gone through the library..." Mr. Havelna began.

"But you're only a couple people," Arana replied. "What if we let everyone from the school look in the library? Have *everyone* look for clues? We all have hours off because we have no magic. We can use that." Once again, she kept her eyes fixed on Revan, as if she wanted to provoke him to respond.

"But everyone will panic," Revan said. Immediately everyone looked at him, and Revan wanted to hide away again. He didn't like being the center of attention, but he had said it more loudly than he'd intended. He might as well voice his whole idea now. "Mrs. Garedna managed to convince everyone with some lies that it isn't nearly as bad as we thought. If we tell everyone the teachers haven't found anything..."

Arana's eyes drilled into his and Revan felt sweat drip down his face. Revan wished he could see what she was thinking, so he could know what she thought about his secret. Part of him wished, in that second, that Arana would say something like, "That's an idea that fits an Else," because then at least he'd be rid of that uncertainty.

"I'm sure we can think of something," Arana said. "Something about looking for alternative solutions. That we want to be as exhaustive as possible."

Revan completely gave up on only listening. "And you think people will believe that? It's a cheap way to make people think something different. The students aren't that stupid."

"I'm not saying they are," Arana replied, "but this is the best way."

"If you even assume all the students will read all the books well. What kind of system are you considering? To throw all the books, among which are ones that are hundreds of years old and very sacred, on one pile? Because if you're hoping to apply some system to the library..."

"No," Arana replied, "but we don't have to. We'll just go shelf after shelf..."

"And imagine one of those books has *the* location, where we'll find *the* solution, but someone from the first year picks it up, isn't quite good at reading, and puts the book away."

It was quiet again. Revan was startled by his own words—he'd said much more than he'd planned to say. But at least Arana was talking to him. In fact, she was still staring at him.

"We can have every book read by two or three students," Mr. Havelna said. "But you're still right, Revan. We're risking a lot. If we let every book be read twice it'll only cost more time we don't have. Does anyone have a solution for that?" For a few seconds, it fell silent. Only then did Arana look away from Revan—he was back to being non-existent to her, filled with uncertainty. "No ideas," Mr. Havelna said. He sighed. "Of course it's safest to not have the youngest students read the oldest books. But the more responsible, older students might be able to do that, or us teachers. I wanted to involve you students because I feel the teachers keep thinking the same thing, and by involving the students we'll stand a chance. Does anyone else have any other ideas?"

* * *

The discussion lasted another thirty minutes. Lots of ideas were brainstormed and shot down again. Hdar suggested letting all the teachers look all day through the library for a solution, but that idea was quickly shot down as just an easy way to avoid having to do work. Strayi suggested they cancel all the classes so that everyone could look through the library as quickly as possible but that was also declined as the teachers wanted to keep regular classes going as long as feasible. Even if everyone went as fast as they could, the library was so big that it would still take much too long to read everything, even if all the students were in the library at the same time. In the end, everyone agreed on Arana's plan, tailored so that they would start looking in the relevant sections of the library. With Revan's adjustment, so every book would be read twice, they'd hope to find the location of the Flow. Or, at least, they'd have an idea of why the magic had stopped.

Revan's thoughts didn't run in the same way when the discussion was over. He was exhausted but stuck around in the classroom. He wanted to break the uncertainty. Yes, he was terrified of what would happen if he talked to Arana, but he *had* to know. What would Arana do with him? When would she start blackmailing him? Revan *had* to know. Arana stuck around as well, but unfortunately, so did some other students.

Finally, after another very long conversation, Arana said she should go. She hadn't looked at Revan even once—she just turned around and left. Revan ran after her.

"Arana, what do you want from me?" Revan almost begged as soon as they were in the hallway, out of earshot of the classroom, but Arana didn't respond. She called the elevator and the doors immediately opened. Revan got in after her—and then they were alone, the doors closed behind them. "Arana, what do I need to do to make you keep my secret?" Revan heard how close he was to begging.

Arana kept looking at the ground until Revan thought she was still ignoring him. But then she said, after a long silence, "Leave me alone."

"...Oh," Revan said sheepishly. "Is that all?"

"No," Arana said. "Never get in the same elevator as me again."

The elevator arrived at the floor Revan and Arana were both sleeping on. But Revan remained fixed to the ground as

Arana walked out of the elevator and didn't turn around. "Is that all?" Revan asked again, but he didn't get a response. He didn't know what exactly he was asking either—whether it was "*is that all it takes to make you hate me?*" or "*is that all it takes to make sure you keep my secret?*"

Revan got out just before the elevator doors closed again. He stared at the ground, crestfallen. This wasn't just anyone, this was Arana, his big crush. Revan had followed her like a shadow. Someone who Revan had thought was amazing; beautiful, intelligent, the best person to be with. But none of that counted as she was a crystallist.

His parents had been right. Revan had to keep his second crystal a secret, at all costs.

Chapter Eight

"So, you're on that committee," Gaveh said, on his way to the library, "because you're an 'excellent scoring' pupil, but I'm not."

Mrs. Garedna had given another speech that morning. It was a day after Revan attended Mr. Havelna's group, and apparently, he had gone straight to the other teachers. They'd all agreed with them, because Mrs. Garedna had opened with, "During magic lessons, pupils have to go through the library, finding answers. We're counting on you." The pupils reacted to it with mixed feelings, and the usual murmuring had filled the room. But the decision had been final, because there was no time to hesitate.

"I'm sorry," Revan said. "I'd asked Mr. Havelna if you could join, but..."

"Ah well," Gaveh said. "I'm not jealous or anything. I was just wondering where the cut-off was. How good do you have to be to join?"

Revan looked at Gaveh, one eyebrow raised. "You're sure you're not jealous?"

"Of course not, I'm happy you're getting such high grades." Gaveh sighed.

Normally they'd have magic lessons from Mr. Havelna. Despite himself, Revan once again made that movement with his hand, allowing him to open a gate, while he tried to imagine his home—but of course nothing happened. The class would meet up at the library, where they'd go through the bookshelves as Mr. Havelna supervised them.

"You're very smart too," Revan tried. "I'm sure the committee would be lucky to have you."

"Yeah, yeah, sure," Gaveh said, holding up one hand. "Whatever."

"All right," Revan said as they got into the elevator and pressed the button of the right floor. "If you need any distraction..."

Gaveh chuckled joylessly. "That's my line."

Revan shrugged. "But you'll feel better too, so I thought, if I propose this..."

"If words fail us, we'll always have sex," Gaveh mumbled. "No, Revan, it's all right, never mind," he said, stopping the flow of the conversation. Not that they could talk a lot anyway, because the elevator doors opened and they walked straight into the library.

The library's floor took up as much space as ten normal floors, and that was noticeable as soon as Revan looked up. The room was enormous, with gigantic bookshelves and a couple ladders so that everyone could get to the right books straight away. The library took up the whole floor, another reminder as to how big the skyscraper was. He couldn't see the black wall on the other side of the room, although the books also made that harder. The only color came from the books, which also spread a musty scent. On the right side, Revan saw a glass wall behind which were the oldest books. He'd wanted to go there for years, but the oldest books were very fragile and so the students weren't allowed there, as they were considered too irresponsible. He had to focus on the other books, although there were more than enough of those. On the left side, Revan saw lots of tiny, illuminated chambers where people could read on their own. Those rooms were now all free.

"Welcome, Revan, Gaveh," Mr. Havelna said. "We can begin. You know what you have to do. Right now, we're going through these bookshelves." He pointed at the bookshelves right in front of him. "This is how we'll do it. I'll take the books from the bookshelves and give them to you all. You do *not* have to read every page, you will not be quizzed. Try and find answers, that's the only thing I'm asking. If you don't think you'll get any answers in the books you have, let me know, and I'll fetch you another book. Any questions?" Mr. Havelna looked around as the rest of the class was silent. "Great. Then I'll get on the ladder."

"How long will it take before we've looked at all the books?" Gaveh asked softly. "All students in the entire college? In this *enormous* library? Particularly if we have to read every book twice? They should've categorized this."

"That's impossible," Revan said softly. "This collection was so big that every attempt to order it didn't last long enough—because then someone else had a better one."

"But there are parts that are ordered," Gaveh said. "Can we not start there?"

"Yes, and we are," Arana said. Revan looked in her direction, confused. So she *did* want to talk to Gaveh. "The Reform of 1168 started here. The idea was to sort them by genre. These bookshelves are ordered entirely like that. Mr. Havelna's looking in the history section. We're ignoring the cookbooks, don't worry."

"Oh," Gaveh said sheepishly.

"I've been here a few times," Arana added, and Mr. Havelna handed her a book.

"You are not allowed to take the books out of the library. Once the lesson's over, I want you all to return everything. If you haven't found anything useful in the book during that time, you won't find it anyway. I want to emphasize, no matter how interesting the book might be, we're looking for *answers*. I will walk around if you have any questions. You're allowed some conversation time, but keep it down for the others and don't slack off too much." He handed Revan a book with a green spine. "Good luck."

Revan opened the book, which was about Samillan's life, and started searching.

* * *

"They're keeping us busy," Gaveh said softly. "That's all it is. It's just to keep us occupied. We will *never* find the right books, not in this enormous collection."

"You're angry because you can't join the group I'm in," Revan replied, just as softly. He didn't look away from his book.

"Of course," Gaveh said. "This is my problem too. I want to help."

"All our lives are at stake, Gaveh, and all you can worry about is that you can't help?"

"I can't and neither can most students. If everyone could join the discussion, that'd be great, but no, instead it's just Mr. Havelna's favorites."

"There are a *lot* of students, Gaveh."

"So, have everyone write down their ideas and put them in a suggestion box, or something. If Mr. Havelna wants to involve everyone so badly, why won't he?"

Revan rubbed his temples. "I'm trying to read, Gaveh, I want to find a solution. I suggest you do the same."

"Yeah, I'm sorry I'm not as smart as you," Gaveh muttered.

Revan frowned. "What?" He looked up.

Gaveh's face was annoyed, angry. "Nothing." He looked back at the book and continued reading.

Revan had half a mind to put down his book and walk to Gaveh, to ask him what was wrong. They didn't fight a lot, because Gaveh usually wasn't as hostile as he was now. Even now, still, he looked at his book with a big frown on his face, and Revan knew only one thing for certain, that nothing he said would help.

It hadn't been often that Gaveh was so angry at Revan that Revan was in this position. They'd always been able to talk it out. It helped that they'd known each other for so long, it was a friendship that had essentially formed during the first days they were both at the college. Revan had always been in Gaveh's corner, particularly when Gaveh had fights with his parents, and Gaveh had even stayed over at Revan's house when the fights had become too much. Of course, Wilan and Javik had joined them in that friendship, but even with them around, Revan had known deep down inside all along he was closer with Gaveh than the others. That friendship had happened before they'd decided to become each other's Kodens—they had already been so close that when Gaveh had asked Revan two years ago if they could start having sex, to Revan it had been a logical step. Though he'd been terrified to reveal his crystals; his mother had come up with the idea of lying that he wouldn't take off his shirt to respect his culture. Once that had been cleared up, their relationship had only intensified.

And now, there was nothing Revan could do to fix the fact that he'd been asked to be on the committee, but Gaveh hadn't been, and that didn't feel great. Particularly not since Revan's mind kept coming back to Gaveh when really, he should've been studying the book about Samillan's life. Still, Gaveh would probably just be a little angry about it, and it would blow over in a couple hours.

Revan tried to go back to reading, but unsuccessfully. Revan knew all about Samillan already, and although he hadn't read this specific book, he knew the main lines enough that the book just retold those things in a more boring way. A farm boy supposed to herd "animals"—living creatures like cows and sheep that had disappeared since—the Flow had approached him to do eleven works, every single one more challenging. Accounts on the final work differed; according to some stories, the final work was to cleanse the Flow of corruption, according to others Samillan was allowed to change the Flow as a reward for having completed all the works successfully. Where in the timeline Samillan wrote those books that said Othercrystalled should be suppressed was also unclear; some said before, saying that Samillan was a very well-read farm boy who had written a couple essays. Some said after, but before manipulating the Flow.

Whatever the theories about Samillan's life were, the book tried to talk about them all, and that made it a bloated, self-contradicting book that was a slog to read through. Revan blinked a couple times more, trying to focus back on the latest sentence, when someone shouted, "I did it!"

Revan looked up, shocked, and turned around. For one moment he couldn't believe what he was seeing. He saw a gate, and right in front was Wilan, his eyes open with shock. "I can do it again," he said. "We can go again. I felt that yearning, and…"

The gate disappeared and Wilan collapsed. "Wilan!" Sanbura, a classmate of Revan, shouted and caught him.

Javik was on the other side of the path but ran to him. "Wilan?" he asked.

Revan immediately started to make a gate home as Mr. Havelna ran to them. Making the gate had apparently cost Wilan a lot of energy. That was no problem, and he'd recover, but Revan was able to go home—but no, he still couldn't make a gate, no matter how hard he tried. "Wilan?" Revan asked.

"He's not breathing," Sanbura said. She slapped Wilan in the face in an attempt to wake him up, but that didn't help.

"Javik, go to the infirmary," Mr. Havelna shouted.

But Javik didn't move. He still stood next to Wilan and pulled his arm. "Wilan? Wilan?"

Sanbura squeezed Wilan's arm, perhaps hoping he'd react, but that didn't help either. Revan felt the creeps sneak up on him.

"...Is he dead?" Gaveh asked.

Sanbura looked up and nodded solemnly. "I think so."

Javik started crying.

Chapter Nine

"Yesterday," Mrs. Garedna said, "two students died, roughly at the same time, just after they were suddenly able to make a gate. Their names were Wilan and Jastre. It's unknown to what place the gate was made."

They were all aware of the news. It had spread like wildfire. They'd brought Wilan to the infirmary, but the doctors had seen the same thing Sanbura had also seen. Wilan was dead, but it was unclear what had killed him. His heart had just stopped suddenly and it was impossible to get going again. Revan had been too shocked to cry and Javik had disappeared: his chair at the eating table was empty.

"Those in classes with Wilan and Jastre have gotten the rest of the day off to process the loss. We're thinking of their families, but we sadly can't inform them. They were both living on another island." Mrs. Garedna's lips were pursed and she swallowed awkwardly—despite trying to keep a strong face, she was visibly affected by the news. "We're working on finding a solution in the library, all of us. I strongly believe we will succeed." It genuinely sounded as if she believed it. Jastre, a first year, died in her class according to the rumors. Mrs. Garedna had tried her best to save her, but a few seconds after the gate appeared she'd dropped dead. Just like with Wilan. "We're not sure why Wilan and Jastre are the ones who passed away. There was no connection between the two. They were not in the same year, didn't live on the same island and even had no friends they shared. We're still investigating it. I want to tell the ones who saw them die that I know it's rough, but try to keep following your classes. And if you can't—at least try to keep looking in the library. We need your help, more than ever. For Wilan and Jastre there will be a service in the dining hall. You don't need to go, but if you go, you don't need to go to class. This is difficult and I understand. You are all grieving, and that's allowed, as this is horrendous. But I want to keep asking you not to panic. We'll find out what's going on. The Flow hasn't turned on us, I'm certain of that. Thanks for your attention."

Students usually talked quietly once a speech was over. But as soon as Mrs. Garedna was done, nobody said a word. Revan bit back tears. Wilan and Revan might have grown apart a little over the years but nonetheless, they'd been good friends in the past and Revan had liked hanging out with him. And Jastre...just an innocent little girl? It made no sense. And if Wilan and Jastre, two apparently completely random pupils, could die under these circumstances, who would be next? Gaveh? Arana? Him? Revan ate his breakfast in full silence, and next to him, Gaveh apparently didn't feel like talking either. Breakfast was no longer porridge, but simply bread—bread was all they had for the next week, until that ran out too.

Wilan and Jastre will be the first victims of a very long list, if we don't get the magic back quickly. It made Revan's stomach churn.

* * *

Revan and Arana walked out of the eating hall together. That wasn't on purpose. She happened to walk next to him, and he wanted to disappear in the crowd, but he didn't quite succeed. Fine—he'd just ignore her, then. Arana seemed to be doing the same.

"Revan, Arana," Mr. Havelna said from behind them. "I need you both."

"Why?" Arana asked. Revan decided it was better to keep his mouth shut.

"I want to call a meeting of the committee. During Wilan's service."

"During..." Arana started.

"I know, it's not perfect. But I have to talk to the committee this afternoon, and this is the best way to gather everyone."

"I actually wanted to honor my old..." Revan said, against his better knowledge.

"I know," Mr. Havelna repeated, talking fast, sounding almost desperate. "Really, I get it. It's your classmate, and I'd rather have been there too. But trust me, this news is *urgent*, and I *have* to share it with you. Tell your teachers you're going to the service, but go to my classroom instead. Please."

It had to be important—and Revan felt like saying no wouldn't accomplish anything, Mr. Havelna would keep trying. Revan had never seen him *this* desperate. "I'll come," he said.

"I'll come too," Arana said.

"Thank you so much," Mr. Havelna said. "I'll see you this afternoon."

Revan left Arana behind and sprinted forward. In the crowd he looked for Gaveh and found him near the elevator. "Gaveh, can you go to Wilan's service? In my name?"

Gaveh lifted an eyebrow. "Are classes that important to you?"

"No, but Mr. Havelna needs me."

"More than your former friend needs you?" Gaveh said.

"I know," Revan said quickly, "and it sucks, and if there was any other way, I'd do that, but...I'll mourn him, Gaveh, I promise you. Some other way."

Gaveh sighed. "I'll let you know how it was. But I don't like it, and Javik will like it even less." There was that look again—the same look he'd had in the library when Wilan had died.

"I know," Revan replied, "and I don't like it either. But Mr. Havelna insisted." Gaveh just shrugged in response. "Gaveh?" Revan begged. "Please?"

Gaveh sighed, still seeming annoyed. "Sure. I'll say something in your stead. Just go to Mr. Havelna's classroom, and I'm hoping Javik won't be too angry at you."

Revan let out a brief sigh of relief. "Thank you," he said, and hurried to where he had to be.

* * *

Revan was the first to show up in Mr. Havelna's classroom, his stomach heavy with guilt. "Sir?"

"Come in," Mr. Havelna said with a sad expression. Revan sat down next to the teacher, as other students entered the classroom. It was indeed the same group as before, although a couple people were missing. Those people apparently would rather be at Wilan and Jastre's service—Revan once again felt like a traitor and just hoped Javik would forgive him.

Arana entered as well. She briefly looked Revan in the eyes, then looked away again, and she took her seat.

"We're all here," Mr. Havelna eventually said—three chairs were empty. When one of the students pointed that out, Mr. Havelna said, "They unfortunately declined. But I'm glad that the rest of you came. I'm going to tell you something the teachers don't want you to know." For one second it was completely quiet again. "There is one thing Wilan and Jastre have in common. They're both Othercrystalled."

Despite himself, Revan immediately grabbed his calm crystal. He corrected himself as soon as he realized, then looked around hoping that no-one else had seen him, but they were all focused on Mr. Havelna.

"Wilan originally had a lit-up central crystal," Mr. Havelna continued. "His family was disappointed and shocked when his skill crystal lit up, and his central crystal extinguished at four years old. The school knew; it was mentioned when he enrolled. We had to keep this a secret at all times. Jastre had no lit-up crystals. That, too, was a secret we kept. Jastre told her teacher, and they told us."

"So, all Othercrystalled are in danger," Arana said. Revan made a conscious effort *not* to look her way. He felt her gaze drilling into his skull. He briefly allowed himself to spare a thought about Wilan. Wilan had kept his secret from Revan very effectively, then. Revan felt a stab of guilt when he realized they could've helped each other, if either of them had shared their secret.

"Well, then there's no problem," Hdar said. "Great. The Flow is just thinning the herd. Let's get rid of all the Elses."

Revan bit back a response, fearing Hdar's reaction if he'd call her out—perhaps she or one of the others would say, "Why are you defending them so hard? Are you one yourself? Let me see your crystals, and you can't say no."

But Mr. Havelna beat him to it. "Hdar, you're supposed to be one of the most intelligent students in this school. Othercrystalled are people too—and they've already had enough trouble." Revan briefly allowed himself to breathe a sigh of relief. "I didn't summon you to confirm your prejudices. I want to know, what can we do to protect these people?"

Make her stop saying that word, Revan begged Mr. Havelna in his mind, but Mr. Havelna didn't seem to understand that "Else" was a slur.

"Assuming it's really Othercrystalled who are picked," Arana said. "Is it possible it's just a coincidence?" Revan still didn't look at her.

Mr. Havelna shook his head. "There are no other similarities. They both had other teachers, other subjects, and so forth. There really isn't any connection between the two of them other than being Othercrystalled—trust me, we tried everything else."

"But that's odd," Hdar said. "If you pick two students at random, there should be at least some similarities. The college is big, but not *that* big. It's almost as if the Flow is trying to send a message." Hdar had a faint smile on her lips and Revan wanted to throw something at her, but as usual, he suppressed that desire. Revan pinched his own neck as subtly as possible, hoping all the blood would flow there—otherwise he'd see red very soon. Revan knew a large part of the students at the college would react in the exact same way, which made it worse. *Oh, the Othercrystalled are in danger. No problem, they're just a burden.* Revan already knew what Hdar's favorite Samillan book was. He thought he knew her—they'd met a couple times—but he'd been unaware these were her views.

"Also," Mr. Havelna carried on as if he wasn't interrupted, "statistically we can't have a lot of Othercrystalled in this college. I believe the estimate was that it would be one in fifty people. Both victims being Othercrystalled is *too much* of a coincidence, so my question to you is, what can we do to protect these people? We're in a crisis—we can't afford to wait any longer to verify if Othercrystalled are the ones being chosen. We have to act *now*. And I'd like to hear a response from someone other than Hdar." He looked at her, his gaze firm. Hdar looked at the ground, frowning and crossing her arms.

"But we don't know anything," a tall, blond guy said—Tavrina, Revan remembered. Someone with a lit-up central crystal. "We don't know how we can find the Flow, and we don't know how to get the magic back. What can we do?"

"Keep an eye on the Othercrystalled," Arana said. Revan couldn't help it; he briefly looked in Arana's direction and indeed found her eyes drilling into his. Revan immediately looked away again. "Do we know of any other students?" she asked. "Did any Othercrystalled report in?"

"A few," Mr. Havelna replied.

"Tell several teachers to keep an eye on them. Don't tell them why, just tell them what they have to do. It's the best we can do. And ask during a speech, 'If you're Othercrystalled, let us know. We won't tell, but we need this information.'"

Mr. Havelna was briefly silent and nodded a few times, and then said, "That was Mrs. Garedna's suggestion too. There's already a whole network of counsellors; we can employ that."

"But what will we accomplish with that?" Strayi asked. "We'll keep an eye on them then, but that's all. That won't improve the situation. Those people will still die."

"Whatever," Hdar said, leaning on her chair, relaxed. Nobody paid her any attention.

"They were both able to make a gate, right?" Strayi asked. "They have that in common too. Well, say in the speech, if you feel you have to make a gate, don't. Suppress that urge.

You don't have to tell just the Othercrystalled. Tell everyone and leave it there. Nobody needs to know why."

"It still seems useful to know," Mr. Havelna said. "The Flow is picking them, somehow, and I don't know why. Things might get worse. Isn't it important to make sure we know who we need to pay attention to? This way, we can still help more people."

"Ask around then, if they want to help," Hdar said, still with that disgusting contented smirk on her face. "Or we just tell everyone that those beloved Othercrystalled are in danger. If you know your best friend, partner or Koden is Othercrystalled, tell us and we'll keep track." She shrugged.

Mr. Havelna held up his hands. "We've already employed our network of counsellors, so Othercrystalled will report in eventually. Maybe I'm asking too much of you, but I just want to know, are there any other solutions for this?" He remained patient, but Revan heard what Mr. Havelna wasn't saying. *We already had this idea, I'm expecting more from you.*

* * *

But that was all that was productive during the rest of the talk. All other ideas were rejected quickly, and soon the service for the dead students would be over, so eventually Mr. Havelna adjourned the meeting, and everyone went back to their own classes. Revan walked out of the classroom as soon as he could without seeming too suspect. He hadn't said anything anymore, not during the whole meeting, while the rest of the committee was discussing his future. Hdar kept getting involved in the discussion, and after the discussion had been going on for a bit, Revan allowed himself to tap out with his thoughts and think about Wilan. Somehow, him being Othercrystalled hurt even more for Revan, because Revan had never known. If they'd told each other, perhaps they could both have felt less alone.

After the whole discussion Mr. Havelna had emphasized again, "What we discuss here will remain between these four walls, don't tell anyone else." He'd taken an extra-long look at Hdar. Revan felt like Hdar wouldn't be invited to the next meeting.

When the meeting wrapped up, Mr. Havelna closed it off by saying, "Thank you all for coming to the meeting on such short notice. I know I'm expecting a lot from you. Perhaps I was expecting too much. I was simply hoping to hear you out, and you have all performed wonderfully."

"Revan!" Revan heard, and he turned around. Arana walked right behind him and gestured to him.

"I thought you wanted me to leave you alone," he said.

"I now want you to follow me," Arana responded curtly.

Ah, Revan thought. *Finally, Arana has thought of something I can do, some way to blackmail me. What would Arana expect me to do? Hopefully it won't be too terrible.* Revan already knew he would do it. Hdar's reactions had only confirmed that feeling. If it leaked that the Flow was picking Othercrystalled, then people like Revan would immediately be considered the source of all problems, and if everyone knew Revan was an Else...No better time for Arana to start blackmailing him than now.

Arana opened the door of an empty classroom. Almost everyone was still at the service downstairs, so a lot of classrooms were empty. "What do you want me to do?" Revan asked as soon as he walked into the classroom and Arana closed the door.

"Report to Mr. Havelna," Arana replied.

Okay, Revan hadn't expected *that*. "Or you'll do it for me?"

"It's fairly obvious the Flow is picking Othercrystalled. If you report to Mr. Havelna, he can at least keep an eye on you."

Revan had indeed considered it, but he hadn't been sure. Of course, it seemed like Mr. Havelna would support him. But Arana's demand came out of left field. "Or you'll do it for me," Revan repeated, but he was no longer asking. He crossed his arms. Arana had avoided his question, and that was enough of a response.

"What…" Arana said.

Oh, she had the chutzpah to seem surprised about it too. Well, as far as Revan was concerned, she deserved everything he was about to say. "I've been waiting for days until you start blackmailing me. I'm happy you finally found something that'll allow you to exercise your power."

"Blackmailing?" Arana asked, confused. It took her a while to realize what Revan meant. "Revan, I don't want to blackmail you, I *worry about you.*" Somehow that was even worse.

"Wait a minute," Revan said. He felt the heat on his face again, but this time it wasn't out of shyness or shame. "You've been avoiding me for days after you find out I'm Othercrystalled. You simply *scare* me because of your actions and keep me at arm's length. You even threaten that I should never talk to you again, or you'll tell other people. But now suddenly you're *worried* about me?! Where have those worries been the past few days?" Revan had to keep himself from shouting, lest the people in the hallway would hear him.

"I never threatened that I'd…" Arana started.

"I asked, what do I need to do, and you said, 'stay out of my way.'"

"I didn't know…didn't want to…" Arana stuttered.

"So, if I get this right," Revan added, "you're blackmailing me, but you're too hypocritical to actually call it blackmail, because you want to feel good about yourself. Come on, Arana."

"People of your kind are in danger!" Arana said.

"My *kind*," Revan said, eyebrows raised. "Now we're a *kind*."

"You know what I mean! You…"

"I know exactly what you mean," Revan said. "I read your dad's book. But apparently this isn't blackmail. Fine, I'm not reporting in then."

"Revan…"

"Please," Revan said. He left the room, slamming the door shut behind him. .

No, it wasn't very smart to talk like that to the person keeping his secret. But he'd be doomed either way, whether he told Mr. Havelna or Arana did.

"I didn't tell Gaveh," Arana shouted in the hallway. A couple students were talking on the other side—they looked up for a second, but carried on with their conversation.

"So you're going to do that too?" Revan asked.

"I didn't mean that, I..."

Revan didn't want to hear it anymore. He got in the elevator and the doors closed before Arana could join him. He was still trembling with anger.

* * *

"Everything okay?" Gaveh asked that night, in their bed.

"A classmate of mine just died and I can't go home," Revan stated bluntly. "How do you think I'm feeling?"

Gaveh shuffled to Revan's side of the bed and put an arm around him. Revan almost automatically shifted closer to Gaveh. He felt nice and warm. "Stupid question," Gaveh said. "Of course nothing's okay."

"And you are okay?"

"I'm more okay than you." Gaveh sighed. "What did the committee discuss?"

"I can't say," Revan said. "Sorry." He absolutely didn't want to lie to Gaveh.

"Oh," Gaveh said. "Shame." Then, after a short silence, he added, "because you're angry and I wondered why."

For a second Revan thought, *I could show Gaveh my calm crystal.* He refused to believe Gaveh would respond the same as Arana or Hdar. Not his very best friend and Koden. But then Revan thought about the plan Hdar had thought up. *If you know your best friend, partner or Koden is Othercrystalled, tell us and we'll keep track.* No. Even if Gaveh was trustworthy—and Revan still wasn't sure—Revan would be endangering himself.

"I think it's unfair," Revan said after a silence that was hopefully not so long it would be suspicious. "That someone like Wilan or Jastre could suddenly die. I don't get it. That makes me angry."

"I understand," Gaveh said. "Me too."

Somehow that was enough for Revan. "Thank you," he said, and Gaveh let go of him.

Chapter Ten

When Revan came down for breakfast the next day—another meal of dry bread—Javik was one of the first ones at the table. He looked tired, pale, but his expression was hard to judge. Gaveh wasn't there yet, as he was still getting ready. Javik looked up and if he'd seen Revan, his expression didn't change much. Yet Revan somehow felt the disappointment anyway.

Because of everything with the committee Revan had kind of forgotten Javik. He hadn't had any room to think of Wilan's death, or him not attending the service. But as soon as Javik looked away Revan knew he'd blown it. So he swallowed, gathered his courage, and walked to Javik. "How are you holding up?"

"It was a nice service," Javik said, avoiding Revan's gaze, instead looking at his plate with dry bread. "Lovely speeches." Javik avoided eye contact, which he did more often. It didn't have to mean that he was angry. But he had every right to be.

"You're not doing well," Revan said.

Javik shrugged. "Wilan used to talk about you, you know? 'Revan, such a nice guy, and he's smart too. We used to be such good friends. I'm so sad we drifted apart.'" His face remained neutral, but the words stung.

"I'm sorry," Revan said.

"One hour for him, that was all that he needed—that *I* needed. Where were you? Gaveh was there. I know you're a smart guy who loves studying, but there's no way that you loved studying so much you skipped the service for that." Javik still avoided eye contact, but he sounded more crestfallen and tired. Even now, he was mostly grieving.

"Mr. Havelna needed me," Revan said truthfully. "He sounded very urgent and asked me if I could miss the service."

Javik nodded briefly. "I'll tell Wilan when I see him again, that hanging out with our magic teacher was more important than your friendship."

Revan sighed. "Really, I'm sorry."

"Okay," Javik said, shrugging again. He licked his lips, then said, "He was my best friend. And lover. And Koden, once," he added, pronouncing Koden with a little disgust, as if he couldn't ever imagine having been a Koden with Wilan, "but we had too many romantic feelings for each other, so we just turned it into a relationship. Once we finished school we'd move together somewhere. And maybe we'd get kids, through a female friend, or something. Out of everyone at school, he understood me the best. And I knew everything about him." He swallowed, his lips trembling.

Did you know he was Othercrystalled? The question entered Revan's mind, but he kept it to himself. "I can imagine it hurts," Revan said. "And I'm sorry he died, and I wasn't at the service."

For the second time, Javik shrugged. "Whatever," he said, exhausted. "I have to keep going to classes, after all." He shook his head a couple times. Then he grabbed his bread, his expression still forlorn. "He's now one with the Flow again, and I have to make peace with that."

Revan felt a hand on his back and saw Gaveh standing there. Gaveh briefly looked at both Javik and Revan, seemingly asking, *everything okay?* Revan said, "We're missing Wilan. Do you want to join us? Then Javik will feel less alone."

"Actually..." Javik said, "if you don't mind, I'd rather be on my own." He finally looked up, first at Gaveh and then at Revan, and for a moment Revan thought he saw hatred in his eyes, but it disappeared just as quickly. Before Revan could reply, Javik stood up, carrying his plate, and walked to another spot at the table. Revan raised his eyebrows, Gaveh just shrugged. It was clear, Javik had no desire for contact, so Revan just grabbed his piece of bread. But once he had done that Gaveh said softly, "You'll have to apologize to him."

Revan sighed. "I did. He just walked away."

"Of course he did, you weren't at Wilan's service." He shrugged. "Maybe he'll come around. But honestly, I can't blame the guy."

Revan heard what Gaveh wasn't saying. Gaveh blamed him for missing the service too. "Sorry?" he asked. "But Mr. Havelna..."

"Has no respect for the fallen students if he's using their service," Gaveh said. Revan wanted to contradict that, but he bit his tongue as Gaveh's expression told Revan nothing he said would be enough.

So instead, he said, "What else do you want me to do? I just apologized; it wasn't enough. Do I need to apologize to *you*?"

Gaveh shook his head. "No," he said. "But maybe you should try again with Javik. When he's a bit more ready than now." He shrugged. "Let's eat our glorious meals," he said, the sarcasm dripping from his voice.

* * *

Once everyone was present eating, they expected Mrs. Garedna to give another speech, but she remained seated. Then, Mr. Havelna stood up from behind the dining table to take the place of the principal. That caused murmuring in the hall, which disappeared once he held up a hand. "Your last principal, Mrs. Dahena, still hasn't appeared, and I have reasons to suspect she won't be coming back either."

The murmuring came back. Mr. Havelna listened to it for a couple seconds. Then he raised his hand again and the murmuring got quieter, but never really disappeared. "We don't know what's going on, but we hope she's all right." Of course Mr. Havelna wouldn't tell the whole school—and least of all her wife, Mrs. Garedna—that he suspected their principal. "But the point remains that she disappeared and has't come back. In these difficult times we need a principal, so after a long discussion, the teachers made me a temporary one. I understand this is usually a moment of joy and peace with a whole ceremony, but we have no time for that. For now, I'll hold the morning speeches instead of Mrs. Garedna.

"I'll try my very hardest to resolve the food situation. We have enough to last us the following week, even if it's more bread than you're used to. After that, we're going to have to see. It might be that some of you have to skip meals. We are all doing our best to ensure that won't happen, but considering how this involves the Flow, I unfortunately have no certainties." Mr. Havelna fell quiet for a couple seconds to give his words more impact, and a grave silence passed over everyone in the eating hall. Nobody was looking forward to a food shortage, but it was to be expected. "I'll also try my very hardest," Mr. Havelna continued, "to find out why the magic stopped and why students died." Mr. Havelna sighed. The murmuring started to return, but it stopped the moment Mr. Havelna opened his mouth again. "Unfortunately, I have news regarding them. We probably know why the Flow targeted those two students. They were both Othercrystalled."

Mr. Havelna let his words land. Revan swallowed the lump in his throat. In the committee they had very clearly said they would *not* do this. Revan didn't want to look at the others in the hall in his shock, but he was too curious for their responses. He saw shocked faces, sad faces, but also a couple relieved and even happy faces. Revan saw Hdar, who was at the same table as Revan. She had a smile from ear to ear, fully relaxed. Revan's stomach churned. Next to her was Javik, who barely showed any reaction at all. Yes, he knew about Wilan being Othercrystalled.

"I understand this causes some mixed feelings," Mr. Havelna continued. "But I want to remind you that Othercrystalled are just people too, and they deserve to follow the same classes as everyone else."

That last sentence caused a stunned silence, almost as bad as if Mr. Havelna had admitted *he* was Othercrystalled. Of course Othercrystalled were just people, but they weren't allowed to be at school, they'd be too lazy for that, most people thought. Of course they weren't prosecuted anymore, but they were still kicked out of school if they were public about their crystals. Mr. Havelna explicitly saying they were welcome was more shocking than admitting Wilan and Jastre were Othercrystalled. Finally, murmuring started up again—Revan couldn't hear what was said, but judging by a few expressions it wasn't too positive. Mr. Havelna held up a hand to goad the students into silence; it worked, but only after a long while.

"I'm therefore asking," Mr. Havelna calmly proceeded, "all Othercrystalled to report to me. I'll keep your status a secret. We're going to try and protect you from the Flow. There might be a way!"

Othercrystalled were mistakes from the high and mighty Flow. To support Othercrystalled was to contradict the Flow's perfection. That's how Samillan wrote it, and everyone had learnt something similar—except for, apparently, Mr. Havelna. Revan started to feel reporting to him might be the right move. Because saying something like that, as the acting principal, to the crowd—that was a brave move. He wouldn't do that if he were a crystallist, right?

"I also would like to request you all to keep looking for clues. We're going to find something, I'm certain. We have nothing yet, but keep searching. We're counting on you all."

It was tradition that the first speech of every principal was met with applause. But it was dead quiet when Mr. Havelna walked away. *This is change*, Revan thought to himself. *Change is never welcomed the first time*. Yeah, Revan had to report in.

"Maybe we should tell Mr. Havelna that we saw Mrs. Dahena," Gaveh said softly in Revan's ear, startling Revan. Gaveh looked at him, questioning. "I mean, we have some important information. You saw."

"But you didn't want to tell anyone else..." Revan began.

"Yeah, that was then," Gaveh said. "But a lot has changed. Are you going to tell him?"

Revan sighed. Lying would get him nowhere. "Mr. Havelna already knows."

"Huh?"

"I told him, right before we went to Arana's."

Gaveh looked at Revan, confused. "Even though..." he stuttered. "We had agreed..."

"I know," Revan said. "But it seemed the right decision, so..." Revan didn't know how to finish his sentence. They just looked at each other for a few seconds.

Then Gaveh shook his head. "I need to be alone."

"Gaveh..."

"I heard enough," Gaveh said and walked away without saying anything, leaving Revan behind on his own. Once again, he had that look that meant Revan knew not to follow.

He looked at the table and his food, insecure about what to do. Should he go after Gaveh? Gaveh was clearly angry at him, and perhaps rightfully so. But it hurt. Gaveh was his buddy—Revan trusted him with anything except that one thing—someone who was always at his side.

Revan looked at Mr. Havelna again, who was back at the table for teachers. Then he let his gaze wander until it settled on Arana, who threw a very demanding look his way. It was clear what she wanted from him. *Report to him, Revan.*

So Arana hadn't gone on his behalf to Mr. Havelna. Apparently, she wasn't blackmailing him then. But still Revan saw, under her gaze, that hatred that had made her want nothing to do with him. She might try to hide it, but she didn't do so well enough. Revan felt the same hatred around himself. It *buzzed* through the whole hall, because the principal did something as ridiculous as protecting Othercrystalled.

If so many people hated him, and Gaveh might hate him too, and the Flow was actively trying to kill people like him...well, the Flow was never wrong, it was perfect. So then maybe the hatred was deserved.

If the Flow would come for Revan, he'd welcome it, he decided. If this was the way the Flow took out Othercrystalled, then that was okay. Revan wouldn't stop it, and neither would he try and look for some protection.

No, Revan would *not* report in. If only because it allowed him to apologize to his old friend Wilan.

Chapter Eleven

Revan stared at the ceiling, trying to find the right words to say to Gaveh. Mr. Havelna had become principal that morning. Revan knew that meant the end of the committee, because as a principal, Mr. Havelna wouldn't have time for them. Revan had tried to talk to him, but of course that wasn't possible. Gaveh hadn't said a word to him all day, not even when they had to comb through books in the library. Javik hadn't said anything to him either, but that was no surprise. Javik didn't talk to anyone. And now it was evening, they were about to sleep, and Revan wanted to break the silence, but he didn't know how. He decided to just keep it simple.

"Gaveh?" Gaveh didn't respond. Revan briefly thought Gaveh was already asleep as he was usually out cold quickly, but no, Revan could tell from his breathing he was still awake. Something had been keeping him up. "Gaveh?" he just asked again, not looking away from the ceiling. Gaveh grumbled something. So yes—he was awake. "We need to talk."

"So talk," Gaveh grumbled again.

"You know what I mean," Revan said. He gathered his courage and then said, "I'm sorry I told Mr. Havelna before."

It was quiet for a couple seconds and just before Revan said Gaveh's name again Gaveh said, "That's not it."

"...Oh?" Revan tried.

"It's that you were right."

The bed shook—Gaveh turned around. Revan took a deep breath and finally looked away from the ceiling. Gaveh looked at him, angrily. "What do you mean?" Revan hesitated.

"Well," Gaveh said. "I told you not to tell anyone else. It's obvious now Mrs. Dahena was to blame, because she's now disappeared, and that means my advice was worth nothing. Mr. Havelna, in the meanwhile, invites you to his beautiful committee. You've also gotten the best grades for a while. In other words—the whole of Samillan College is at your feet. And me? Oh, I'm just some random dude who happens to have sex with the Great Hero. I'm not important. And that makes it worse when I give you the wrong advice and tell you not to tell anyone else, because I'm the one who screwed up."

Revan hadn't seen that coming. He hesitated, his mouth open, trying desperately to find the right words. "But we got there because you wanted to have sex there," he tried. He didn't know what he'd wanted to say with that.

"Yeah, I got there because of dumb luck. You got there because you did the right thing."

"You're jealous," Revan said. Gaveh kept silent for a long while, which was as good as a yes. A couple feelings went through Revan. He partially understood, because Revan did get higher grades and was a very good student—that part wanted to reply with, "you're also great in your own way." The other part was anger, and anger won. "You think I'm not struggling? I can't see my parents anymore. I can't see my sister anymore. There's no-one in this entire college I can trust. And students are dying and..."

"Oh, so not me either," Gaveh replied softly.

"...What?"

"You can't trust me either," Gaveh said. "I'm not good enough for you. Good to know."

"It's not easy for me either," Revan said. "The whole world's on fire, and you're mad about *this*?!"

"Yes!" Gaveh replied softly. "Because everything's easy for you here! You can expect a wonderful future with all your good grades and..."

"Nothing's easy for me at the..." Revan had wanted to say more, and he would probably have shouted it so loudly the people in the bedroom next to them would be woken up, but Revan stopped in the middle of his sentence. He felt an incredible need to make a gate.

Wilan and Jastre had died once they'd made that gate and Revan had suspected more Othercrystalled would follow in the same way. He had wondered how it had felt for Wilan and Jastre to make that gate. Now he knew. The urge to make a gate was *irresistible*. There was nothing more important in the whole wide world than Revan making a gate right now, to a different place in the world. He felt the pressure through his whole body but in particular his right arm, which he normally used to make gates. It even started to make the first move, no matter how hard Revan resisted. Even if he would die in the process, Revan *had* to make that gate—and as he had already decided he could die because he was Othercrystalled, he decided to welcome it.

"Revan?" Gaveh said.

"Gaveh," Revan managed to say. Because he'd been arguing with Gaveh, he just remembered. "I'm sorry. Stay safe, without me, and tell my family I love them." The moment had arrived. Revan braced himself. He'd welcome his death.

"What do you mean..." Gaveh said, shocked. Revan made a gate. It happened very easily—how had this ever been impossible? It was even easier than normal. Revan made the movement with his hand, and a gate to another place appeared. He didn't even have to visualize his destination, which normally took the most effort. The compulsion immediately went away, its goal accomplished.

Gaveh screamed, his jaw dropped as he looked at both Revan and the gate. Revan saw it through the light of the gate. Revan closed his eyes, awaiting his death.

Gaveh embraced Revan tightly, squeezing him firmly. "No," he said. "Not you, not now, not here..." His hug was so firm it almost felt like strangling. Revan felt tears run down his face and understood vaguely that Gaveh would be heartbroken.

They remained lying like that. After a while, Revan thought, *I should be dead now, right?* After a bit longer Revan said, unintentionally dryly, "I think I'm still alive." Gaveh immediately let him go and looked at him, aghast. Revan put his hand on his chest, just to be safe, but his heart was still beating. "I'm still alive," he confirmed.

"You're still alive?" Gaveh repeated. "You..." he barely seemed to get it. "You can make a gate?"

"Yes," Revan said. "But..." Keeping a gate open took energy and Revan's was running out. It had been a long day. "There's a gate."

Gaveh kissed him, intensely relieved. Revan briefly kissed him back, but then let him go. Gaveh was still on top of him in that embrace. "I'm sorry, Gaveh," Revan said. "I would love to talk this out with you. But there's a gate in the middle of the room and I want to go through."

Gaveh held on to him, still befuddled. "You were so certain you would die..." he said. "So you are..." Revan couldn't respond. He couldn't go through that again, losing another great friend because he was who he was. But he couldn't deny it either. "That's why you kept your shirt on," Gaveh said. "Tied at the hem and everything. You're just like Wilan."

"Gaveh," Revan said. "I *have* to go." He shoved Gaveh off him and stood up, looking for answers. Normally when you made a gate you knew where it was headed—but Revan had no idea and felt compelled to walk through. Gaveh shouted something as he was leaving, but Revan wasn't listening. He walked to the gate and went through.

He didn't recognize the island. He'd never been there before. Normally you knew exactly where your gate would go. You kept the destination in your head, and you created the gate. The better you kept the destination in your mind, the better the gate was—and the bigger you could make it. Depending on the distance it was important to visualize the destination more and more precisely. But Revan hadn't visualized anything. He just had to make a gate, like back when he was a first year and only learning. Back then you had to focus on the movement first and making the gate before you started to visualize. That kind of gate didn't go anywhere, but this one did.

The island was clearly a bit further to the east because it was still dusk there, instead of the complete darkness that was now at the college. In the distance Revan saw a quickly constructed building. The remaining light of the sun was strong enough that Revan recognized it as a house, but clearly a house made by somebody who had materials lying around and had strung them together haphazardly. It was an abandoned island. Revan realized he recognized it. He'd seen it the day he'd gone with Gaveh to the uppermost floor. But something like that made no sense—space was incredibly necessary if islands were the only places to live. Why would somebody leave an island abandoned?

An arrow flew through the sky, just past Revan's ear. Revan dove away and looked around in shock for where the arrow came from. There he found a woman with gray hair, her face above a cocked and loaded crossbow. Despite her hair color, she looked relatively young. Revan wasn't welcome here; he shouldn't be here on his own. And despite having been ready to die before, Revan wouldn't speed the process up now.

Revan immediately made a gate back to the college. Normally visualizing a specific place was hard because visualizing it had to be as realistic as possible, but making a gate back to his bedroom was, once again, very easy and he didn't have to visualize anything. Revan made the gate and ran through it without looking over his shoulder. The woman didn't fire another arrow.

Gaveh was still on the bed, looking gobsmacked. He gasped for breath as soon as Revan appeared. "Revan?" he said.

Revan shook his head. "I have to leave *now*. This is important."

He ran to the bedroom door when he realized what he'd discussed with Gaveh. He turned around just before he was gone and said to Gaveh, "And we'll talk this out later. I'm sorry."

So Gaveh knew and that wasn't great, and Revan would've done anything he could to reverse that. But he couldn't, and right now, there were more important matters than whether or not Gaveh was still his friend. Revan shut the door behind him and ran to Mr. Havelna's room.

Chapter Twelve

Revan pounded on the door of Mr. Havelna's bedroom, hoping he hadn't changed bedrooms, now he was in charge of all Samillan College. The principal had a different room, but so far Mr. Havelna had neglected to follow all ceremonies in this time of crisis, and in his own words, "People have other things on their mind than who's in charge." The principal's room was always strictly off-limits to students, so if Mr. Havelna had moved there Revan could forget about this whole plan.

But to his relief the bedroom door opened, and Mr. Havelna appeared. Not yet in his pajamas, apparently he hadn't gone to bed yet. Revan did wear his, but that didn't matter.

"Revan?" the principal said. "It's nighttime, go to…"

"I made a gate," Revan replied. His words tumbled over each other. "And I'm still alive."

Mr. Havelna fell silent. Revan was panting, to his own surprise. Mr. Havelna quickly looked over Revan's shoulder. "Come in." As soon as he was in, the principal asked, "You made a *gate*?"

Revan nodded. "It's impossible," he said. Revan knew he was talking too fast, but he couldn't stop. His heart was pounding. "I know, and I thought I was dying, but…"

"Are you Othercrystalled?"

"No," Revan lied before he could think about it—and he didn't have the guts to change his answer.

"You made a gate and you're still alive."

"Yes, to an island," Revan said. "An abandoned island, very weird, without any buildings except for an abandoned house, and it was dark, so I couldn't see a lot and I'm still alive and what happens now and why me and not Wilan or Jastre or…"

"Revan," Mr. Havelna said, and he took a hold of Revan's shoulder. "Slow down. Do you need a drink?"

"Why me?" Revan asked. "Why not Wilan or Jastre?"

"Slow down," Mr. Havelna repeated. "I'm going to get you a glass of water. I'll be right back. This will work out." He let go of Revan, about to leave the room.

"No," Revan said, suddenly realizing something important. "There was someone there, on that island. A woman with grey hair but who didn't look very old. She shot at me with a crossbow when she saw me. Maybe she's dangerous. Maybe she's the reason why this happened."

Mr. Havelna had the doorknob in his hand but froze. He turned around slowly. "A woman with…"

"…Grey hair who didn't look very old. She wore wealthy-looking clothes, like she had a lit-up central crystal. I couldn't quite tell, because it was dusk, and…"

Mr. Havelna let go of the doorknob. "Erchina?" he asked. Revan knew who she was—the preceding principal, but she'd left before Revan had started at the college. On the highest hallway, near the principal's room, there were portraits of all preceding principals—but Erchina's portrait had never hung there. As far as Revan had heard, she was let go in full honors, supposedly having said that she'd had enough of the job. Mrs. Dahena had taken over from her.

Revan wasn't sure if he heard right, and it sounded like the principal's voice was trembling. He hadn't said "Mrs. Erchina"—"Mr." or "Mrs." was an honorific and dropping it made Mr. Havelna sound disdainful.

"Could be," Revan said. "I don't know. I didn't know her."

Mr. Havelna took the doorknob back in his hand. "Revan, I'm going to get you a glass of water, and we'll talk about this then." He left the room. Revan barely believed what he was hearing, because this time he was sure there had been a tremble in the principal's voice.

* * *

The principal eventually returned with two glasses of water, once Revan had calmed down a little. But he was still tense—as soon as he saw Mr. Havelna he said, "Erchina?"

Despite not knowing why Mr. Havelna had said her name in such a disdainful way, Revan dropped the "Mrs." too.

Mr. Havelna sighed and handed Revan the glass of water. "What else did you see?" he asked. He sat on the chair and Revan on his, the way they used to.

"Not a lot," Revan said. "I was in bed with my Koden, we had a fight, and then suddenly I felt the irresistible urge to make a gate." He briefly explained what he'd felt and seen. Mr. Havelna listened to it all while nodding, without saying a word.

Once Revan was done, Mr. Havelna said, "It sounds like Erchina."

"But she'd quit, right?"

Mr. Havelna nodded. "And we thought she was dead. Once she left, we never heard of her again."

"Is it possible she's the one behind this all?"

Mr. Havelna sighed and was quiet, seemingly hesitating. Then he said, "What I'm going to tell you has to remain a secret at all costs. You can't tell anyone, not even your Koden. Understood?"

Briefly Gaveh's words wandered through Revan's mind. About Revan always being right and always being in the foreground. Revan briefly thought, *I want to be able to tell Gaveh.* But no. This was the principal, Revan wouldn't say no to him. "I'm listening."

"Erchina didn't leave voluntarily," Mr. Havelna began. "We forced her to step down because of corruption."

"Corruption?"

Mr. Havelna nodded. "She'd been principal for a couple years when she suddenly started firing teachers. You have to understand, a couple teachers are in the council, those teachers decide what the future of the college will be—they have a bit more power than the others. The principal isn't the only one in charge, but we have dozens of teachers, so not everyone's votes can weigh equally."

"I know," Revan said.

"Erchina forced the whole council to quit, and she replaced them with people she knew, that she could bribe.

This way she could push through plans that benefited her. She also tried to control who was accepted to the college. Only pupils she liked would be allowed to enter the college."

"Scandalous," Revan said. Everyone was accepted to the college—it was one of the ground rules. It wasn't always followed in practice, and it didn't apply to any Othercrystalled, but this was the theory.

Mr. Havelna sighed. "You can guess what kind of pupils she liked the best." Revan's heart sunk. *People with the right crystal.* A bit further than just Othercrystalled—they were hated, but if you had, for example, a lit-up force crystal, you were still welcome at Samillan College. You didn't adhere to society's rules either. It was tolerated and even accepted far more, but some people still felt everyone should stick to their own crystal. You weren't Othercrystalled if you didn't stick to the roles that belonged to your lit-up crystal, but it was a little harder compared to having the "right crystal" lit up. "We were busy taking the power away from her when it turned out she'd repeatedly kept money for her own benefit. Once that was discovered, she *had* to step down. We had no other choice than to keep it a secret to prevent ourselves from losing face. She never got in touch again. Once she'd stepped down, she disappeared and was impossible to find. Which is why we assumed she had died."

"Instead, she's on a secret island," Revan concluded. "Where nobody found her."

"Exactly," Mr. Havelna sighed. "And that might not be strange. Erchina is a very capable magician who can create gates that cross a very short distance." He pointed to the other side of the room. "Erchina loved to deceive you by making a gate to the other side of the room, and then suddenly stand behind you. She also used her strong affinity with gates to listen in to people, as you can hear everything that people say at the place you made your gate." Mr. Havelna shook his head. "As far as we know I was the only other person capable of such short-distance gates."

Revan knew what Mr. Havelna's next assumption would be. "And if anyone could've found the Flow..." Mr. Havelna nodded, still holding that glass of water. His hand was trembling, but barely noticeable. "But does she hate Othercrystalled *so much* that she wants to kill them all?" Revan was too curious; he couldn't hold back now.

"She hates Othercrystalled so much that, when her own daughter turned out to be Othercrystalled, she killed her herself."

"What?" Revan said, shocked.

Mr. Havelna nodded. "She was very close with her only daughter, who was even regularly allowed into the principal's room. She had been talking to her daughter in that room when suddenly a second crystal, her calm crystal, lit up. Erchina responded by making a gate appear, to a place we don't know. There she dumped her daughter and let her starve, then claimed to no longer have any kids. She told me that herself." Revan bit back the urge to touch his own calm crystal. He couldn't say another word. "Now you understand why she's so dangerous. She's very capable and unpredictable, after killing her own daughter—that might have made her unstable. She *hates* Othercrystalled. If there's anyone capable of manipulating the Flow to make their lives worse..."

"But why isn't she here yet? If she wants to kill, why won't she come herself?"

"I don't know," Mr. Havelna said. "Because she can't? Because maybe Mrs. Dahena manipulated the Flow at her request? Because she disappeared as well."

"So, she's also in on it," Revan said.

"It's all speculation," Mr. Havelna replied. "I'll admit to you honestly I didn't think Mrs. Dahena would do such a thing, but then she used magic."

"Then the question is, why doesn't Mrs. Dahena kill us all? Why did she run away?"

"Probably," Mr. Havelna sighed, "because the Flow has blocked her in some way? The Flow is a reflection of all our wants and needs, it can't be manipulated easily."

"But we can't get to Mrs. Dahena, and we can get to Erchina," Revan said. He gasped when he realized what the next step would be. "So we have to go to her. Confront her, stop her, question her..."

"Yes," Mr. Havelna said. "With a couple extra people. If she's still as capable as she used to be, I wouldn't want to confront Erchina on my own, or even with the two of us. If we're with ten, we'll stand a chance to capture her. She should be past fifty by now, about as old as I am, but if I recall she was always very fit."

"But why *me*?" Revan said.

"The Flow has a will of its own," Mr. Havelna said, "and picked you. Perhaps because you have a good heart. Perhaps it fought the will of Erchina, or Mrs. Dahena."

"But..."

"You're capable too. You're a good magician and very intelligent. The Flow thinks you can handle her. Can you summon another one of those gates?"

Revan nodded. He already started to make the gesture—but the principal stopped him. "I believe you," he said. "Let's not take any other risks. I'll talk to the right people tomorrow, and once we gather everyone, we'll go to Erchina. We'll interrogate her and end this nightmare. I'll meet you in the eating hall downstairs tomorrow afternoon. All right?"

"All right," Revan said.

It was quiet for a couple seconds. Revan wanted to leave, but then Mr. Havelna held up a hand to stop him and said, "What do you make of Othercrystalled, Revan?"

The question seemed to come out of nowhere and Revan had to ponder before saying, "Um...they're also just people?"

"Lazy people, like Samillan said?"

Revan hesitated. "I don't know," he finally said. "Maybe?" *Maybe I'm lazy.*

Mr. Havelna sighed. "Thanks. Sometimes I don't know what to do. We'll see. Get some sleep."

"Thanks," Revan said. He lingered for a couple seconds. It would be so easy, confess to Mr. Havelna that he was Othercrystalled too, that maybe they could keep him safe somehow. Mr. Havelna would take him under his wing and make sure nothing would happen to Revan.

But what could Mr. Havelna do, in the end? He was powerless against the Flow. Even then, Revan could tell the truth. But no—he'd already blurted out that he wasn't an Othercrystalled. To walk it back was too complicated for now, and it wouldn't change a single thing anyway.

So after those few seconds, Revan walked away, his head full of questions.

* * *

A lot went through Revan's mind as he took the elevator. He could use magic. All right, he couldn't go home, he could only go to that island—but he *could use magic.* He *was still alive*, even as he'd been ready for death. And Gaveh knew he was Othercrystalled.

Suddenly, Revan felt ten pounds heavier. The elevator was back on his bedroom's floor, and he struggled to lift his feet. So their friendship and Kodenship was over. Who'd want to have sex with a dirty *Else*? Gaveh had probably already left, telling everyone at school that the brilliant Revan, one of the best students of his year, was Othercrystalled. Revan was a goner. Could he maybe weasel out of it? Go back to Mr. Havelna and ask if he could have another Koden? Or at least another bedroom? Switching Kodens required a medical inspection to prevent transmitting diseases between Kodens, but Revan would just undergo that then. He could do that while leaving his shirt on, as the medical inspection would just focus on his sexual organs.

But no, he couldn't do that to his very best friend. So, Revan opened the door of his bedroom, expecting humiliation. Gaveh was on the bed, his legs crossed, still above the sheets but fully nude. The weak green light of his skill crystal lit the room a little. "Welcome back," Gaveh said in an inscrutable voice.

"Hey," Revan said. He looked away, at the floor, ashamed.

"So," Gaveh said. "You're Othercrystalled." No questions about what Revan had just discussed with the principal. No questions about the gate. No, there were more pressing things to Gaveh.

"Unfortunately, yes. What are you going to do about it?"

"*Do* about it?" Gaveh asked. "Revan, what could I do?"

"Well," Revan said, looking up again. Gaveh seemed compassionate, but Revan was cautious. "I'm lazy because my crystals get up to weird stuff, Samillan wrote it himself. It's my fault that..."

Gaveh stood up and before Revan could say anything else Gaveh embraced Revan. "I'm sorry," he said in Revan's ear. "It must be so hard for you to hear all of that. I shouldn't have claimed you had it easy."

Revan needed a couple seconds to understand Gaveh's reaction. "You mean...you...accept me?"

"Of course, you idiot," Gaveh said, squeezing Revan closer to him. "I don't think the crystals mean as much as we think. And I think Samillan was just a human being who was wrong sometimes."

Revan still had trouble with what Gaveh was saying. "Just a human being," he repeated, still in shock. So many people claimed Samillan was much more than that. Gaveh had said similar things before, but it still stunned Revan to hear them every time.

"Yes," Gaveh said. "That's what us Marans say, at least. Arana knows?"

"Yes," Revan said, still baffled. "And her reaction..."

"I can guess it," Gaveh laughed joylessly.

Revan gathered his thoughts—and realized Gaveh had fully accepted him. He could only respond to that in one way—he finally embraced Gaveh back, sighing deeply, feeling relieved and ready to cry. They embraced for a while, until Gaveh let go. "Can I ask you something?"

"Of course," Revan said.

"When we're having sex, can you keep your shirt off?"

Revan hesitated, but ultimately nodded. "As long as no-one else sees."

"Good," Gaveh said, and an awkward silence fell. But then, as if he'd just gotten the idea, Gaveh asked anyway, "Can I see them now?"

"My crystals?" Revan asked.

Gaveh nodded. "If you want," he quickly said. "Unless you want to wait for marriage."

A voice inside Revan said, *This is all fake, he'll turn against you once he sees.* Another voice said, *Mr. Havelna said he'd ask the Kodens. You can still go back. You can't if you take off your shirt now.* But Revan didn't listen to either voice. He'd lied to Gaveh for so long, Gaveh accepting him now without a doubt meant he was entitled to the truth. Revan untied the knot at the end of the rope in the hem of his shirt, as he sat down at the edge of the bed. He took a couple deep breaths. Gaveh didn't say anything, he just waited.

Revan was going to show someone else his crystals. Not by accident, but fully voluntarily. That wasn't easy.

"You don't need to," Gaveh said when the silence had lasted too long, but Revan ignored him.

He swallowed one more time, gathered his courage and took off his shirt. The faint green light lit up the room a smidge, but the tape blocked his other crystal. Revan's hand shook as he took off the tape, but there the red light of his calm crystal appeared. Revan had to pull twice to take off all the tape, but then it was off, and the very faint light in the room became a little more orange. Revan thought it was an ugly color, but Gaveh visibly disagreed. He looked at Revan's crystals, fascinated.

"Can I ask you one more thing?" Gaveh asked softly.

"All right then," Revan responded in the same volume.

"It's weird, but...can I touch them?" Revan nodded. Gaveh touched Revan's skill crystal very carefully, with his index finger, then across from that his calm crystal. "Beautiful," he said. He looked Revan in the eyes and smiled. Revan looked back and also smiled.

They had slept with each other often—sometimes even multiple times a day—but they'd never been as intimate as now. And as Gaveh touched Revan's calm crystal with a second finger Revan thought, *Arana, the girl I had a crush on, had a completely different reaction.* Gaveh was his Koden, his buddy, his best friend—but despite all that, suddenly Javik and Wilan went through his mind. They had been Kodens at first, but then had turned the relationship into a romantic one because there were too many feelings between them. As Revan maintained eye contact with his own Koden, that story went through his mind again, together with the thought, *Perhaps I was going after the wrong person.*

The thought was unexpectedly uncomfortable. Possibly because Gaveh might not feel the same way about him.

Chapter Thirteen

The next morning, one of the teachers knocked loudly on the door, doing their wake-up service rounds. Revan jolted awake, as usual. The first thing he did when he had opened his eyes was put tape on his calm crystal.

"Do you have to?" Gaveh asked drowsily, rubbing his temples.

"I don't want to get caught," Revan replied without looking up. "Particularly not now. Not everyone's as accepting as you."

Gaveh sighed and mumbled something Revan couldn't hear, then got out of bed. He took off his pajamas and grabbed his clothes, thrown over a chair. "Do your parents know?"

"Yes, and so does Fenna," Revan replied as he inspected the tape. Unfortunately, he'd been careless, and a little bit of light still leaked through. Revan sighed, ripped the tape off, and reattached it to the crystal. The skin around the crystal had hurt when Revan had begun doing this, but by now he'd done it so often he didn't feel a thing.

"That's why you're so eager to go home."

"Yeah," Revan said. Now the tape was properly on his crystal. Revan put on his shirt and tied it at the hem again, then put on his pants. Just in the nick of time, because suddenly the door flew open. Revan jolted up and looked straight into Hdar's eyes, who had walked into his bedroom unannounced. "Good morning," she said and smiled at him.

"How do you know I'm sleeping here?" Revan asked, startled.

"From back when we both went to Mr. Havelna." Hdar smiled, ear to ear.

"Most people knock," Gaveh said angrily. Revan was grateful to him. "That's the polite way."

"Sorry," Hdar said, smiling again. "I just wanted to tell you another Else has been found."

Revan gasped. "...What?"

Hdar's smile transformed into a grin that showed her white teeth. "Fifteen years old, Dajanda, had three crystals that were lit up. She didn't have a Koden yet, so they found her this morning. The Flow is doing its job, Revan, whether you like it or not."

"And you're telling him this because?" Gaveh said.

"Because I want to let him know things are changing, and it's best to be on the right side of history. See you later, Revan." With that remark, Hdar closed the bedroom door again.

Revan could only stare at the door. Gaveh put a hand on his back. "Oh, Flow," he said.

Revan bit his lower lip and said, "Tonight we'll solve it all."

"I'm glad you're still here," Gaveh said. "What's happening tonight?"

Revan shook his head. He wanted to go to Mr. Havelna immediately, but he suppressed that feeling. He'd agreed with the principal on this, he was going to stick to it. And yet, his mind raced. If Revan had immediately gone to Erchina, maybe it would've ended differently...maybe Dajanda would still...

No, they'd solve it tonight. Until then Revan couldn't think that way. He'd do that later. "Doesn't matter," he said. "Let's go to class."

* * *

The day went by incredibly slowly. Whatever Hdar had meant by her jibe, Revan had thankfully seen little of it. Rhetorics, History, Culture and Magic were his classes that day, and that meant by the end of the day he could scour through the library again, looking for answers. They were working on the same bookshelves, and as they still didn't have any answers, Revan was losing his courage. In the meantime, he continued to stay as far away as he could from people who said all Othercrystalled should die. Javik continued not to look at him, and during magic classes when they were all going through books in the library, Javik stayed far away from him. Though he might have been staying far away from everyone; Revan heard the word *Elselover* being thrown at him by students who walked by.

Hopefully tonight everything would go right. That thought got Revan through the day, and he waited in the eating hall once he could. There weren't a lot of people. Dinner hadn't been served yet, that would only come in about an hour for the youngest pupils.

"What are you going to do?" Gaveh said softly. He sat next to Revan with the excuse he didn't have anything better to do anyway. Revan knew what was actually going on. Gaveh was very curious about Revan being Othercrystalled and wanted to ask him all kinds of questions. And he was curious, too, about what would happen tonight.

"Mr. Havelna's going to join me," Revan replied, "when I make a gate to the spot where the gate led to last time. Hopefully the principal has a whole slew of people along with him."

"Why?"

Unfortunately, Gaveh remained curious, which meant Revan needed time to think about what he could best say. "The gate leads to the solution, to the one who caused all this. We're going to solve that now. Then we'll all get our magic back and everything will go the way it's supposed to. I hope." Revan had wanted to tell Gaveh, but Mr. Havelna so far had insisted on keeping Gaveh out of the loop. Revan understood why; the fewer people who knew, the less likely it would leak. As much as Revan trusted Gaveh, he never wanted to go against the principal's wishes.

"Good," Gaveh said. "I hope you're right. And you can do that?"

"Not on my own," Revan said, "but I won't be."

"Great," Gaveh said, and said something else too, but Revan didn't hear because Arana had entered the eating hall, tears in her eyes.

As soon as she was there, she saw Revan and Gaveh. Gaveh hadn't noticed her, but she made eye contact with Revan for a couple seconds. Arana seemed surprised he was there, but also very emotional. About Dajanda? No, that couldn't be, she was only an Else after all.

Gaveh took Revan's hand and squeezed it, seemingly still not knowing what was going on. Revan only had eyes for Arana. Just for a second, while they locked eyes, everything was forgotten, and Revan very briefly allowed himself the fantasy again of being with her, kissing her, and just talking to her like they cared about each other. *Despite everything, she's still absolutely beautiful.* But then the moment was gone. Arana sighed and looked at the floor, clearly doubting where to go. Finally, she turned around and walked out of the eating hall, slumping.

"Yeah," Gaveh said, shifting Revan's attention back to him, "she knows. She wasn't like this before." He'd finally caught on.

"Do you see why I didn't want to tell you?"

"Completely," Gaveh responded. "Even though Arana seemed to be such a good match for you. I'm sorry for you." He hadn't let go of Revan's hand. Revan didn't know if he wanted him to.

"Ah, well," Revan said, feeling funny on the inside. He hadn't forgotten his thought yesterday and hated himself a little for it. He had no romantic feelings for Gaveh, they were just Kodens. Right? "At least we can keep having sex," he added. He didn't want to stop that either; sex with Gaveh felt good, something that was part of their friendship. Of course, that had to stop if Revan started something with Arana. That thought, since their moment yesterday, suddenly made him feel all kinds of weird, conflicting feelings on the inside.

* * *

Even with Gaveh keeping Revan company, it still took way too long before the balding, friendly head of Mr. Havelna appeared. Revan jumped up as soon as he appeared in the doorway. "Revan! I heard about Dajanda—I'm so sorry to hear that!"

"Now," Revan said. "We're going now, right?"

Mr. Havelna sighed. He walked closer to Revan, until they were enough within earshot that they could speak softly. He threw Gaveh a strict look, then looked at Revan. "You didn't tell him?" he asked.

"Nothing secret," Revan said. "I needed some company. He can't know, right?"

"Sorry, but that doesn't seem wise," Mr. Havelna said. "I don't know if he'll tell other people. I trust you, but I'd rather keep this information away from the students."

Gaveh sat close to him, Revan took his hand and squeezed it. "I hate sending you away," he told Gaveh, "but..."

"I get it," Gaveh sighed. "Good luck." He shrugged, stood up and walked away.

"We can go," Revan said once again to Mr. Havelna once his best friend was gone. "Right? Where are all the others?"

"They're not coming," Mr. Havelna said.

Revan growled. "Because? It's not enough to prevent the death of more Othercrystalled and having the magic return?"

"It is," Mr. Havelna said. "But not today. Erchina's got access to the Flow. She can cut you off at any moment."

"...So?"

"So you might make a gate there, then find yourself unable to return. We don't know. And then you're trapped."

"That's worth the risk," Revan said.

"The teachers are voting right now on who can join you. Tomorrow we'll have a task force ready, with teachers willing to join you and willing to get trapped, if the situation arises. Then we'll be all equipped."

Revan didn't hear what else the principal said. Mr. Havelna wanted to wait one more day. In the meanwhile, somebody else could die, another Othercrystalled he could've saved. Another person dying, another family that would never talk to their Othercrystalled child...but Revan would have to live with the knowledge he could've done something if only he had talked. Erchina was the one behind all this, she was the one who had manipulated the Flow, and they couldn't afford letting the situation continue a moment longer.

"No," he said softly. "Tomorrow's too late." His own words startled him.

Mr. Havelna was apparently startled too. "Excuse me?"

"Someone else will die," Revan said. "We have to do it today. We have to do it now." His legs were shaking. He knew Mr. Havelna could punish him for insubordination easily, as this kind of behavior wasn't tolerated—even if they knew each other that well. Students didn't disagree with the principal.

"Revan, if you don't make it, or if we both don't make it…"

On the inside Revan screamed to himself, *Shut up, you're sticking out like a sore thumb!* But he ignored that feeling. "If things start to look dicey, I'll have us both out of there before anything happens."

"Unless Erchina cuts you off."

"So far, I've felt it when I gain access. If I'm cut off, I can make a gate before things get that far. I can feel that. Or you shout at me the moment Erchina disappears through a gate of her own, and I'll make a new gate as quickly as possible."

"Okay," Mr. Havelna said, "but even then, we don't know what she's capable of. She could get violent or have manipulated the Flow into getting some powers herself. I'm just worried the college will lose another principal. I have to think of all the students, Revan. Not just the Othercrystalled ones."

"I will protect you," Revan said. It sounded laughable, Revan knew. Mr. Havelna was a far more capable magician than Revan could ever dream of being. Plus, he was an adult, and Revan was just a scrawny, insecure eighteen-year-old. But in Revan's mind, there was no version of this conversation where they wouldn't go. "We will be out of there the moment anything is in danger. We have to do it or someone else dies."

"You can't protect me, Revan," Mr. Havelna said. "I have to confront her, preferably together with other teachers. I don't want you there. Whatever happens, I can't afford to put you in danger. *I* will protect *you.*"

Revan frowned. "Why am I more important than the principal?"

"Because right now, you're the only person in the college who's capable of making a gate," Mr. Havelna shot back. "Whatever the outcome, you might very well be our way out of this. But Revan, you *can't*…"

"Or I'll go myself," Revan said, now properly feeling chills. "I can make a gate. You can't stop me. I'll confront her myself. It is that or losing yet another Othercrystalled."

Mr. Havelna's expression contorted briefly into fury and anger, but it disappeared just as quickly. "You can't do that."

"I can. Leave me to go to her myself or join me. I can't wait another day."

Mr. Havelna stared at him for a couple seconds, then he swallowed. "All right then," he said reluctantly. "You may have a point. Maybe the Flow is trying to tell us something, and we ought to listen," he said, sounding less than eager about it. Revan felt weak in the knees. He'd just talked back to the principal—and had managed to convince him too.

* * *

Revan was back with Mr. Havelna in his original room, apparently still not having moved to the principal's room. "The rules, then," Mr. Havelna began. "You're making a gate. We're both going through there. The moment we're through, I go to her. You're staying put. Hide, if you need to. I don't know what Erchina will do. She might use magic against us. Now normally magic means making gates and nothing else, but Erchina might have changed the rules by manipulating the Flow. We don't know, and so, we can't take the risk.

"Do not attack her, do not follow me, do not engage in conversation. We're both very valuable to the college, but you might be more valuable than me." Revan nodded, feeling the tension build inside of himself. "The *moment* you feel anything change in your magic, you make a gate as fast as possible and hop through. Don't worry about me. Okay?" Revan nodded again. "Last time you went through, you made a gate back to your bedroom, right?" Revan nodded. "We don't know the rules here, but I can imagine your bedroom is the only other place you can make a gate to. I'm hoping your Koden won't be there."

"He'll probably be hanging out with some other people," Revan said. "He usually does that at this hour."

"Good. You'll make the gate when I give you the signal. All right?" Revan nodded again. "Then go ahead." In the middle of the room Revan made a gate appear, and Mr. Havelna and Revan walked through it.

It was day, so Revan could take in the mysterious island. He'd been right; there were no skyscrapers anywhere, just hills and even some lakes of water. Nature everywhere. And right in front of him was a small house that looked like it had been constructed quickly. Revan expected another crossbow bolt to be launched at him—but Erchina wasn't ready yet. Through the windows, he saw someone move and got a quick glimpse of their face. A woman with grey hair, but still fit.

"Erchina!" Mr. Havelna commanded. "We need to talk!" He stormed towards her.

Erchina shouted something Revan couldn't hear, turned around and ran. Revan was going to stick to their agreement no matter how much he wanted to help, which meant staying put. He looked around and saw he could hide under one of the windows of the house—which was made out of some brown material Revan didn't recognize—and he could maybe hide in one of those lakes of water but he didn't know how to swim. There weren't many hiding places. There usually weren't many outside. Revan didn't dare go in.

He ran to the window and crouched under it, waiting, as he heard shouting and noise from the inside. Revan hoped and prayed Mr. Havelna would be safe, but he was second-guessing himself. Had coming here been a good idea in the first place? Revan could only wait until the principal returned and he'd captured Erchina. Just a few minutes and it'd be over, and everyone would be safe...

Suddenly Erchina was right in front of him, her crossbow cocked and loaded again, aimed at him. Revan immediately raised his hands. "I'll say this just once," Erchina said. Her voice was rough and loud. "You're going to make a gate to the college, or I'll shoot." Revan couldn't answer, shocked, trying desperately to think up some way to stall her. "Are you listening?" Erchina said, pushing her arrow right in Revan's face. That gave Revan only one chance, and he decided to take it. He slapped away the crossbow and turned around, ready to run into the house. But Erchina recovered quickly. Before Revan could take a step, Erchina dove at him, forcing him to the ground. He twisted around and there was Erchina, her crossbow still loaded, now sitting on top of him. Revan couldn't go anywhere.

"Last chance, boy," she said.

Revan couldn't go anywhere and Erchina didn't seem to be a person for empty threats—there wasn't any room for anything else in Revan's mind, just Erchina's crossbow and him knowing, if he didn't obey, he'd be dead. So, he made the gate without even thinking about it.

Erchina immediately jumped off him and disappeared through the gate. Revan hated himself for obeying—it was just him, the gate, and the knowledge of what he'd just done. He hoped with all his heart that Gaveh was indeed in the library.

The tears flowed down his cheeks, but as soon as the first fell from his chin, Mr. Havelna appeared, looking at Revan, shocked. "What happened?" the principal asked.

"I have...I have...I have..." Revan tried. Then he gathered himself and barely managed to say, "I have let a murderer into the college."

Chapter Fourteen

It was the first time Mr. Havelna had to give an emergency speech. The moment he came back, he'd immediately summoned the necessary people and had ensured the doors of the college were firmly locked to prevent Erchina from getting away.

Revan had apologized heartily. Mr. Havelna had said coldly, "We'll talk about this. First, I have to deal with the consequences."

Revan had made a mistake that might cost a lot of lives. Once again, the eating hall was filled with students, quite a few were sitting on the ground. Revan could barely hear all the chattering. Gaveh sat next to him and tried to talk to him, but Revan couldn't look at anything that wasn't the ground. He was *so tired*. He just wanted to be in bed and never wake up.

"I'm going to tell you all something that we until now had successfully kept a secret, and that's about our previous principal. Not Mrs. Dahena. This is about Erchina." No "Mrs." Mr. Havelna had never used that with her. Revan knew what he was going to say and didn't feel like listening. He could only keep staring at the ground.

Mr. Havelna talked about Erchina's history, her being a previous principal who hated Othercrystalled and got kicked out because of corruption. He talked about how they had to get rid of her, because it was the only option.

"She's dangerous," Mr. Havelna ended his story. "The school could only conclude that she didn't have a conscience, so we had her exiled to a remote island. Somehow, she's found her way back into the college." Mr. Havelna kept quiet for a few seconds to emphasize his point. "She managed to intimidate a student who was harboring her in their own bedroom. They finally confessed it to me."

Even now he protects my identity, Revan thought bitterly. *Even as I screwed everything up this much.*

"Erchina ran off afterwards. And now we need your help to bring her in again. That's why the college doors are locked—because we have good reasons to assume she's responsible for the magic disappearing." There was silence as the crowd processed the news.

"Erchina's a very good magician, as are most who become principals, and she's incredibly stubborn. On top of that, she despises Othercrystalled for a reason I'm not at liberty to divulge. Her appearance all of a sudden and hiding here is reason enough to suspect she has something to do with our crisis.

"We *have* to talk to her if we want this situation to end. I don't know why she's here and I shall refrain from speculation, but we need her to end all of this.

"So that's my assignment to all of you. The moment you see her, approach your closest teacher and let them handle it. Don't listen to her; she can be very manipulative. But we have good reasons to assume she can only use magic to access the Flow—she can't leave the college with the doors closed, and the keys are in a place where she can't find them.

"This evening, the teachers will go past all the bedrooms, trying to find Erchina. Don't try to stop or hinder us. I understand you all want your privacy, but in times like these, privacy is a luxury, not an obligation."

It had all started with the magic disappearing, and Revan had thought it couldn't get any worse—he'd been wrong then, and wrong every time he'd had that thought since. And now it was Revan's own fault, which hurt so much more. He felt like crying.

After Mr. Havelna's speech was over, most pupils stood up in sullen silence and went back to their bedrooms, and Revan stayed put, feeling sad. Mr. Havelna would indubitably have a very nasty punishment lined up for him, and Revan would welcome it. After all, he was an Else.

Revan saw many weren't as sad as he was. No, a couple people even seemed relieved. Revan feared the news that Erchina hated Othercrystalled would only help her.

"Shouldn't you report to the principal?" Gaveh asked softly in Revan's ear. "As Othercrystalled?" Gaveh almost breathed that final word, barely audible, fearing others would hear him.

Revan squeezed the bridge of his nose and shook his head. "I escaped the curse," he replied softly. "I don't think it's necessary." He sighed. "I don't want anything. Just leave me." He nodded to Mr. Havelna, who had sat down at the teachers' table. "I'll stay here and await my punishment."

"Revan..." Gaveh began, "you're taking on all the blame. Maybe you should..."

"Gaveh," Revan groaned. "Leave me alone. Just go upstairs or something. Just let me be."

"You're feeling awful, Revan, I..." Gaveh tried, but Revan held up his hand, and Gaveh sighed and nodded. "Best of luck," he said and walked away.

Soon, only a couple students remained seated. They stuck out, like Revan did. The teachers were still at their tables, with the principal in the middle. Mr. Havelna looked at Revan once or twice, but his look remained neutral and inscrutable. Revan just hoped that what he was trying to convey would come across well. *Whatever punishment you're planning, I'll take it.*

When the teachers got up to leave, Revan still didn't bother moving. When Mr. Havelna walked by, he asked with his eyes, *What kind of chores will you assign me to repent,* but Mr. Havelna's gaze settled only briefly on him, then the principal moved on. He didn't even say anything like "Follow me, we have stuff to discuss," so Revan just remained seated, tired and forlorn.

Across the table, Revan found Javik sitting there. "Hey," Javik said.

"Hey," Revan replied, flabbergasted. "Shouldn't you be leaving, like the rest?"

"And go where?" Javik said and sighed. He seemed exhausted. A couple students walked right past him with disgusted expressions on their faces, and Revan was once again certain he heard the word *Elselover* in there. Then they looked at Revan. Revan decided not to reply, but to sit down across from him. Javik sighed and said, "Just get it over with."

Revan frowned. "What?"

"Elselover," Javik said. "Everyone's been calling me that already all day long anyway. That, and worse. Just get it over with. I know how you feel about Wilan anyway."

"I don't think you are that," Revan said quickly.

Javik finally did look up, and looked him in the eyes, for the first time since Wilan's death. "Really?"

"Of course not, and for what it's worth, I'm genuinely sorry I didn't attend the service."

Javik was taken aback and finally broke eye contact to look back at the table. "Oh," he said. A small smile broke through, and despite the visible exhaustion it seemed genuine, peaceful, even relieved. "Even knowing that Wilan was an Else?" Revan nodded and didn't know what else to say. "Don't you regret ever having been friends with him?" Javik kept prodding.

"No," Revan said. "Not one bit. He couldn't help it if he was Othercrystalled."

"Wow," Javik said, maintaining a smile. After a while, he said, "Remember when it was the four of us against the world?"

Revan smiled with him. "We got along great, didn't we?"

"All of us," Javik said. "I think we played a stupid amount of Island Hopping."

"Almost every evening," Revan laughed.

"And we told each other everything," Javik said. Then he added, "What happened?"

Revan was a bit taken aback. After some thinking he said, "I think you just drew more towards Wilan. And I drew more towards Gaveh."

Javik gave a sad smile and said, "Yeah...I'm not good at making friends."

"I'm sorry to hear that," Revan said.

"Yeah." Javik swallowed. "Can we be...friends again?" Revan needed a moment to process what Javik had said. He had moved quickly from "call me an Elselover" to this, and because it was so unexpected Revan wasn't able to answer too quickly. In that moment, Javik seemed to realize he'd gone too far. His smile disappeared into a forlorn look. "Never mind. I'm sorry I was so forward."

Revan wanted to talk again, but Javik got up and walked away quickly before Revan could say anything else.

* * *

That evening someone knocked on the bedroom door as Revan was lying on his bed. Gaveh wasn't there, as he'd said he wanted to go to the library to do his homework. School just carried on, even during crisis. Once Revan opened the door, five teachers stormed in, all cautious. Mr. Havelna wasn't one of them.

They looked under the bed, knocked on the door trying to perhaps find a hollow compartment—Revan didn't know why—and even looked out the window to see if Erchina was hiding somewhere on the outside. They were *very* thorough in their search and even went through the closet in the corner. Of course, afterwards they didn't clean up everything, and Revan's and Gaveh's clothing was spread out across the room. To Revan it didn't matter. He crashed down on his bed and closed his eyes. He'd clean up later.

It was very dark, possibly after midnight, when Gaveh joined him. Revan realized it vaguely but he was too sleepy to say anything. He said a dull "hi" to Gaveh, then turned over and went back to sleep.

Chapter Fifteen

The next day—after he'd heard Mr. Havelna's speech in which he mourned the death of another Othercrystalled named Seku—Revan decided to apologize to Mr. Havelna. He was still tired and sad, but at least sleeping allowed him some clarity. If the principal threw him out and never wanted to see him again, then that was inevitable, but Revan still felt he should at least get the chance to say sorry. He felt incredibly guilty and the death of Seku, which he'd hoped to prevent, only hit him harder. Revan hoped that by apologizing he'd relieve himself of at least a bit of that guilt.

Revan went to Mr. Havelna's private room after breakfast. Once at the door, he gathered himself and took a few deep breaths. He would accept whatever punishment he was given, but he wasn't looking forward to it. Once he'd gathered his courage, he knocked on the door.

It took a while, and Revan heard some shuffling in the room, but finally the door opened and the balding head of Mr. Havelna appeared. "Who's there...Revan?" He seemed surprised.

"I'm sorry," Revan immediately said. "I screwed up. I suppose this is where you punish me."

"Ah," Mr. Havelna said. He gestured to Revan he could come in. Revan took another deep breath and followed the instruction. The principal closed the door behind him. "Sit down," Mr. Havelna said, and they both took their usual seats.

"I screwed up," Revan said again the moment he'd sat down. He didn't want to look at Mr. Havelna, so he looked at the ground instead.

"You did, kind of," Mr. Havelna said.

"I barged in, forcing you to come with me as I made a gate. Thanks to me, there's a murderer in the college. It is completely, utterly, my fault and I take full responsibility."

"No, it's not."

Revan had his next sentence ready when he realized Mr. Havelna's answer. He stuttered, "Huh?"

"I shouldn't have listened to you," Mr. Havelna sighed. "I should've done anything in my power to prevent you from making a gate. Perhaps I should've had you locked up. Or maybe, if that failed, I should've gone to the other teachers so you wouldn't have been alone. Yes, you overstepped your boundaries—but I let you force my hand, and that's on me."

"Oh," Revan said. "I still forced your hand, though."

"I suppose we're both to blame," Mr. Havelna said, his lips curving into a small smile before he shook his head. "Playing the blame game doesn't help anyone, though. Right now, we've got a problem, and it needs fixing."

"So, no punishment?" Revan asked, uncertain.

Mr. Havelna shook his head. "It's clear to me you've already learnt from your mistake. I might need your help in future, though, as you're able to make that gate."

"Noted," Revan said, feeling relieved despite everything. "So, what happens now? What's Erchina going to do? Why is she here?"

Mr. Havelna pondered, thinking over his answer before he said, "I miscalculated. I thought she wouldn't need to get off her island, because she's got access to the Flow, she can do anything she wants. Why would she come here? If she just hates Othercrystalled, then she can kill them with the Flow without ever coming here. And yet here she is."

"So, she wants something here..." Revan said.

Mr. Havelna nodded. "Something she can't get from the Flow." He looked at Revan, challenging him with a look to figure it out.

Revan frowned. "If it's not killing, then maybe it's...followers? She wants people to follow her and hate Othercrystalled as much as she does. For that she'd need to be...oh." Revan clasped his hand in front of his mouth. "You're in danger."

"I think she's trying to right the wrongs we've done to her," Mr. Havelna said. His smile told Revan he was proud, and Revan felt happy for a brief moment, despite the circumstances. "If she becomes the principal again, she can gain all the followers she wants."

"She's going to try and kill you," Revan said. "Sir, you need to..."

"Increase security," Mr. Havelna said. "I'm moving to the principal's room. The door there is more secure. And when I'm not in that room, I'll be with other teachers at all times." Revan saw he didn't like that decision. "I'll be guarded far better in general. And that's right and proper. Erchina's after me, it seems."

"Not after me..." Revan said.

Mr. Havelna shook his head. "This is now my problem. And it's time I start acting like the principal, instead of just a substitute who lucked into the position." He looked at Revan for a second, with a look that made clear what the consequences of that would be. The principal wasn't seen buddying up to students, not like Mr. Havelna had done with Revan in the past. This might be their last conversation for a while. Mr. Havelna added, "In the meanwhile, I need to fix this together with the teachers. This is grown-up business, Revan, and you've done great, but now we have to fix it. Don't get involved like you did before. You might make it worse, despite intending to do good. Erchina's not after you."

"Yeah," Revan said. "I've learnt that lesson."

"Good," Mr. Havelna said. "Want to help me start packing?"

"Sounds like an appropriate punishment," Revan said, with a chuckle.

"Let's say it's that, and not an excuse to spend some final moments with my favorite student." Mr. Havelna winked. The principal was above favorites, to the point where regular students weren't supposed to be seen in the principal's room except in the most dire exceptions, so Revan was never going to see him there. This was the end of their relationship as Revan knew it.

So Revan helped him. What else could he have done?

* * *

As much as Revan still wanted to be involved with Erchina, he understood what Mr. Havelna told him. He decided to lay low, let it happen. He'd contributed, and now it was time for the grown-ups to take over. Revan still couldn't go home, so he took the elevator back to his bedroom. Gaveh would probably be there as well, after all; Gaveh had told him he'd study today. Gaveh was struggling with being stuck at the college as well, that was clear—he'd been more easily angered lately, and even he would probably be missing his parents by now. Maybe they could distract one another today, which could help both of them to chase the bad thoughts away.

But Revan was completely distracted when the elevator doors opened and Hdar was there—her upper body fully nude. Her breasts and all five crystals were visible, and it was immediately clear that her skill crystal lit up.

Revan was barely able to get out of the elevator. He looked at Hdar, shocked, trying very hard to just look at her face. "Hdar...what?"

"Hi, Revan," she said with a smile. "You okay?"

"You...it...what?"

"Oh," Hdar said, still with that terrible smile. "You're probably confused about my crystals. I thought I'd show them to the outside world. After all, I have nothing to hide."

"But...but..." Revan stuttered. "Everyone can see..."

"So what?" Hdar asked. "That's their problem. It's not illegal to walk around with an exposed upper body. Trust me, we did our research."

That might be true, but it was still very awkward. You were supposed to at least wear a T-shirt, you didn't show your stomach, except for close relatives, and for most people, Kodens. But there was one word Revan struggled with the most. "We..."

"Yeah, we. I'm not the only one, and you might've known that if you'd paid attention." Hdar smiled. "There are more like us. The Flow picked us, Revan. Just you wait, we'll cleanse the college, no problem." Revan swallowed. He had been about to walk into the elevator but his feet wouldn't budge anymore. "So, take off your shirt, what are you waiting for?" Her smile still didn't go, as if she knew and wanted to cleanse him right there.

"I...um..." Revan said. "No," he finally managed.

Hdar shrugged. "Your choice," she said. "But I'm not the only one. Sooner or later we'll all have to do this, so you'd better get used to it." She got out of the elevator without even looking at Revan.

Revan watched her disappear, his head full of thoughts. The feeling of relief Mr. Havelna had given him had all but disappeared. There were people walking around with their chests exposed. Those people expected Revan, and everyone else, to do the same. They thought they were on the right side of the Flow and a small part of Revan agreed with them. On top of that, Mr. Havelna was in danger. Revan was personally safe—for the time being—but he was scared, and with good reason. He decided to do what usually cheered him up.

* * *

Gaveh was indeed at the desk of their bedroom, reading a book, but he looked up when Revan entered. "Hey," he said.

"Hey," Revan replied. He immediately wanted to say something, but Gaveh interrupted him.

"Could you help me out studying in the library sometime soon?"

Revan was briefly taken aback. "Um...why?"

Gaveh shrugged. "You get good grades, I don't, maybe you can help me?" He added, "I suddenly got the idea when I was in the library this afternoon."

"Um...fine," Revan said. "But um...I want sex." There, he'd said it. "If you want to, of course."

Gaveh frowned. "Now?"

Revan sighed. "I let a dangerous murderer into Samillan College, I can't fix it myself, and now a couple students have decided to walk around shirtless so that they could show their crystals to everyone. I talked to Hdar, and she said everyone would have to do that eventually."

"...Ah," Gaveh said.

"My head is full," Revan said, swallowing away some tears, "and I need it empty."

Gaveh closed his book and lay down on the bed. "Go ahead," he said.

Revan got on top of him, and their lips smashed together as they kissed furiously, hungrily.

As they had sex, the bad thoughts left Revan's head one by one, as he had hoped; there was only Gaveh and him, doing together what they'd been doing for a while. Erchina wasn't after him, Hdar wouldn't care about what Revan was doing with his Koden, everything was fine.

And yet, that didn't mean his mind was quiet, because it felt different from how it did normally. Gaveh's looks seemed to be just a bit hungrier, his kisses just a bit more romantic. Revan couldn't put his finger on it, and somewhere in the act he realized it was all probably just in his mind, which didn't make it any less confusing. He hadn't forgotten asking himself what would happen if he ended up with Gaveh, and minding it increasingly less. Revan didn't know his feelings for Gaveh and just couldn't figure them out.

And when they were done and their panting filled the room, Revan was too scared to ask if Gaveh reciprocated his feelings. And yet, there was nothing he wanted to know more desperately.

Chapter Sixteen

Hdar was indeed not the only person to walk around without a shirt—more students than Revan was expecting were walking around shirtless. After Gaveh distracted him, Revan had gone downstairs, and there he'd found about twenty students walking around topless. Most teachers watched the students desperately, and a couple tried to convince them to put shirts back on, but nobody wanted to listen. They all said the same thing Hdar had told Revan—as far as Revan could hear—but Revan heard something else twice, and it scared him.

Now that Mrs. Erchina is here, everything will go the way it's supposed to, was the first. The second was, *Everyone with a different crystal has to go. Not just the Othercrystalled.*

They called themselves the Bared. Bared because they had nothing to hide, and because they felt that what they were asking was the bare minimum. *At least nobody died today,* Revan thought.

The next day he woke up with a very bad feeling—had more Othercrystalled died? Whatever the Flow set out to do, it wasn't done, and neither was Erchina. Mr. Havelna was still alive, as Revan found out at breakfast where the principal was at the teacher's table. Two teachers were seemingly more alert for any gates appearing out of nowhere. He was being guarded well. Revan was alone, as Gaveh had wanted to lie in bed a little longer. Breakfast consisted of the usual dry slices of bread, and Revan had come to expect them. They weren't very filling, but Revan barely noticed that through all the stress.

He hadn't even taken a bite before he'd already heard names of two other students. Ekar and Yvtan, both Othercrystalled. This time the rumors were ahead of the principal, and everyone already knew before Mr. Havelna even started his speech.

But once he'd started the whole hall fell silent. "I understand," Mr. Havelna said, "that you're already aware of the dead. I'm still naming them: Ekar and Yvtan, both of them Othercrystalled. We wish their classes, and their friends, all the help they can get in this difficult time, and there'll be a service for them here, like with all the previous victims. But I'd like to warn you about a movement that has apparently started recently." Mr. Havelna shook his head. "I understand a few of you have decided to walk around shirtless, your crystals visible to everyone. That is a choice you've made yourself, but not one I'm supporting. I would like to tell you to stick together and pay particular attention to those of you who have undergone a loss like the friends of the deceased. We should go through this as a unit, because we from Samillan College support one another. Don't pay attention to whose crystal lights up when."

Not for the first time, Revan's heart sank. He'd expected Mr. Havelna to openly judge the Bared and make their goal impossible by, for example, making a uniform mandatory or adjusting the rules so that an exposed upper body was illegal. But he did this instead. Revan wasn't sure if that was because he was unable to, or because he didn't want to. Knowing Mr. Havelna, it was probably the former somehow, but that wasn't much consolation. Revan's *kind* was killed, he thought bitterly. He kept thinking about that when someone gently shoved him. For a moment Revan thought of Gaveh, but he hadn't left his bed yet as it was the weekend. When he turned, he saw Arana next to him. At least she was still wearing her T-shirt.

"Can we talk?" she asked.

Revan rolled his eyes. Yeah, that was a great plan, totally something he could handle. "Or else you'll report me?"

Arana made an annoyed sound, but that quickly turned into a sigh. She didn't say anything, expecting him to say something, but when he didn't, she asked, "Could you please come with me, Revan?"

"Or else...?" Revan asked.

"Or else nothing," Arana replied. "I just want to show you something." Arana seemed to almost beg, her eyebrows lifted, a desperate smile on her face. "Please, Revan. I want to talk to you. After this, you never have to listen to me again, and I'll leave you alone for the rest of your life, if you want. But please, come with me now." She stood up and walked to the eating hall's door.

Whatever, Revan thought. He wasn't particularly hungry anyway. He followed Arana.

* * *

Arana didn't say anything when she got into the elevator and pushed the button for the highest floor. Revan wanted to say something but held back. Why were they going to the highest floor? Last time Revan was there...that couldn't have been Arana's purpose, she had a Koden herself. But then what did she want? So he just said nothing and waited until they were at their destination. Arana was the first to get out of the elevator, and she opened another door to an empty room. It had a table in the middle, and one chair on each side.

Revan walked after her; Arana closed the door behind him, after which she reached for the hem of her shirt. Revan knew what she would do before she did. "Wait..." he began. But Arana had already taken off her shirt before he could protest.

He immediately saw what she'd wanted to show him. Arana's legs trembled, and she looked away from him, avoiding eye contact. "I know your secret. It makes perfect sense for you to know mine as well."

It wasn't Arana's skill crystal that was lit up—the crystal between her right shoulder and her chest—but her *art* crystal, the crystal between her *left* shoulder and her chest. It shone a faint blue. Revan looked at her dumbfounded, still having no idea what to say. "Why is everyone showing me this stuff nowadays?" he blurted out.

"What?" Arana asked.

Revan shook his head. "Nothing," he said. "But...why?"

"I want to be your friend again," Arana said. "I want to apologize, without you accusing me of blackmailing you. Now you can blackmail me back, so we're even." Arana should've had a creative job, and because she was here, she was a minority. Plus, she very obviously dressed like someone with a lit-up skill crystal—people might be shocked and feel she was lying to them, and in a way, she was. She would never be as hated as Revan would be if her secret was out, and yet...it was a secret.

"What..." Revan said, still baffled. He briefly lost control and his gaze wandered downward, away from Arana's face. Then he got a hold of himself. "Could you put your shirt back on?" Talking to Arana this way was harder than he could bear.

Arana shrugged. "Of course." She put her shirt back on, her expression uncaring. Revan looked away out of respect. A lot of emotions were going through his body. Anger, disappointment, but also affection—Arana had that effect on him. Another question came to him. Once Arana had put her shirt back on, Revan asked, bluntly, "Why can't you leave me alone?"

Arana looked back at him, her face pained. Yes, Revan really liked her, but Revan had made very clear he didn't want any contact and yet she kept trying.

"We're classmates," she said, "and I like you, and feel you understand. But if that isn't mutual, okay. Sorry."

She prepared to leave. Revan held up his hand and shook his head. "Sorry," he said. "That came out wrong. After everything that happened you're showing me this...I don't *mind*, but I just want to know...*why*? Do you like me that much?"

"Yes," Arana said without a doubt. "I invited you to my home, remember?"

"You invited Gaveh as well."

"And if I'd had a fight like this with Gaveh I'd want to make it up to him as well."

"But..." Revan said. "You have plenty of friends to talk to, right?"

Arana laughed piercingly, without any humor. "No, I've been feeling alone at this college for a while. Most students don't really want to talk to me, don't think I'm that interesting. I'm mostly into books, and nobody knows about my crystals."

"But..." Revan said, "you pushed me away."

"I know," Arana said, looking apologetic. "And I'm very sorry about that. I guess I was scared. I still am, a little."

"Yeah," Revan said bitterly, "most people are scared when they find out." The last person Revan had told—before Arana and Gaveh found out—was Fenna, his little sister. She'd been worried and distant for a day or two before coming around, but she did eventually. She'd said, "You're my brother, I love you any way you are."

"I don't know a lot of people like you," Arana said, "and that's my fault. I can't take back the words I said the first time around, but I can give it a second shot. So. I'm sorry. When I heard about the Bared...that's when I understood what you felt."

"I don't think so," Revan said. Arana raised an eyebrow. "Most people with a different crystal are accepted. If you show your crystal to the whole world, it wouldn't do as much as if I showed mine."

"You're right," Arana admitted. "I still have a lot to learn."

"So, I don't understand why you kept it a secret. You even dress like someone with a lit-up skill crystal. Why...?"

"I wanted to become a magician," Arana briefly said. "And I was very stubborn, so my parents said, okay, but hide. So I started doing that, and I worked hard to prove myself. I've always thought nobody would understand. But Revan, please. Can we talk again? I don't have a lot of friends. I know I ruined it, but please give me another chance."

Revan smiled. "Why me?" he asked again, though he had a pretty strong hunch.

"Because I feel like you're one of the few people who understands," Arana replied.

Revan nodded, still smiling, but he hadn't forgotten how they'd gotten here. "Okay," he said. "We'll talk again but...I don't know if everything's all right. At least I won't be scared you're blackmailing me."

Arana's face fell. "Did you really think that?"

Revan nodded. "You're the only one who knows. Well, except for Gaveh, and I've been scared."

"You told Gaveh?"

"Not really, but he found out." Revan decided not to discuss the details—he didn't need to involve Arana more with their problems.

"How'd he react?"

Revan grinned softly. "He wanted to touch my crystals. I'm glad he knows. But..." He shrugged. "I don't know if, what...I like you. But I have a lot going on right now. I'm happy talking to you, but not any more than that, okay?" *No friendship*, Revan meant. But at the same time, he also thought, *no relationship. Because apparently, I have feelings for Gaveh, and I don't know what they are.* "I just have to...go through some stuff."

Arana smiled. "Fine." Revan almost drowned in her smile. He shook his head before that could happen. "But you don't need to be scared of me."

"I'm not," Revan said. *But it would be unfair to leave you hanging while I'm confused about Gaveh.*

And yet he felt unexpectedly comfortable about a relationship with Arana.

* * *

As the elevator took him back down Revan felt something change, as had happened the first time. He knew immediately he was able to make a new gate, to a new destination, though he had no idea what that destination would be. Once again, it was an irresistible temptation that completely overwhelmed him. Nothing was as important as making a new gate.

But just as he realized that, the elevator doors opened and two other students got in. They said hi and nonchalantly waited for their floor.

They'd see Revan make a gate. His feelings told him that wasn't important, he had to make a new gate *now*—why would he be interested in those other two people?

I'm dying, Revan thought to himself, *this time the Flow is actually coming for me.* Simultaneously he thought, *Maybe this time I'll have something to explain to the whole school.*

Revan bit his fist to suppress the temptation. People were probably looking at him funny, but he didn't care. Just as the temptation got so strong that Revan couldn't hold back, the elevator doors opened on his floor.

Without even looking at the other students, Revan ran out of the elevator, into the hallway, finding his own bedroom. He hoped he just looked like he really needed to use the bathroom. He also desperately hoped the Flow wasn't coming to kill him for good this time, fixing a loose end it had left on the table. Revan slammed the door behind him way too loudly. Gaveh wasn't there—he'd probably gone down already. Shame. Revan made a gate.

He closed his eyes, awaiting death. A death that once again didn't come.

Revan opened his eyes again and looked through the gate before he stepped through. The destination didn't seem familiar—it was a small room, but Revan couldn't see everything through the gate. The walls were brown and seemed to shine, as if they were made of some kind of gem.

Should he try and get Mr. Havelna? It made sense, but as the principal, he was plenty busy. No, Revan was on his own. He walked through the gate, hesitating. He'd expected to get shot as soon as he walked through, but nothing happened this time. Now that he was through, he saw the room was a little bigger than he'd thought, and there was a hallway on the other side.

He looked around. Where was he? He couldn't be *too* far, as making the gate didn't take that much energy. Revan didn't see any sky, no windows, no indication whatsoever where he could be. He had so many questions.

Revan let his gate disappear. He looked into the hallway, searching for other people, but nobody was there. Revan walked into the hallway, uncertain of what to expect—scared, even. Where was he and how did he get here? Did the Flow do this, or Erchina for whatever reason, or somebody else entirely? Part of him wanted to ask if anyone was there—but he didn't know what their intentions would be.

In the distance, a big room appeared, and he ran towards it, his steps echoing through the hallway. If there was someone else, they'd know Revan was here, right? He'd already given himself away, right?

Revan was almost in the room and started to sprint. He didn't quite know why. But once he arrived, he immediately recognized what was inside, though he'd never seen it before.

There were two big metal bars coming out of the ground, reaching to about his waist. Between them was some kind of blue energy flowing from one bar to another. It wasn't water, it was just pure blue energy.

Revan flinched backwards, slamming against the wall, and cried out in simple confusion. He was seeing the Flow.

Chapter Seventeen

For a couple seconds Revan couldn't do anything but stare dumbly at the magic power.

This was the Flow. The books Revan had read all said something different about what it would look like. Samillan knew, of course, but he'd only ever talked about it vaguely, lots of people interpreting his words differently. Some people said it was a gigantic waterfall. Others said, no, it's a flow of lava, like what's surrounding us.

But everyone agreed, the Flow had been here since the world was formed, long before the first people came into existence, and it would still be here when the last human was dead and buried. The Flow *was* the world. Nobody ever knew where it came from, but the Flow knew everything about everyone and was the source of the magic that made people able to form gates. But at the same time, it didn't understand individual people. Why would it? The Flow was leagues above them. The Flow was a force of nature and at the same time a god. It was above everything. After all, as far as people knew, only Samillan had ever interacted with the Flow. It must be uncaring about most individuals. And yet, if Revan was here, that was because of the Flow's will, and now Revan was alone with a god. What could he say? How could he talk to a god responsible for everything and everyone?

All those sources that talked about the Flow and whatever Samillan had said about it had agreed on one other thing—once you saw the Flow, you *knew* it was the Flow.

Revan knew.

He wiped away his tears. "Your Godness?" Revan tried uncertainly. He immediately wanted to laugh. It sounded so stupid, but he had to do *something*. "What am I...doing here?" He stuttered. Immediately it sounded way too rude.

The Flow kept flowing, but changed color—from blue to green. Did that mean anything? Was this an answer? The motives of the Flow were impossible to guess.

"The magic..." Revan tried, "has disappeared?"

The Flow changed colors again, this time to red, and it seemed to whirl harder—the waves in the energy between the two metal bars became stronger.

"What do I do?" Revan *really* didn't know what to say.

The Flow changed back again, from red to green, and stayed that color for a couple seconds until it changed back again to red. Then back to green. It oscillated faster and faster until it was constantly changing.

Why those colors? What's it...

When he realized, Revan put his hand on his calm crystal, shocked. Those were the colors of *his* crystals.

"What do I do?" he asked again.

The Flow changed color again to white, and Revan didn't understand anything anymore.

He looked around himself, to the walls made of that brown gem, looking for a clue, something different than the Flow, but he didn't find anything. "What do I do?" he asked a third time, focusing back on the Flow. And because that hadn't helped before either, he asked again, "Why am I here?"

The waves became calmer, now the Flow was barely flowing at all. Revan thought it almost seemed inviting. The color was blue again, like that of the sky.

The Flow was inviting him.

Change me.

Revan gasped when he realized. "No," he shouted. That wasn't possible. The Flow couldn't be asking *him* to change it. First, because he was only a student. Second, because nobody *could* change it, unless they had been part of the Flow all along. Everything and everyone except for Gaveh had told him so. Revan must've misinterpreted it somehow. "What do you want?" he asked. But the Flow kept flowing in the same inviting way, and Revan realized it knew what he was thinking. The Flow knew how Revan had interpreted it. "That's not possible," Revan said. "I can't do that. Nobody can. I'm not Samillan. I'm just...some student."

The Flow kept flowing, and for a brief second Revan entertained the thought of putting his hand in it, just to see what would happen. Revan gasped when he realized. "No," he said again. "I can't...do that. That makes no sense." He must've misinterpreted it; there was no other possible explanation.

Revan turned and started walking away, and once he'd started, it became running. His footsteps echoed through the mysterious hallway. Revan had contradicted the will of the god, but he *must* have misinterpreted it somehow. *Nobody can manipulate the Flow.* It was a mantra Revan said in his head, because the alternative was ridiculous. The alternative was that a god had appeared and asked some student at some school to change it, even when almost everyone Revan knew said that was absolutely impossible.

Revan ran back to the first room, and there he made a gate to the college, to his own room. Once he was there, he hid in a corner, breathing heavily.

* * *

Once Revan calmed down, everything only felt worse. *I just want to be normal*, he thought. He hid his head in his hands. *I am just simple, regular Revan. Who goes to his classes, does his homework, has his meals, maybe has sex with his Koden somewhere along the line, and then goes to bed. And who visits his family on the weekends and on vacations. I just want to be regular Revan, who isn't worth paying attention to.* Why was he here? Why did the Flow have to pick *him*? He wasn't Samillan. He hadn't undergone eleven works of any kind. Revan was just the kind of guy who let things happen to him. Like being Othercrystalled and being discovered by Arana. He wasn't a big hero; he wasn't the very best of the best. He just had some good grades.

Nonetheless, he was still able to make a gate to two places: Erchina's island and the Flow. Against his better knowledge, Revan tried to make a gate back home, hoping maybe he could access everything else as well; but he couldn't. The magic was still locked and somehow, he was the one with the key. But...*how*. Why *him*?

Revan remained there, his arms wrapped around his knees, trying to calm himself down, then the bedroom door opened. There was Gaveh. "Ah, there you are," he said. "You okay?"

Revan didn't know what to say. *Yeah, I'm fine, I just ran into an all-knowing, all-present god that wants me to solve all problems although I'm so certain it'll kill me in the process. Anyway, want some sex?*

"I...it...we...they..." Revah stood up and rubbed his temples. "I just did..." he tried again. "I can now..." Nope, that didn't work either. "Sorry," Revan gave up, "I just went through something, and I can't talk about it, because I'm so utterly confused." He shook his head and wanted to cry again.

The principal had to know about this—Mr. Havelna was one of the few magicians who could deal with Erchina, and if someone out there could change the Flow back, it was him. Suddenly everything was clear again. He *had* to find the principal now. He'd just have to go to the principal's bedroom, even if that wasn't allowed. Mr. Havelna would solve all this. Revan only hoped he'd be there. "I have to go to Mr. Havelna," Revan finally said. "Now."

Gaveh frowned. "Because?"

"Can't tell you," Revan said. "But I have to." He wanted to run away, but Gaveh grabbed his arm. Before he could say anything, Revan sighed and said, "I'll tell you later, just not..."

"Come with me, Revan," Gaveh said, suddenly serious.

"Gaveh..." Revan started, "I have to..."

"Please," Gaveh said. "You said you'd help me in the library."

"Huh," Revan blurted out, and then said, "Yeah, but not *now*."

"You said you'd do it today."

"Gaveh," Revan said, completely befuddled, "something *very important* is going on and..."

Gaveh held up his free hand. "Okay. That's important, I get it. This is too. Please. Follow me to the library."

Revan blinked a couple times. "But...what's important about..."

"Not studying," Gaveh admitted. "Trust me."

"But..." Revan protested, but something in Gaveh's tone of voice crumbled Revan's defenses. "But..." he tried again.

"Important," Gaveh repeated.

Revan sighed. "Okay, I'll follow."

Gaveh let go of his arm but grabbed his hand, as if he was scared Revan would run away. He walked out of the room, almost dragging Revan behind him. Gaveh seemed very agitated—it was more like he was holding on to Revan than just holding his hand.

"What's wrong?" Revan asked, but Gaveh didn't reply. Gaveh wasn't just agitated, he was tense too, Revan realized. Whatever Gaveh was going to show Revan, it wasn't very easy. He even seemed...*scared*? Could Gaveh make gates too? Could he access the Flow as well?

"Where are we going?" Revan asked once they were in the elevator. They were indeed going to the library. "Did you find a book? Gaveh, did you find the solution in a book?"

"Something like that," Gaveh said, not making eye contact, almost as if he was feeling guilty. This wasn't like him.

"You shouldn't discuss it with me then, but with Mr. Havelna," Revan persisted.

Gaveh laughed without mirth but didn't give any other reaction, and everything fell quiet. "Gaveh..." Revan tried again.

The elevator doors opened again. Gaveh grabbed Revan's wrist and sped up his walking to almost a run.

"Gaveh, *what's going on?*" Revan asked desperately. He didn't like Gaveh acting in such a way, it was like Revan didn't know him. Gaveh walked to a corner on the other side of the library, a place where Revan had never been and where he'd never expected to be. Once he got there, Gaveh looked around and moved a tile that was loose, then grabbed some kind of bar.

"What..." Revan said.

Gaveh opened a hatch and pointed in there. "Get in," he said.

It wasn't like Gaveh to be so commanding. But what else could Revan do? Apparently, this was important. Revan jumped into the secret room. It was just low enough that he didn't need a ladder.

He looked around and saw a couple chairs, a table and a bed. The room was just big enough for one person to survive. On one of those chairs was a woman with grey hair who seemed very fit. She wore red garb and had a necklace around her neck.

Erchina.

Gaveh jumped in after him and closed the hatch.

Chapter Eighteen

"Help!" Revan shouted. He stood in front of the person who was responsible for everything that was wrong, someone who had already tried to kill him. If he was going to die, it wouldn't be without a fight. Gaveh put his palm over Revan's mouth, muting the sound. Revan mentally cursed him. Gaveh had betrayed him, had thrown away their Kodenship and friendship as if it had meant nothing to him. He tried to struggle to get free, but Gaveh's grip was too firm. After all, he knew exactly how to keep Revan in his grip. Revan shouted again, but it didn't help.

"I'm sorry," Erchina said. Revan stopped struggling. Well, this was it. Gaveh had betrayed him, how *could* he? Now it was over. "We need to talk." She raised her hands in an attempt to calm him. "The room should be soundproof, but the hatch lets through some sound, and I don't want to take risks." Revan cursed the Flow, but it all evaporated into Gaveh's hand. Why did Erchina want to talk to *him*? "I understand you're angry," Erchina said calmly. "I know you're not going to believe me, so I called him in to help. Revan, I need you."

Gaveh trembled. It was barely noticeable, but Revan felt it because Gaveh was holding on to him so firmly. "Revan," Gaveh said, the same tremble in his voice, "we're best friends, we're Kodens, we might be more than that. If that means anything to you, I have to ask you, keep quiet and listen."

Listen while a mass murderer tells me a story? Revan thought.

"I know you don't trust her, but I hope you'll trust me. I'm going to take my hand away from your mouth. Stop shouting, or I'll have to put my hand back. Nod if you understand."

Would protesting help? Erchina was a mass murderer who would kill Revan without a second thought, considering what he was. He was going to die anyway. So, Revan nodded.

Gaveh let go of Revan's mouth but still held him in that firm grip with his other arm. His legs surrounded Revan's own, keeping him firmly locked in place. It would've been sexy in any other situation, but now Gaveh was apparently—rightfully—scared he'd run away.

"Why should I believe you, mass murderer?" Revan asked. He'd promised Gaveh he wouldn't shout, so he controlled his volume, but that didn't mean he couldn't talk. "You caused the magic to disappear. *You* manipulated the Flow. *You* randomly kill people for not having the right crystal. Or because they're Othercrystalled! Why should I listen to *you*?"

Erchina sat on the chair, her arms crossed. She stayed calm throughout Revan's angry outburst. That only made Revan angrier and almost made him forget to talk softly.

"Are you done?" Erchina asked. Revan said nothing, narrowing his eyes. "I'll assume that's a yes. Good. My turn. Everything you say is true, but you're shouting it at the wrong person. Your beloved Mr. Havelna wants everything you're accusing me of right now."

Revan's jaw dropped. After a beat, he laughed—first loudly, then he kept it under control. "That's ridiculous. We're going to get you, Erchina, whether you like it or not. I see you for what you really are. You have no proof. And why would I believe you anyway? You attacked me and forced me to make a gate back. You fired an arrow at me. You..."

"That's correct," Erchina said calmly. "And I'm sorry. I had to act quickly, and I didn't know you were Othercrystalled."

"You *told* her?!" Revan asked, staring daggers at Gaveh. "Are you kidding me? My secret, and you're telling it to...to..."

Gaveh said nothing, he only looked tense and guilty. Revan wanted to get out of his grip, but Gaveh held on too firmly.

"If your Koden lets you go, could you listen to me calmly? I'm glad Gaveh told me, otherwise I never would've tried to talk to you. I would've thought you were just another follower of Mr. Havelna."

Why would Revan trust Gaveh if Gaveh had told Erchina *everything*? Revan's expression must've betrayed more than he thought, because Erchina sighed. "Gaveh, can you hold him a bit longer?"

"Will do," Gaveh said.

"Good. Then maybe you can tell him how you discovered me."

Gaveh swallowed with difficulty. He seemed to have to fight something before he could say it. "I can make a gate too," he then said.

Revan's jaw dropped for a second time. "What?"

"You weren't in our bedroom, and I suddenly felt I could also make a gate. I originally thought the same as you did, that I was going to die. I'm not Othercrystalled, but that feeling was still there. I made the gate, walked through and ended up here. Mrs. Erchina was very confused to see me." Mrs. Erchina. Gaveh called her *Mrs.* Erchina—that was only a title for respected people.

"The will of the Flow," Erchina said, nodding. "The Flow led him to me."

"Once she'd figured that out, Mrs. Erchina started talking to me. She told me all the things she's going to tell you. Then, she told me she was planning to end Mr. Havelna's life. And yours, if you stand in her way. I had to protect you and saw no other way out. So, I told her you were Othercrystalled so she would spare you. To show her you weren't just a slavish follower. Flow be thanked, Mrs. Erchina believed me." Revan still wanted to hate Gaveh—it still felt like a betrayal— but he understood Gaveh's reasoning a little bit. Not enough to forgive him, but still, a little.

"I know I shouldn't have," Gaveh said, still slowly and calmly. "I know we trust each other through and through. I ask you to do that now as well. Revan, please, can I let you go?"

Revan let Gaveh's words sink in before he nodded, without saying anything. Gaveh let go of him. Revan didn't do anything. He stretched himself, happy his limbs were free, and sat down on the chair across Erchina, his arms crossed. "What's this room?"

"A secret room," Erchina replied. "Something only principals know of. If the college is under attack, it's important the principal can hide somewhere. The library is large and impossible to fully keep track of. After Samillan, when the skyscrapers were built and the college was founded, this room was also built, exactly for cases like this. Mrs. Dahena didn't tell Havelna before she died, so the secret was lost."

"She died?" Revan asked. "How?"

"She died because she resisted Mr. Havelna," Erchina said. She sighed. "I have reasons to believe that Mr. Havelna has manipulated the Flow, putting us all in this position."

Revan blinked a couple times. "That's not possible," he said.

"And yet, I think it's true," Erchina replied. "Mr. Havelna manipulated the Flow in order to kill Othercrystalled."

"Nobody can manipulate the Flow except the Flow itself, and if anyone were to manipulate it in order to kill Othercrystalled, it would be you," Revan spat to her.

"I don't want to kill Othercrystalled."

"Lies. Come on, you hate Othercrystalled so much you killed your own daughter when her second crystal lit up."

Erchina's face fell. "Havelna told you that, didn't he?" Revan nodded. "My daughter killed herself. Trust me, I had no hand in that." Then Erchina's face softened, and Revan saw a flash of sorrow. Gaveh took a seat next to him, listening, but also watching Revan intently. "I don't know when her crystals changed. I saw her naked often enough when she was young, and only her art crystal lit up then. But when she died, she had two lit-up crystals. She left behind a suicide note wherein she told me she didn't want me to have the shame of having an Else as a daughter." Erchina swallowed. "I'm sure she had other issues, but that was the only one she wrote down. She'd made a gate, to somewhere in the distance, and I was certain she wouldn't come back." Revan shook his head. He found it hard to believe.

"The second worst thing is that she was right. If someone else had caught wind of my daughter being Othercrystalled, I would've been forced to step down. The worst thing is that my first thought was, nothing of value was lost." Erchina sighed. "I still regret that. Because at the time I too was so certain they were a mistake from the Flow. Lazy, the way Samillan had proclaimed, the whole thing." She gestured vaguely. "Sure, they maybe shouldn't die like we used to believe, but they didn't deserve an equal status. And then my daughter became Othercrystalled, and only then did I look into it. Just after her death, I'd considered stepping down to process the loss. I'd already taken a few weeks off where Mr. Havelna could take over. I trusted him most of everyone to take over that job from me." Suddenly looking tired, she shook her head. "Once I realized what was going on, I knew I could use my position to incite some change in the world. To make sure that what I had to feel—what my daughter had to feel—that no-one else had to feel that ever again. I wanted to have the college accept Othercrystalled, openly."

"The college already allows Othercrystalled..." Revan said, but he knew that wasn't true.

Erchina put his thoughts into words. "As long as everyone keeps mum, yes. But you have to keep your mouth shut, don't be open with it, or you'll get kicked out. And that's already a lot better than in the past. In the first days of the college..."

"People were expected to walk around bare-chested." Revan knew.

"Exactly," Erchina said. "I'd undergone a change and naively, I had assumed the rest of the world saw the same thing. Suddenly I realized how the world worked, and that we couldn't afford to keep going. We couldn't treat a whole population this way. So, in my enthusiasm, I started making changes. But just before I did that, I discussed my plans with the teacher I trusted the most." Erchina's gaze hardened. "Your beloved Mr. Havelna." She shook her head. "He heartily recommended against it and said things I hadn't expected him to. He said, 'your daughter deserved that, why don't you realize that. Lead the college the way you're expected to. We're already going in the wrong direction, let's not degenerate any further.' It caused me to doubt again. I trusted Mr. Havelna, why would I go against him?" She shrugged. "So I decided to take it slowly. I tried to hire more people who had different lit-up crystals. Yes, people with lit-up skill crystals, but also people with a lit-up art crystal, calm crystal, and force crystal. I thought I was being subtle. I slowly started to replace the teachers in the council once members wanted to leave and slowly started to talk about equality among crystals.

"I took my time. Five years I spent slowly trying to turn public opinion. I think I did a pretty good job, and I could've done more if my old friend hadn't betrayed me then by discussing my intentions with the council. Of course I couldn't get away with it, the council thought, but they were worried firing me for that actual reason would put them in a bad light. So, they quickly made up a financial scandal to get me out. I *had* to leave. Mr. Havelna tried to take over from me, but Mrs. Dahena outmaneuvered him somehow, sly as she was."

"The abandoned island?"

Erchina shrugged. "I don't know why nobody built anything there. I am reasonably good at magic—as I think you know—and I was looking for a spot where I could withdraw and make new plans, just after I'd gotten fired. I somehow found the island, maybe through luck, maybe because the Flow wanted me to." She smiled briefly. "I stayed there for longer than I'd expected."

Revan didn't want to believe any of it. He still had his arms crossed. Mr. Havelna would never say the things Erchina claimed he'd said, and the whole story about her daughter could be an easily made-up explanation.

But part of him started to trust Erchina, and he hated that.

"Why would Mr. Havelna say that?" Revan asked. "He's trying so hard to gather all the Othercrystalled, and observe them, trying to find a solution, to find..."

"He's the one manipulating the Flow," Erchina repeated.

Revan shook his head. "Not possible."

"Look around, Revan," Gaveh said quietly. "Othercrystalled people are dying left and right. All of a sudden, nobody can make gates anymore. You have to admit something has happened to the Flow. It's not that much of a stretch to imagine someone having manipulated it."

Revan sighed. "Suppose I believe that," he replied, "Mr. Havelna somehow manipulated the Flow to kill random Othercrystalled kids at school. Why, then, is he trying to protect them?"

"How do you think the Flow picks Othercrystalled?" Erchina asked dryly. "You think the Flow has a list—that one's Othercrystalled, that one isn't—and this is how you kill them?"

"Well...yeah?" Revan said.

Erchina shook her head. "I don't think that's how the Flow works. The Flow is above all of us, isn't aware of our own consciousnesses. I don't think the Flow knows who is and isn't Othercrystalled. I think Mr. Havelna found the Flow somehow and learned how to manipulate it. Then he picked two pupils who he knew were Othercrystalled, and told everyone he was a friend of the Othercrystalled to make sure he would get to know more and more names. I suspect the Flow has no idea how our prejudices work. Mr. Havelna had to have chosen them consciously, each individually. That's why you escaped the attack. You never told anyone, except Gaveh."

"But then why can I make those gates? How could Mrs. Dahena make that gate?"

"I don't know," Erchina said and it seemed honest. "I guess maybe the Flow has some will of its own after all."

"Do you hear how shaky that sounds?" Revan asked. "The Flow doesn't know how our own prejudices work, but it has a will of its own somehow. It's not responsible for all the

Othercrystalled children dying left and right, but it *is* responsible for Gaveh and I being able to make gates out of nowhere."

"I don't know how the Flow works, Revan," Erchina said, sounding tired. "I don't think anybody does, in the end, because all we know is what Samillan told us. I know it sounds hard to believe. But I know Havelna, your current headmaster. If there's anyone responsible for all this, it has to be him."

Revan shook his head. "That makes no sense." He shrugged. "But I'll indulge you. How did Mrs. Dahena die, then?"

"You saw her make a gate, right?" Revan nodded. "That gate was to me. She suddenly felt she was able to make one; she knew where she had to go, but she knew she was only able to go there by actually seeing her destination. So she went to the uppermost floor, where you and Gaveh..."

"I get it," Revan quickly said.

"Mr. Havelna caught wind of her being able to do that. He manipulated the Flow, so that the next time she made a gate to my island, she thought she was going there but the gate actually led into lava."

"Again," Revan said, "shaky."

"I know what it sounds like," Erchina said, "but this is the way it's gone."

Revan looked at Gaveh and said, skepticism dripping from his voice, "And you believe this?"

"Yes, because I saw proof."

Revan said to Erchina, "Go ahead."

"Not again," Erchina said, suddenly crestfallen. Revan was curious about what she'd show him, despite himself. Erchina gave in after a few seconds, then took off her necklace, which apparently had a small locket. Erchina opened it.

Inside, Revan saw the painting of a young woman. "Your daughter?" he asked.

Erchina nodded, avoiding eye contact, seemingly having aged ten years in a second. "And a hair of hers, if you look carefully." For the first time since Revan was in the basement, Erchina seemed to have lost control over the situation. Revan looked inside the locket and indeed saw a small black line on the edge of the painting, which must've been the hair.

"I know what it sounds like," Gaveh said. "But I trust her. You know I'm right with this kind of stuff. You can't trust Havelna, Revan. Truth be told, I never liked him." Gaveh almost spit out *Havelna,* with so much hatred Revan pulled away from him and could barely stop himself from correcting Gaveh with, "You have to say *Mr. Havelna.*"

"But..." Revan started to protest. "Mr. Havelna is so...pro-Othercrystalled..." It sounded weak, and Erchina's sceptic look said enough. *It's all fake.* But it didn't make sense with how Mr. Havelna had acted towards him. Open, accepting. The committee he'd created had been diverse too. At the start there had been many people with different lit-up crystals. Right?

Yes, a couple, but Revan didn't remember them coming back after the first meeting, Mr. Havelna had said he hadn't been able to find them. What if he hadn't bothered to? What if he'd just invited the others to ensure he looked a lot friendlier than he actually was?

"But..." Revan still said. He could only stare at the floor, doubting more than he wanted to. Erchina knew he was Othercrystalled, but didn't treat him with the disdain that crystallists usually treated people like him. She did seem comfortable with his crystals, but that could all have been an act.

Gaveh put an arm around him and embraced him tightly. "I was shocked too."

"But..." Revan repeated, because a lot of things were going through his head. Mrs. Dahena, who'd made a gate, and Revan, who'd immediately gone to Mr. Havelna. Mr. Havelna had probably understood everything immediately and had taken steps to ensure Mrs. Dahena wouldn't stop him. That wouldn't have happened if Revan hadn't been so stupid as to go to Mr. Havelna. If everything that Mrs.

Erchina had said was right...Flow, Revan had just called her *Mrs.* Erchina in his head. Revan didn't know who or what to trust, didn't understand anymore.

"Revan, I need you on my side. We need to think about how to fix all of this. We..."

"Don't need to do anything," Revan replied. "I still don't trust you." He let go of Gaveh's embrace. "Your story sounds weak, though some parts make sense. There's definitely something odd going on here, I'll admit that." He swallowed and felt like all of a sudden everything depended on him. Who would he trust? He'd have to make the right decision, when all he wanted was to just be himself.

"We have to make plans, fix the Flow somehow."

"Or you're lying to me," Revan responded. "I don't know that. I need time."

"Another Othercrystalled could die..."

"And if I act rashly, so many more could die instead," Revan replied. "Making rash decisions is how you got here in the first place. I'm not making that mistake again. I don't know who I can trust. Your story makes some sense, but not enough."

"He'll see the light," Gaveh said to Mrs. Erchina. "I'll talk to him. But we need him."

Mrs. Erchina sighed. "I hope you're right about this, Gaveh." She looked at Revan. "What do I need to do to make you trust me?"

"I'm going to talk to Mr. Havelna first," Revan said.

Gaveh and Mrs. Erchina flinched. "Revan, if you do that..." Mrs. Erchina said.

"I will not tell him you're here," he said. "You have my word. I need to hear his side of the story. When I'm done, I'll go back to Gaveh, and we'll make plans. He'll take me back to your secret room and we'll take it from there."

"Revan, we have to act now, or..." Erchina tried one last time.

"Or you could be the schemer Mr. Havelna makes you out to be," Revan countered immediately. "I don't know that. I have to go talk to him."

"And what do you intend to say to him?"

"That is not for you to know," Revan said. "These are my conditions. Go ahead and kill me if you don't trust me." Both Erchina's and Gaveh's eyebrows rose in surprise. "Yeah, I'm not stupid. That's probably crossed your mind. You being here can't leak, right? I presume you still have your crossbow here somewhere, and it's too risky to let me go if you can't trust me." Revan was going to protest if he suddenly found a crossbow in his face—but he gambled on Erchina not being that bold.

"Nobody's going to kill you," Gaveh said quickly. Erchina, however, had a look that screamed that she had been caught red-handed. Revan saw it, Gaveh didn't, and Revan decided to not mention that.

Eventually Mrs. Erchina sighed and said, "Okay. Go to Mr. Havelna, then. But come back to me as soon as you can."

"Will do," Revan said. He looked at Gaveh. "Could you make a gate back to our bedroom?"

Gaveh shrugged. "Sure." And indeed, out of nowhere, a gate appeared, in the same way Revan had been able to summon them. So that part checked out. Revan looked over his shoulder at Erchina looking displeased, then went through the gate. Gaveh went after him, and made the gate disappear.

Back in his bedroom, Revan crashed on the bed, his heart beating, his head throbbing. He groaned softly. Gaveh sat down next to him and rubbed his shoulder, probably trying to calm him down. It didn't work as well as it usually did, and Revan was having trouble pinning down why.

Until it clicked, suddenly. "You told her I'm Othercrystalled," he said.

"Yep," Gaveh said.

Revan rubbed his temples. "It's the biggest secret I have, one that is so big not even you were meant to find out. And you told her."

"I had to try and keep you alive, Revan," Gaveh said calmly. "I had no choice."

"You could've told her I was secretly trying to overthrow him, or something."

"Chances are high she wouldn't have believed me then," Gaveh said.

"But you could've tried."

"Revan, who are you angry at?" Gaveh said calmly.

Revan stood up, breaking his contact with Gaveh, and said, "You. Me. I don't know. I have to go." He looked at Gaveh, Gaveh looked back at him, and Revan wondered if he should tell Gaveh that he'd been able to access the Flow.

But no. Gaveh was absolutely in Erchina's corner, and Revan didn't know who to believe yet. He was supposed to go to Mr. Havelna—that was what both Gaveh and Erchina believed. But there was another option.

Apparently, it *was* possible to manipulate the Flow. Revan had come to realize that in the conversation. Whatever theology Samillan College was espousing, it was wrong, and people could manipulate it. Mr. Havelna had apparently manipulated the Flow well enough. If he could, so could Revan. He'd run away before. He wouldn't run away again.

"Good luck talking to the principal," Gaveh said.

Revan nodded and left the room. Then he looked around, making sure that nobody else was in the hallway, but thankfully he was completely alone. Revan made a gate appear, to the Flow, went through it and made the gate disappear as quickly as he could.

He wouldn't have to wait another day. Everything depended on Revan? Well, it didn't matter who had manipulated the Flow. Revan would manipulate it right back. He'd fix all the mistakes he had made, if the Flow would allow him. He'd make sure Othercrystalled wouldn't be killed anymore and Havelna, or Erchina, or *whoever* was guilty of this mess would immediately get the punishment they deserved.

Revan started running. He'd been too afraid the first time. But now, he'd actually make everything back the way it was supposed to. He entered the room where the Flow was. He had no idea how he was supposed to do this, but he was going to—the Flow was oscillating between his two crystal colors again, seemingly calling for him. Good, the Flow wanted this as much as he did. So he ran to the Flow, focused on that. How did people manipulate a flow of lava? They'd stick a rock in it, maybe—so it seemed to make sense for Revan to put his hand into the Flow to change everything that way.

Revan was at the energy flowing between the two metal bars, in the middle of taking a deep breath when he heard, right behind him, "Revan, wait!"

Revan turned around and looked into the eyes of Mr. Havelna.

Chapter Nineteen

Mr. Havelna stood perfectly poised, as if he'd planned to meet Revan right there. He wore a smile that was perfectly regular, brimming with kindness—just the kind senior teacher Revan had gotten to know over the years. Revan was frightened beyond belief and felt he'd been caught, but Mr. Havelna didn't show any emotion but friendliness in his posture. Revan was right at the Flow, ready to change the world back again—and if Erchina was telling the truth, the perpetrator was right behind him.

Revan still couldn't believe Mr. Havelna was behind it all.

"Revan," he said with a smile, "I'm so glad you're here. Exactly according to plan. How about you move away from the Flow and talk to me?"

Revan still had his hand at the Flow and stared at Havelna, doubting, unsure.

"That's going to kill you," Havelna said. "You have to have a very strong will to manipulate the Flow. Only the elites can do that, and I'm very sorry, Revan, but you're not among them."

Revan swallowed. "What do you mean by 'very strong will'?"

"You have to be very determined that this is what you want. You have to want something despite everything, and everybody telling you something else. Then you have to show that determination a thousand-fold, because that strength of will is what you need when the Flow goes through your mind. That's why only Samillan and I have survived it. That's not you."

"So what if I touch it?"

"You die," Havelna said plainly. "The moment you touch that Flow, you'll be swept away and absorbed into it. You have to be able to resist."

"Oh," Revan replied. That made sense. The Flow was a god after all. Revan was just a common mortal, and that wouldn't be enough to change it. But he'd be ready to die for the cause, right? Revan's hand trembled. The Flow had asked him to manipulate it—but what if it didn't know? What if it would kill him too, with nothing changed? And what if Havelna was lying?

"Think of Gaveh," Havelna continued. "He's going to miss you. The magic is going to return eventually—wouldn't you like to be here for that? Seeing your parents again? Seeing your sister again? What was her name again—Farna?"

"Fenna," Revan corrected him almost immediately, and bit his tongue.

"Fenna," Havelna repeated. "Come on. Put your hand in that Flow, and it's going to kill you. I haven't seen it happen, but I know that's how it works. You won't accomplish anything."

It can't be him, Revan thought to himself. *This kindly man, who's helped me for so long*. Revan remembered all the times he'd seen Mr. Havelna in his office. All the times they'd discussed home and family. The teacher was a good man, Revan knew. And even now, he was trying to keep him from killing himself. Havelna had been a sort of father figure to him sometimes, when his own father was at home and not reachable. And yet, Havelna was here, with him, with the Flow, somehow. Erchina told Revan Havelna was behind all of this, that Havelna was a ruthless murderer, if he needed to be one. It made no sense. Revan kept doubting—until his hand moved away. He had too many questions, but Havelna couldn't be the bad guy, there had to be some kind of rational explanation for this that didn't involve Havelna being a murderous monster.

Havelna grabbed him from behind in an embrace—it seemed kind, but Revan realized Havelna was pulling him away from the Flow. "I'm so glad you're here."

"What..." Revan began. "What are you doing here?"

"How about we sit down," Havelna said, but he made no move to do so and instead pulled Revan away until there was a reasonable distance between him and the Flow. Revan wanted to go back, but something was stopping him. He needed more information before he'd act.

Havelna turned Revan away from the Flow, putting himself between them, and then gestured Revan should sit down. Revan, shakily, proceeded to do so.

"What are you doing here?" Revan repeated, his voice shaky, and he prayed to the Flow that he had made the right decision. It was weird, praying to an entity that was in the room with him.

"I'm so glad you're here, Revan," Havelna repeated, and the smile felt a little bit off, somehow. Revan had seen the teacher smile often enough, but it was never mean, and this smile hid a dagger. "I need some help, which is why I picked you."

"...Me," Revan said.

"Yes, you." Havelna gestured around himself. "Why do you think I'm here?"

No, Revan thought. *No, not him, anything but him.* "To...kill all the Else," Revan managed to squeeze out.

Havelna nodded. "Indeed I am. Do you know why?"

I've made the wrong decision. I've trusted the wrong person. Revan very quickly calculated if he could still make it to the Flow, but he realized—Havelna was sitting between them, still fully alert, ready to jump if necessary. Havelna would be there faster.

Revan wanted to cry again.

"Because we, as a society, have forgotten what it's all about," Mr. Havelna said. He shook his head. "Everyone's forgotten their place. People whose skill crystal and central crystal are lit up should become magicians—and *only* them. The rest have their own roles to fulfill. When the college was founded, it didn't let in any other lit-up crystals and Othercrystalled were *killed.* Nowadays if you're a lazy Othercrystalled, we like to keep it a secret and pretend nothing's going on. If your crystals change, or if you've got more than one lit up, the Flow has abandoned you and you have nothing to live for. We used to know that. We used to respect the Flow's will. But now? We actually hire people with different crystals." The principal made a disgusted noise. "In extreme cases you're *kicked out of the school.*

That's just grabbing the lava with paper gloves. Your hands are on fire, and you haven't fixed anything." Mr. Havelna sounded meaner the more he spoke, and with every word, the kind man Revan had gotten to know disappeared more and more into...whoever this *monster* was.

"But..." Revan said. Mrs. Erchina had been right.

"People with a lit-up central crystal are supposed to be leading. People with a lit-up skill crystal are supposed to be magicians. And the rest need to do as their crystal commands them to. If you don't want to do the role the Flow assigned you, too bad. Don't go against the will of the Flow."

"So you're the one behind all of this..." Revan said.

Havelna nodded and smiled proudly. "The Flow chose me itself," he said. "I know, because I suddenly found myself able to make a gate. I realized I could manipulate it after testing it once or twice. It knew I was strong enough."

Just like how I found the Flow, Revan thought. *Or rather, the Flow found me. The Flow found both of us.* That felt like it made no sense. "I set all of this up. Made sure the magic would stop, so that people would be suspicious of minorities again." Revan's stomach turned as he remembered how, all throughout history, Othercrystalled had been only tolerated if everything was going well. Havelna had ensured things wouldn't be going so well now. "And then I gave those people a scapegoat by having the Flow off all the Othercrystalled. People are surprisingly easy to understand, sometimes."

Revan had to get himself together, he had to hide his surprise, Havelna still trusted him... "so why am I here? For the same reason as you? The will of the Flow?"

Havelna laughed. "You're here because you know your place, Revan. I'm pretty certain the Flow doesn't have a *will*. I didn't find any of it for sure when I accessed it. The Flow is just a reflection of the people that live on this world. No god, just a mental reflection of all of us. *I* gave you that access, Revan."

"But the Flow gave you access to itself..." Revan said, trying to process what Mr. Havelna was saying. The Flow wasn't a god. The whole religion they'd built up was a lie. The

Havelna Revan had come to know would never have said such a thing and saying it in front of him would earn you a nasty look at best.

"Yes, and I'll admit that puzzles me as well. Maybe there are random events every once in a while where someone gets access to it. Truthfully, I don't know. All I know is that it knew my will was strong enough. The Flow simply doesn't have a will of its own.

"I got to know you in our earlier conversations, back when you missed your home so much. You love authority. You're one of the meekest people I know, as you're supposed to be. You get excellent grades but you'll never vie for a profession where you have to lead. Because you know you don't belong there, without a lit-up central crystal. When Mrs. Dahena suddenly turned out to use magic, you came to me again, knowing your own place. There was no better test. You're very intelligent and very meek, and that's a very rare combination. Unlike, for example, Hdar, who would probably discard any orders I gave her in a heartbeat if she felt like she had a better option."

The Flow *had no will of its own.* "So...this was your plan?"

"Well, I wasn't expecting you to stick your hand in the Flow immediately, Revan!" Havelna laughed. "That's a level of fanaticism from you that was new to me. I was expecting you to make it here, and then I'd appear and we'd talk, but you were a lot faster than I was expecting you to be." Havelna patted him on the knee. "I'm glad you made the right decision." He smiled.

Revan smiled back, through tears. Havelna would hopefully interpret those as happy tears, but Revan was wishing he could run to the Flow and fix everything, nonetheless. Or at least try to. But Mr. Havelna would stop him before it got that far.

"Then how did Mrs. Dahena still have magic?"

"I'd forgotten to lock her out of it," Havelna said. "Not a smart move. I did that later, and dumped her body at Erchina's. But that's why I gave you the gate, to send you to Erchina's island. I had to get rid of her. I'm sorry, I'll admit that she threatened you. I'd never meant for that to happen. I knew I could trust you. And you showed it to me again just now. You're my lieutenant, Revan. I can trust you. You went against my wishes once, but you got punished for that immediately, and now you know your place again. I'm so proud of you."

The words hit him like a punch in the face. Everything Mrs. Erchina had said was right—even though he didn't want to believe it, still desperately wanted the truth to be a lie. But maybe he was lying about the Flow, and the Flow actually had a will of its own?

"I know everything," Havelna said, and smiled—it wasn't the kindly smile, this one was all grin and daggers—and Revan felt his last hope vanish. Mr. Havelna knew about Mrs. Erchina. Mr. Havelna had given Gaveh access to that gate, somehow. To test him? To move Mrs. Erchina in the right direction? "So, shall we head out?" It still sounded so friendly.

"But...I was here earlier..." Revan still tried. "The Flow was flowing so calmly then. It seemed to tell me I had to change it."

"The Flow is a reflection of everyone, Revan," Havelna said calmly. "You were close. Your emotions were the most powerful for the Flow to feed on. It responded to that. You were why it flowed so strongly."

"And that's why it's so calm now?"

"Exactly." Havelna reached out his hand to Revan. "We have so much more work to do." In that hand, Revan still saw a little bit of hope.

He doesn't know I'm Othercrystalled. Or he wouldn't have reached out like that.

The Flow didn't know who was Othercrystalled, Mrs. Erchina had been sure of that. Maybe that meant Revan had a little bit of time left. He took Havelna's hand. Inside of Revan, a small flame of hope flickered as it fought another thought, one Revan hated. One he'd been having his whole life.

What if Havelna is right? What if the Flow somehow wanted *this to happen, as it gave Havelna access to itself?*

Once they returned to the college, Revan could still make gates to Mrs. Erchina's island and his bedroom—but he was no longer able to make a gate to the Flow.

Chapter Twenty

"I can access the Flow," was the first thing Revan said when he was back in his bedroom. Gaveh was there, sitting on the bed, waiting for him to return. Gaveh's jaw dropped as soon as Revan said it. "Or rather, I *could*," Revan added.

He sat down on the bed. Gaveh wrapped an arm around him, clearly seeing the emotion on his face, and Revan told his story about how he was supposed to go to Mr. Havelna but went to the Flow instead, finding Mr. Havelna right there, telling him everything. Gaveh listened without a word. Revan's story wasn't without pause, occasionally Revan was interrupted by tears. He hadn't seen it. He *hadn't seen it*. In all those days, weeks since the magic had disappeared and Othercrystalled were killed, Revan hadn't seen who was to blame.

And with each day Revan hadn't seen it, he had furthered the plans of the mass murderer. He had brought Havelna to Mrs. Erchina. He had talked to Havelna instead of sticking his hand in the Flow, and that was how he'd killed the only solution they had. If he'd shown it to Mrs. Erchina, everything would've been solved now. If he'd actually followed through on changing the Flow, he might have died but at least he would've tried to change it, and if he'd succeeded, perhaps no-one else would've died and Revan could've gone home. Only when Revan was done and said, "Then I arrived here and I'm unable to go back," did Gaveh start talking.

"The Flow does have its own will," he said calmly. "How else could I have made a gate to Mrs. Erchina?"

"Havelna says he knows everything," Revan replied. "Havelna says the Flow isn't a god. He's put his hand in it, he knows what's up." Revan tried not to think about all the religious implications that had, tried not to think about how that affected everything he'd been taught before.

"Havelna's lying."

"But he said so..."

"Havelna knew nothing at all," Gaveh said. "He can claim whatever he wants. Him allowing me to be with Mrs. Erchina makes no sense at all, by any stretch of the imagination. You *have* to see that."

"I don't know, so far I haven't seen anything. And when I assumed I knew Havelna, I turned out to be wrong. I just don't know anymore." Revan shook his head. "I'm an idiot for not seeing it."

"I only got it when Mrs. Erchina approached me. You're smart too, in your own way."

"Well, I don't feel it," Revan sighed. "I made everything so much harder. I should've gone back to Mrs. Erchina and..." He shook his head and sobbed again. "I hate myself. Everyone who's going to die now is my fault. We lost, Gaveh."

"We haven't," Gaveh said calmly. "We can still do a lot. You need to calm down, Revan. Catch your breath."

"Then could you get me a glass of water?" Revan said. He smiled, despite everything. The last person who'd gotten him a glass had betrayed him. Gaveh never would. How could he ever have doubted him? Beautiful, sweet, intelligent, sexy Gaveh. His best friend and maybe even more. But Revan didn't allow himself to think more about that.

"We have to go to Mrs. Erchina," Revan said as soon as Gaveh returned, with the glass that Revan gladly accepted.

Gaveh shook his head. "You took longer than we expected. We can't go there anymore."

"Because?"

"It's late. Around this time the cleaners in the library get to work. They'll hear when there's sounds coming out of the hatch, and they'll ask questions we can't afford."

"Ah." Revan rubbed the last tears out of his eyes. "Is he right?" Revan asked.

"Havelna?" Gaveh asked. Revan nodded. "Why would you ask that?"

"Because I don't know," Revan sighed. "Because I trusted him for such a long time. Because the Flow apparently gave him access itself. If he's winning...is he right?"

Gaveh responded by putting his hand on Revan's calm crystal, above his shirt. It was still tied at the hem. He looked Revan straight in the eyes. "Revan, you're one of the smartest guys I know, despite what you just claimed. You're also a sweetheart, and good in bed."

"But Havelna…"

"Havelna can jump in lava somewhere. You know he's wrong. You're you, and I'm very happy with you. I don't care about which of your crystals lights up or why."

It helped—a little bit. Gaveh said the best thing he could've said, given the circumstances. And yet, Gaveh had told Erchina about his crystals. It wasn't that Revan was angry anymore—because Gaveh had been right, it had been the right thing to do. And yet, Gaveh telling her showed Revan that there was a part of himself that Gaveh didn't understand.

He needed to talk to somebody who *did* understand, more than Gaveh, at least.

"I want to tell Arana," he said. "Show her the hatch and show her Mrs. Erchina. I think she can help us."

"Because?"

"She'll have to tell you that herself. Trust me."

Gaveh shrugged. "Sure. Let's go to sleep? We can't do anything else anyway."

Revan nodded. Yeah, that seemed like it made sense. That was Gaveh—great with people, understood everyone, and always right in the end.

A brief silence fell between them, both of them breathing in the silence. Gaveh seemed to be waiting for something. Revan too, but he didn't know what that was. Would he jump Gaveh and ask him for some consolation sex? No, because that would feel like something different, something Revan couldn't put his finger on. Revan didn't know what he wanted and still didn't allow himself to think about it too long. Finally, he turned away. "Good night," he said, standing up to head to the bathroom.

"Good night," Gaveh said, the moment gone.

* * *

But Revan couldn't sleep. After two hours he woke up again and stared at the ceiling. Havelna's words kept going through his mind, and the paradox of the Flow not having a will of its own, yet allowing Havelna access to it. The fact that Havelna, and indirectly Revan himself, was responsible for all those deaths wouldn't to leave his head. So he decided to get up, and when that didn't help, he decided to head into the hallway, hoping none of the teachers would send him back. Considering recent times, they'd become more lenient about students leaving their bedrooms, but some teachers would still send back any students they caught. Revan thankfully didn't see anyone, because he really needed to get out, walk around, and think. Get everything in order.

He decided to walk to the eating hall. The doors would be shut, but that didn't matter. Maybe he would run into other students. He surely wasn't the only one having trouble sleeping—but to Revan's surprise, the doors weren't shut when he got there.

Arana sat at the table, her eyes red from crying. She saw Revan coming. Even though the lights weren't on, the light of the moon made everything a bit more visible. She quickly rubbed her eyes and cursed. "Revan?" she said softly, but Revan heard it, as there was no other noise to drown it out. "What are you doing here?"

"I could ask you the same thing," Revan replied.

Arana swallowed away a lump in her throat. "I think we both have the same problem?" She yawned.

"Yeah," Revan said. "But Gaveh's out cold. I don't get how he does it."

"Havelt is asleep too. He doesn't understand why I'm so scared." Arana shook her head. "Your advice didn't help, I'm still worried."

"So am I," Revan said. "So, hi."

Arana laughed. Revan walked over and sat down next to her. This felt right, more right than when he sat down across from her. Arana needed consolation and Havelt wasn't going to give her that. But Havelt didn't get it.

"I hate myself," Revan said.

"Me too," Arana said. "I mean, I hate myself too. Not you. I don't get why anyone would hate you."

Revan nodded. "Exactly. Same with you, by the way. Stop hating the smartest, most beautiful girl I know."

Arana grinned, wiping away some tears. "I thought, maybe the Flow will come kill me tonight."

Revan looked at her, surprised. "Why? The Flow is only coming for Othercrystalled."

"Now," Arana said. "But maybe it'll come for more different people later. I'll be a goner then."

"I know that feeling."

Arana sighed and laughed. "I'm sorry, my mind's being weird. You must have a harder time than me."

"Could be," Revan said indifferently. "Did you tell anyone, apart from Havelt and I?"

Arana shook her head. "I'd mentioned that, hadn't I?"

"Havelt won't tell anyone?"

"No, he just thinks the whole thing with crystals is overrated and he'd rather stay out of it. He won't tell anyone."

"Then you'll live."

Arana looked at him, disbelieving. "Nice that you're so sure."

"I have a good reason," Revan said. He considered telling Arana right there, but held back. It was better to wait until tomorrow. He wasn't sure if he could convince Arana that Mrs. Erchina was on their side, and Havelna was the cause of all the problems. Mrs. Erchina could do that better herself.

"Well, thanks, I'll just go back to sleep now that you've solved all my problems in one go," she said sarcastically. "Didn't know it was so simple."

Arana had given up. Revan had been like her not that long ago, but Gaveh had talked to him and was still working on getting his hopes up. His attempts had helped a little. "I get it, you know."

"What?" Arana asked.

"Having a Koden that thinks the whole crystal business is overrated." Revan smiled. "Gaveh's like that too. He's trying to be kind, but...I don't think he gets it either. He's always had the right crystal; he's never had to struggle with keeping his crystals hidden."

Arana sighed. "Havelt just says, you're you to me, I don't care about what color your crystals have."

Revan nodded. "Exactly. But you do."

Arana nodded. "I've been different my whole life, you know? It's so easy to say that the whole system doesn't matter if you're the one benefiting from it. But the system's here, and even if it's screwed up, it's still making me suffer." She looked at Revan. "And you."

"Gaveh's the best," Revan said. "But he doesn't get it."

Arana wrapped her arm around him, hugged him close to herself, and Revan smiled and hugged her back. Gaveh was perfect—but this conversation would've gone very differently with him. Arana understood this, even if her first response had been off—she'd redeemed herself sufficiently. He knew Gaveh through and through, there were no surprises there, which was lovely, but Arana's mystery was also very alluring.

"Arana?" Revan asked once the hug was over.

"Hm?"

"Could you come to my room tomorrow evening? I want to show you something."

Arana laughed, differently from before—her laugh was beautiful, genuine and lovely and for a second it did solve all Revan's problems. "If you want to hook up you can just be direct about it."

Revan immediately wanted to deny that vehemently. But Arana turned to him and smiled that wonderful smile once again, and Revan forgot everything around him, including what he'd wanted to say.

Arana was *beautiful.* Not in the way Gaveh was beautiful. Gaveh wasn't just his Koden because they had such a good connection—but Gaveh's attractiveness was more in a sexy way. The kind of attractiveness that made Revan want to do things with him. In addition to that, he had a great personality, making him attractive in an accessible way. But Arana was beautiful in a way that made Revan feel lucky to be there with her. Beautiful in a way that somehow revealed how intelligent she was. Through their eye contact, Revan felt like she revealed everything about him, and he was comfortable with that, which was a new feeling. Revan barely remembered them having been in a fight where he might have been right. Arana was a friend. Arana was...maybe more than that.

It was completely silent in the eating hall and once again Gaveh's words went through Revan's mind, with a small addition. Revan both agreed and disagreed strongly. *In another world Arana and I might have become a couple. But we might still become one.*

Revan realized he'd been quiet for a very long time and was staring at Arana. Arana stared back at him, and the silence between them felt heavy. Revan wanted to say something to break the silence, and yet he squeezed his lips shut, fearing sound would come out. Arana's face came closer and for a second time in a very short time Revan's heart was pounding the hardest it had ever pounded. He had to go, needed to be somewhere else, and yet he wanted to be nowhere else but with her. His mind decided for him and closed the last bit of distance between their mouths. The kiss didn't take long, a few seconds at best, but in that short time a very heavy burden fell off Revan's shoulders, and the part that wanted Revan to leave vanished.

Once the kiss was broken Revan nervously blurted out, "Mine isn't as big as Havelt's."

Arana immediately chuckled and Revan hated his own mouth. "I know," she said when she paused for breath. "I saw it, you know."

"Oh, yeah," Revan said, getting redder. He really shouldn't have said that. They weren't there yet, this was just a kiss, Revan was still involved with Gaveh, he was going way too fast...

"I have to admit I like you a lot more than I like Havelt," Arana said, still smiling. "So I don't really care about size. If you want to show me something in your room..."

"No," Revan blurted out. "No, no, no. Not that. I shouldn't..."

Arana's face fell. "That's a very firm rejection."

Revan swallowed. "Sorry," he said, trying desperately to keep his dignity as he threw it away for the second time. "I do want to show you something in my room, but...not in *that* way. It is *actually* important."

"Oh," Arana said sheepishly. "And I thought you and me...ah."

"I do like you," Revan quickly added. "Really, I do, but I have so much on my plate..."

"It's okay," Arana said. "You're right. The world's on fire, and I'm thinking of sex."

"No, I don't mean that either, otherwise it would've been fine to visit my room for..." Revan didn't know how to finish his sentence because he didn't have the guts, but also because he just didn't know how to end it. *What* could he say? He had *no* experience with romantic relationships. A Koden was great for figuring out what kind of sex felt good, but there was no romantic Koden. Everything Revan could say now only seemed to sink him further into the lava.

"It's okay, Revan," Arana said calmly.

"No, sorry," Revan stuttered. "I don't want to reject you but there's a lot going on and I don't know how or what or..."

Arana put her hand on his leg and smiled. "It's okay. We'll discuss this later." She patted him on the arm. "I'll see you tomorrow in your bedroom. Not for sex."

"Great," Revan said. His heartbeat dropped slowly. Had he done the right thing, said the right words? He hoped so.

"But before you go, one thing. Were you already interested in me?"

"Yeah," Revan said immediately. "Gaveh knew."

Arana looked at him, confused, then laughed again. "I thought you and Gaveh would hook up."

"What..." Revan said. "Huh?"

"Yeah, it happens more often. Kodens falling in love. Such a relationship can be very intense and deep, for some people." Arana rolled her eyes. "Whenever the two of you are together you seem to disappear into each other, somehow. When Wilan and Javik turned their Kodenship into a relationship I saw it coming too. So I thought, if you guys upgrade your Kodenship, that's great, I'll just step back. I really thought I didn't have a chance."

That remark somehow hit Revan right where it hurt, right where he kept on wondering, *Can I become happy with Gaveh?*

"I...um...we" Revan tried to say something, but he still didn't know what to say.

But Arana kept talking as if she didn't hear him. "Which is why I reacted like that when I saw your crystals. I was so shocked...it made me say the wrong things."

"Wow," Revan said. Arana had liked him for a while. Even though he was so confused, that felt very good to Revan. They both fell quiet, Arana seemed to expect him to say something, but Revan just dumbly said, "See you tomorrow." He stood up. "And about the whole liking thing..."

"We'll discuss that later," Arana said. "See you tomorrow." She winked. "And thank you. I feel a lot better."

"Same," Revan said, smiling back at her. Arana liked him too, which was fantastic, and before his feelings had become a mess, Revan would've killed to find that out.

Now, though, he'd only grown more confused.

Chapter Twenty-One

Gaveh made a gate in their bedroom, with Arana and Revan watching. "What…" Arana said once she saw the gate. "How can you…but…"

"Trust me," Revan said, "that's not the most shocking thing you're going to hear now." It seemed like Arana wanted to run away and tell everyone what she had seen, but she noticeably held back, looking pale. Gaveh had made sure Erchina wasn't visible; the gate was looking at a neutral wall.

Arana walked through the gate. Revan and Gaveh jumped after her and Gaveh closed the gate.

"Hi Arana," Mrs. Erchina said. "I'm the one your school's been looking for days."

Arana screamed.

* * *

Thankfully nobody needed to hold her. "I know this is hard to believe," Revan said to Arana the moment she'd seen Mrs. Erchina, "but listen to her, this was a struggle for me too."

And Arana listened. Reluctantly at first, but as Mrs. Erchina kept talking, it was clear Arana started to get it, at which point Revan thought to himself, *How could I have missed it for so long.* In hindsight, it all seemed so clear. At the end she was completely shocked, but also fully convinced—to Revan's relief. He had needed more time.

"I've been on that committee," Arana said, her hands in front of her mouth, shaking her head. "I went with it. I thought he'd just had good intentions with all of us, also because he kept talking about how young people have the future, that we're far more flexible…"

"I fell for it too," Revan said. "If you think this is weird, realize how weird it was for me to hear this all from Havelna. I talked to him. If he found out I'm Othercrystalled…" A shiver ran down his spine. He realized he'd just openly said he was Othercrystalled to a group of people that wasn't his family. They all knew about Revan's true nature. He didn't have to hide who he was to these people.

"What are we going to do now?" Arana asked.

"Kill Havelna," Mrs. Erchina said.

That remark sucked all the air out of the room. Revan asked, "Is that the only solution?"

"Havelna's not going to give up," Mrs. Erchina said. "We don't understand the Flow, but we understand he can manipulate it. He's the only one who can get to the Flow right now, so we need to kill him. If we kill him, he can't tell the Flow who else to kill. And no more Othercrystalled die."

"Can't we get to the Flow in some way instead?" Arana asked. "Can we undo the changes Havelna made and lock him out of making gates, the way he's done to us?"

"How do you want to accomplish that?" Mrs. Erchina asked.

The guilt returned. "I could have," Revan said.

"Excuse me?" Mrs. Erchina asked.

Revan explained what he'd been up to, how he'd gone straight to the Flow to fix everything, but how Havelna had unfortunately managed to talk him out of it—and how Havelna had taken the gate away from him once Revan had come back. "He said himself this was all his own doing, the Flow doesn't have a will of its own and he gave me that magic, by means of testing me. But the Flow does have its own will, right?" He looked at Mrs. Erchina, but she avoided his gaze. "Right?" Revan asked again, desperate.

"Mrs. Erchina?" Gaveh asked, also worried.

"The Flow is a mysterious force," Mrs. Erchina said after a silence that was too long. "Lots of people have written lots of books on it, guessing at the motives of the Flow. Everything I say is guesswork. Everything Havelna says too, I think. Someone being able to freely access the Flow is a very recent thing. Samillan is the only one who could, and he wasn't exactly clear about it."

"So he could be right?" Revan asked, cursing to himself.

"He has more experience with the Flow than me..." Mrs. Erchina said.

"But it's not possible," Gaveh said. "It doesn't make sense that Havelna gave Revan access to the Flow, right? He wouldn't risk all of his work to 'cleanse' the world being undone, right?"

"Or he doesn't feel Revan's will is strong enough to change the Flow," Mrs. Erchina said. "After all, he told you someone needs a strong will to manipulate it. I'm sorry, I know you're expecting encouraging words, but I'm just being honest."

"Okay, but then we have the conundrum that the Flow gave Havelna access itself..." Arana began.

"Which might be a will, it might not be, we don't know," Mrs. Erchina replied.

"But..." Gaveh growled in frustration. Then he made a gate to his bedroom appear. "He would never do *that*. He doesn't know you're here."

"I'm assuming that," Mrs. Erchina said, sighing again. "I genuinely don't know how the Flow works, and I just want to prepare you for the worst. I'm just going to assume the Flow has a will of its own. If it doesn't, then...we already lost the moment something gave Havelna access to the Flow. Whatever it was."

"Or," Arana said, "we manipulate him into making a gate to the Flow, so that you"—she nodded to Mrs. Erchina—"can walk through, and then manipulate the Flow as quickly as you can."

"Havelna will be there to manipulate everything back the way it was," Mrs. Erchina replied. "It'll be about who has the strongest will. I don't know if that's me."

"But that's a better option," Arana said. "We can always kill him after."

Mrs. Erchina sighed. "How do you envision that? Havelna just suddenly making a gate that I can walk through? He'll never do that willingly. He knows how dangerous I can be for his plans."

Arana sighed. "I'm talking about killing the principal..." She looked at Revan. "This is such a mess."

"Sorry," was all Revan could stupidly say to that.

"Havelna makes a gate to the Flow," Arana went on, "and Revan distracts him before he can close it off, and you'll run through it? Revan attacks Havelna as he tries to stop you?"

"Havelna will probably want to make that gate in his private room," Erchina replied. "How am I supposed to get there? He will never allow me in there and there's no secret entryway I can crawl through."

"Flow," Revan cursed, then he realized something. "What if I told Havelna there's a hidden room in the library? I want to show it to him, and then I'll ask him to make a gate to the Flow there." Everyone looked at Revan and Revan realized he'd agreed to the plan, so he might as well continue. "I tell him there's a room here, he comes here to check it out, together with me. Somehow, I'll try and convince him to make a gate to the Flow. Once he does so, Mrs. Erchina somehow appears and runs through the gate." He realized how nebulous this all sounded—a lot of "somehows." But he might as well continue. "Havelna will run after her, but I'll run after him and try and stop him somehow, so that Mrs. Erchina has enough time to change the Flow." Revan sighed. "Never mind. That was a silly idea."

"Not really," Mrs. Erchina said. She pressed a brick in the wall, and a dark space opened. It was just big enough for a bed and a small toilet. "I can partially open this wall and hide behind it. If you distract Havelna while he's here, he might not notice I am too, and I can get through the gate. But what then?"

"You run to the Flow, Havelna will have to run after you, and I attack him from behind. You change the things that need changing." Revan's hands trembled as he realized that he had to be the one.

"I can do it too," Arana said.

Mrs. Erchina shook her head, voicing Revan's thoughts. "The room behind here is too tiny for two. If we have to take care of two people, chances are higher it'll fail. Revan, you're the only one who can delay him. If he puts his hand in the Flow, you stop him. It'll be two against one, Revan. It's our best hope." Revan nodded, very reluctantly. Erchina must've seen that, because she added, "I'd rather it have been a grown-up, but he trusts you, which makes you the only one who can pull this off."

Revan nodded. "Then let's do it this way."

* * *

After they'd talked to Mrs. Erchina and Arana, they all went their separate ways. Revan's nerves were killing him. Tomorrow they'd have to strike—the longer they waited, the more Othercrystalled could die. The plan wasn't the best, but there wasn't another option, except maybe kill Mr. Havelna—and who was going to do that? Revan wasn't. It could all go wrong so easily.

That evening, when Revan and Gaveh were in the same bed again, Gaveh asked, "Are you and Arana a thing now?"

Revan was still thinking about tomorrow. "Eh?"

"You two were standing kind of close together. You looked at each other a few times." He studied Revan's face carefully; the light was still on. "At the very least, you two got over your fight very well."

"We talked," Revan said. "And...well, she has a secret of her own. That made it easier for her to understand me." He shrugged, feeling like that was all he wanted to share.

"Okay," Gaveh said. Then, "Did you guys kiss?" Revan opened his mouth, then closed it again, and that was apparently enough of a giveaway. Gaveh's face fell, and his expression was heartbreaking. "Okay," he said. "When are you moving out?"

Revan was briefly overwhelmed, unable to respond, before he finally answered, "We're not starting a relationship yet. We have enough on our plate as is."

"Okay," Gaveh said, his voice breaking. "I'm happy for you."

"You don't sound happy," Revan said. *Or look happy*, as Gaveh's eyes were welling up with tears.

Gaveh swallowed and shook his head. "I'm going to miss you, that's all."

"We can still be friends," Revan was quick to respond. "That will never change." *But it won't be what we both want,* Revan's thoughts supplied.

"Yeah," Gaveh said, and he turned off the light. Revan heard him turn around, and he realized Gaveh was probably quietly sobbing to himself. Revan wanted to comfort him, talk about his crying, but he knew Gaveh would probably deny it completely so that he could pretend he was happy for Revan. So, Revan didn't do anything but lie there and stare at the ceiling, bewildered and sad over a choice he hadn't made yet. Even if Gaveh felt he had.

Chapter Twenty-Two

Revan didn't belong here, for multiple reasons. One of them was that regular students were never welcome in the private room of the principal, except at the direst exceptions. A principal wasn't allowed to play favorites and couldn't invite students for that reason. Only teachers were allowed.

Revan knocked on the door, his heart pounding, while he prayed to himself that Havelna wasn't there, running an errand of some kind. He knew the principal's room had extra protection, but Revan didn't see any guards at the door.

However, his question was answered when he heard a muffled voice through the door. "Revan? You're not allowed in here." That was Havelna's voice, distorted through the thickness of the door. Even with that distortion, though, it still sounded firm.

The door remained shut. "Sir? I need to talk to you."

"Students aren't allowed here," Havelna said.

"It's urgent," Revan said. "And I can't say it here."

"Revan, we talked about this. Talk to a teacher. Unfortunately, I..."

Time to bring out the big guns. "I found where Erchina is staying, probably." Revan had hoped to not play this card until absolutely necessary.

It was the right card to play, though, as the heavy door opened and Havelna stood in the doorway, looking shocked. "You're kidding."

Revan shook his head. "Follow me please, sir." He hated how his voice trembled.

Havelna stood there, pondering for a second or two, before he nodded. "All right, show me. This might be an exception. But remember; students are normally not welcome here."

* * *

Once he was in the elevator, Revan pushed the floor's button with a finger that shook a little too much. The elevator was quick, but even the few seconds it took were way too long. Revan felt like his whole plan was written on his forehead and the principal had read it already, but was just playing along.

Finally, the elevator arrived at the library's floor. "Follow me," Revan said, his voice still trembling, and he walked ahead of Havelna. He knew exactly where he had to go, and once he got there, he recognized the tile that was loose. Just in case, he looked around, but there were no other students.

So, Revan took the hidden handle and the hatch moved. Havelna blinked a couple times. "What?"

"Very weird," Revan said. "I was here and suddenly found this tile was loose. Once I pulled it up, I noticed a hatch was attached." He swallowed. "I think that Erchina might be staying there."

Havelna nodded. He looked ahead, into the hidden room. Revan looked with him and saw Mrs. Erchina had opened the hidden wall and was probably standing behind it. She was ready. Havelna climbed down the ladder, Revan walked after him and closed the hatch.

Havelna leaned against a wall. "She's not here," he said, looking around.

"Maybe she's somewhere else," Revan said. "But I wanted to mention something else first."

Havelna frowned. "Another thing?"

"Yes," Revan said, trying to keep his nerves still. So far, he hadn't stuttered, to his own surprise. "My Koden can make a gate."

"Your Koden? Gaveh?" Havelna asked, eyes wide open.

Revan allowed himself a brief sigh of relief. Havelna didn't know of Gaveh's gate. So either the Flow had a will of its own or something else was going on.

"I don't get it either. But I thought you'd want to resolve it. And I didn't want to mention it over at your room, because I didn't know who'd be listening in." It was borderline miraculous that he still wasn't stuttering.

"Resolve it how?"

"Make a gate to the Flow?" Revan asked conversationally.

"Fix it now, before Gaveh ruins our plans." Havelna looked around, but as far as he knew there was only him and Revan. "I won't tell," Revan quickly added.

Havelna hesitated, nodded, then made a gate. He watched Revan in front of the gate, appraising. Revan waited for Erchina to appear, but she didn't, probably afraid Havelna would get her before she made it through. "Come along," Havelna eventually said. He walked through the gate.

Revan stood up, as slowly as he could sell to Havelna, stalling. He allowed himself one look over his shoulder and was certain he saw a pair of eyes in the wall, as if Erchina was looking through some second tiny hatch. Then he walked through the gate.

Just before the gate disappeared a shadow ran through. That shadow bumped against Revan, then against Havelna and shoved him to the side.

Havelna cursed and looked ahead. He must've drawn the right conclusion already. For one moment he looked over his shoulder at Revan, his face an angry mask. Then he sprinted away, chasing Erchina, who was thankfully ahead of him.

Revan ran after them, through the long hallway, and despite the Flow apparently not being a god, he still prayed to it while running. At least Havelna wasn't catching up to Erchina, to Revan's relief. That meant Erchina was the first in the sacred room. If she was impressed by the room around her, and being in the presence of a deity, she didn't show it. Revan was the last to appear in the room and saw Erchina put her hand in the Flow. He felt a change in his magic that he couldn't explain. For a second, Revan thought, *We'll manage, we've saved everyone.*

But then Havelna got to the Flow and put his hand in it, and Revan could only watch helplessly as he tried to run as fast as he could. But Havelna seemed oddly nonchalant about putting his hand in the Flow given the circumstances, and Revan knew why as soon as he looked at Erchina. She was in pain, her eyes open wide, her mouth opened in a soundless scream. Revan wanted to act, to jump Havelna and stop all this, but before he got close to the Flow, Erchina disappeared, together with all her clothes. Her body, and everything she was wearing, changed into pure energy that the Flow seemed to absorb. Revan's hope died with her, and the feeling Revan had in his magic had disappeared again. He was now at the Flow, but it was too late. He had been too slow.

Havelna turned around, his face fully calm, not a trace of the earlier anger. "Traitor," he said surprisingly calmly, as if he hadn't just killed someone. He had figured it out.

A thousand thoughts went through Revan's mind in a second. Could he run to the Flow and try and fix things? No, Havelna was blocking his way, and he'd be faster, and even if Revan could reach the Flow, Havelna would probably do the same thing and have him get absorbed by the Flow somehow. Punch him, shove him aside? Mr. Havelna was strong enough that he probably wouldn't budge, and he would see that coming from a mile away.

You're the only one he trusts, Revan, Mrs. Erchina's voice said in his head. He didn't know whether that was actually Mrs. Erchina talking to him through the Flow somehow, or his own thoughts. But he had to put a stop to this still, and that meant staying alive. If he couldn't reach the Flow, then he had only one alternative.

Revan kneeled and shouted, "She forced me!" Tears rolled over Revan's cheeks that meant something completely different than how Havelna would hopefully interpret them. "She found me, overpowered me, and told me I had to try and get the Flow back right again!" Revan cried as hard as he could as he felt so cowardly. He bowed his head to Mr. Havelna. He just hoped, with all his might, that Mr. Havelna would fall for it, so he could think up a different plan.

"She *made you*?" Havelna asked.

"Yes!" Revan said. He wished he had time to think, but he knew he'd be dead if he waited too long with his answer. Havelna simultaneously looked completely calm, and murderous, like he'd kill Revan without a second thought or even a feeling of guilt. "She forced me!"

Havelna watched Revan for a few horrible seconds, long enough that it made Revan think it was all over. *Gaveh, Arana, take good care of each other* passed through his mind.

"You could very well be lying to me," Havelna said, still calmly—but he was doubting, apparently. It was Revan's duty to seize that doubt.

"Please..." Revan sobbed. He looked up, looked the murderer in the eyes, and felt his last shred of honor die. He was bowing to the guy who was murdering his *kind*, after all. Part of him wondered what would happen if he were to stand up to Havelna now and keep his honor. But he knew the answer. What good was honor if the world was on fire, if your *kind* was being systematically murdered? What good was being honorable if losing that honor was the only way to keep people alive?

"She forced you, but it was your choice to send me here," Havelna said. "You could've come to me instead."

"I'm sorry," Revan sobbed.

Havelna grabbed Revan's shoulder and pulled him up. "I know," he said, his voice cutting. He stood right in front of Revan.

And Revan finally saw through the principal. While Havelna seemed calm at the surface, Revan saw the man was actually furious. Although the rest of his body moved as if nothing was going on, his lips were pursed and his eyes hard. "The college has a prison," Havelna said. "In the golden age those who were perverted were locked up there. Now it's sometimes used for students who act out. I assure you, Revan, you'll get to know the prisons a lot better. Follow me."

Despite everything, Revan breathed a sigh of relief. He was still alive. He could still help people. He'd squandered everything to sabotage Havelna's plans some more.

But he'd just kneeled to Havelna, a man who had freely murdered so many people like Revan. It had been a gambit and so far, it was working, at least a little.

That was some consolation as Havelna led him to the prison. Revan felt like he might throw up at any time, disgusted by himself.

He just hoped this would all be worth it, in the end.

Chapter Twenty-Three

The prison turned out to be on the lowest floor of the skyscraper, far from the floors that were assigned to the college. That was done so that students couldn't visit the prison by accident. It was fully empty; the floor probably wasn't in use anymore, or was used for other purposes.

"You're staying here," Havelna said to Revan as he threw him in the cell. "You're going to repent while I try to fix everything you've broken. I hope you realize you've made a very big mistake." The cell was everything Revan had expected it to be—three walls, and the fourth wall was just bars. There was also a small window to the outside—but it was too high for Revan to look through—and there was a small bed in the corner that didn't look very comfortable.

That evening someone brought him some dry bread, which was normally a punishment but it was the only thing the college had to offer in the first place. Revan ate it thoughtlessly, then slept on the bed.

Revan didn't know if Havelna was aware that he could still leave at any time. He still had two gates he could make, and they hadn't been taken away from him. One gate to his own bedroom and one gate to Mrs. Erchina's island. Perhaps Havelna didn't know, and otherwise he would've taken Revan to a cell made of a special material that made gates impossible. Revan had heard of those cells, but this wasn't one of them.

Or perhaps he did know, and he knew that Revan wouldn't and couldn't use that opportunity. After all, what could he do? If he made a gate to his own bedroom, then he'd appear there while everyone assumed he was still in a cell. He'd have to explain how he got somewhere else all of a sudden. And if Havelna spotted him, he'd just be thrown back in prison.

As for the gate to Mrs. Erchina's island, there probably wouldn't be enough food to last long enough, and he'd be all on his own. At least here he'd still be fed.

But, more importantly, it would make Havelna trust him less if Revan tried to escape, and particularly now Revan needed his trust. Revan didn't know how he could save the Othercrystalled, but one thing was clear: he was on his own now, the only grown-up who had assisted him was now part of the Flow because her will wasn't strong enough, if Revan understood Havelna correctly.

Revan hated the position he was in—he never wanted to be Havelna's lieutenant, and now he was trying to be. But at the same time, he still wanted to save other Othercrystalled, people like him, and if that meant hating himself, he'd take that. He wanted to stop Havelna's plans, at all costs, including his own self-worth.

Revan at least still had some trust left as there wasn't anyone standing guard at his cell to prevent him from escaping. Maybe because they knew Revan wouldn't try something like that, or maybe because Havelna didn't want anything to leak, or maybe for some other reason Revan wasn't aware of.

But that got Revan thinking about what Havelna knew or didn't know. It made him realize Havelna might know more than he was letting on. If you made a gate to some other place, you could hear what was said on the other side without being there. Havelna could have caught a lot more than Revan knew.

Just after that unsettling thought, Revan fell asleep. When he woke up from his bad nap—the bed genuinely wasn't very comfortable—Gaveh and Arana were at his cell.

Revan made a surprised noise and jumped up. "Good to see you," Arana said, smiling. "Mr. Havelna sent us." She put extra emphasis on the Mr. and yet somehow made it sound disgusted too. "He told us you might be alone. Didn't tell us what was happening."

"Yeah," Gaveh said. "We're very worried, though. I guess it's all gone very wrong."

Revan put a finger on his lips and shook his head. Gaveh frowned. "There's no-one..."

Revan pointed to all the cells around him and made the gesture for a gate. Gaveh looked confused for a second, but then nodded. He understood the message, Havelna might be listening in.

"Did Havelna send you guys?" Revan asked.

"He told us you were in a cell on the lowest floor," Gaveh said. "And if we wanted to drop by that was okay. But we didn't agree on a time or anything." He shrugged. "But, you know, I don't know anything. All I hear is that you're in prison—so something must've gone very wrong."

Revan held up a hand—Gaveh sounded so fake that Revan was worried he'd add a sentence like, "And we didn't plan anything with Erchina at all". "What did Havelna say this morning?" Revan asked.

"He warned us about food shortages," Arana replied. "A week has passed since he told us about the food situation, and we're running out of wheat from the supply stores. He's warned us that starting tomorrow, we're going to have to skip meals and students will have to go hungry. He's tried everything to make sure all the supplies are delivered as they should, but he's got no other option. He mentioned he prays every day to the Flow, waiting until the magic gets restored." Arana gave him a look that said everything. This was Havelna's plan, and as far as the principal was concerned, it would take ages before people could make gates again. "But he's also seen the light." Arana sighed. "He mentioned that maybe the Flow is just undoing some kind of corruption, after which he explicitly referred to the Othercrystalled. Maybe, he said, this is the way the Flow finally takes the souls it wasn't supposed to release in the first place." Arana's voice trembled with grief. Revan wanted to put his arm around her.

"What did the crowd say?" Revan asked, vicariously hoping for negative things.

"He was cheered," Gaveh said. "Some people said afterwards, 'hurray, he's finally seen the truth, fantastic!' A couple didn't agree, but nobody wanted to listen to them. He also announced Erchina had died and now the gates of the college can open again. Arana's going home tonight."

Revan nodded, but he wanted to start crying. Havelna was celebrating, and it felt like his fault as he'd decided to join him. The plan he'd made with Erchina had gone perfectly, it just hadn't been enough.

"I hate myself," Revan said softly, more to himself than to his friends, softly enough that Havelna probably couldn't hear it anyway.

"Hey," Gaveh said just as softly, causing Revan to look up. "It's not over yet."

"No," Revan said. "But Erchina's dead, and...if I ever go free, we need to plan." He swallowed. "For what it's worth." He didn't say what he needed to say in fear of Havelna listening in; but he didn't need to. Gaveh understood the message and nodded. *I will oppose Havelna with every breath I have.* And sometimes opposing meant looking like you supported them.

Revan looked at Arana and saw she had gotten the message too. She nodded. "We'll find a way," she said softly. "Try and get out somehow."

Revan smiled at her and suddenly felt deeply grateful she was on their side, planning with them. It was hard to believe, and Revan wouldn't have wanted it any other way. "How's Havelt?" he blurted out at a normal volume, despite the poor timing.

But Arana didn't seem to mind. She shrugged. "Things'll all work out, he says. He's been very absent-minded. He doesn't seem to care all that much."

"Hey," Gaveh said, "we can't stay for too long, but we'll come back some time, okay? Every day if we must. Until you're free. We're your friends. No matter what."

"Yeah," Revan said and he smiled. "Thank you."

He really needed to hear that.

* * *

Hours slowly passed and Revan was alone with his churning thoughts. At one point, he became so depressed he'd been certain everyone was doomed and he couldn't do anything. At another point, he'd been so certain he was going to save all Othercrystalled. Home, Gaveh and Arana, they all went through his mind, and Revan hoped a little more, with every passing second, that he would be given a way out soon. Being so on his own was driving him mad.

Eventually, he just decided to fall asleep again, since he had nothing to do anyway and he couldn't leave, even though it was just barely afternoon, probably. Revan closed his eyes.

A shuffle woke him up. He opened one eye, then suddenly opened both in shock. Javik noticed him waking up and said, "Hey."

Revan sat up straight. "Hey," he said. "What are you doing here?"

Javik shrugged. "Just curious as to how you're doing."

"How do you even know I'm here?"

"Gaveh told me," Javik said nonchalantly. "I'm curious why you're here." Revan didn't expect to have to explain the situation to anyone, and he was briefly taken aback. When Revan didn't say anything for too long, Javik said, "You didn't murder anyone?"

No, and that's the problem. "No, I just did something unfortunate. And since there wasn't really any way to punish me right now, they just put me here." Revan thought it best to leave ambiguous who "they" were.

"When will you be free?"

"I don't know," Revan said.

"Hm," Javik said. For a couple seconds they both fell quiet.

Then Javik started to cry. Revan perked up in shock. "What's wrong?"

Javik hid his face behind his hands, unable to answer because the tears stopped him from talking. Revan wanted to reach through the bars and put a hand on his shoulder, but Javik was just a little too far away. He just cried soundlessly for a couple seconds before finally saying, "Mr. Havelna spoke about...Othercrystalled."

"Ah," Revan said. "I heard. It must suck to hear...well...all of that, when Wilan was, you know..."

Javik didn't say anything, he just nodded, his face still hidden from Revan. He finally put down his hands, revealing his face was red from crying. "And that just allowed everyone to be nasty. About Wilan, to me, to my face. Plus, the whole Elselover thing." He swallowed. "And suddenly, I'm just so, so tired. But you were nice to me, and I didn't know where else to go."

"I also didn't show up to the service."

"But we were friends," Javik said. "Once. That still counts for something, right?"

Revan didn't have it in him to pretend it didn't, in case Havelna was listening in. "It does."

"Exactly."

"Gaveh and Arana also would've listened."

Javik sighed. "Maybe, but I feel like you would understand." He shook his head. "I just feel like we still have a connection, somehow. I don't know why. Maybe it's the Flow telling me this." Javik laughed joylessly. "If the Flow even likes me."

"Why wouldn't the Flow like you?" Revan asked.

Javik fell quiet for a couple seconds. The sobs stilled, Javik's face a bit more neutral. Then he said, "Because I'm not an Elselover."

Revan frowned. "What?"

"I never had sex with Wilan." Javik swallowed, hard. "Oh, we had a relationship, sure. I loved him, sure. But we never made love."

"But you were..."

"Kodens," Javik said, and the sobs began again, though Javik didn't hide away his face this time. "I know. Because everyone told me to get a Koden, and that I'd be a prude if I didn't get one. Everyone told me I needed to grow up and have sex, like all teens do. Because it was the will of the Flow, and I needed to obey it." Javik swallowed, pushing away the sobs. "But I wasn't ready to have sex. It just felt weird to me. So Wilan said, 'Just make me your Koden. I won't touch you anywhere, but we can pretend we're having sex.' He even offered to make some noises in the night so that people wouldn't call me a prude." Javik cried. "He gave up sex just to be with me. What else could I do but fall in love with him?"

Revan felt clumsy and awkward in the face of such a confession, particularly considering the circumstances, and for a couple seconds he was unable to say anything while Javik spilled out his secrets. "Why me?" he finally blurted out.

"Because I'm boiling over and I needed *someone* to know, and Wilan's dead, and if you hate me and judge me now..." Javik swallowed. "Then whatever. The Flow hates me anyway."

"I don't hate you," Revan said. He added, after a little silence, "But I don't get it. Sex is fun, right? It's a good way to get to know your own body. Kodens are perfect for that. It's just pleasure. Why would you ignore pleasure?"

Javik sighed. "I know. I didn't get it either. But I knew I didn't...want to. Not yet. I wanted to wait. But now..." The sobbing started again, and Revan decided to wait until Javik talked, and Javik finally said, "But I realized yesterday that I'm ready to have sex but he's dead and I waited too long." He took shallow breaths in and out at a quick pace, and Revan recognized the emotions were getting the better of him. He had to be shaken out of it somehow.

So, through the bars, Revan grabbed Javik's foot, and it immediately felt awkward. But it helped in grabbing his attention. "Hey," Revan said, looking at Javik. "I still don't get it. But I don't need to. I'm your friend." He smiled at Javik.

Javik smiled back, through tears. "Thanks," he said and it sounded clumsy, but tender. "It's nice to have one again."

* * *

Javik left soon after that, and just a few minutes after Javik disappeared Revan felt another change in his magic. He realized he could make a third gate and immediately knew where it would lead to. He *had* to make it. Not just because he was feeling the urge he felt every time he could make a new gate, but also because it wasn't just a place. Revan was able to make a gate home.

The walls of his bedroom were painted light blue, there was a light blue bed in the corner of the bedroom, two big closets, and a window. Right next to that room was his sister Fenna's room. Hopefully she was all right.

Revan stared through the gate and hundreds of thoughts went through his mind. *I can go home. It's over. I can leave.* He could finally get what he had wanted since the very first moment. Why? Had the Flow granted him this? Had Havelna offered him the option? But why would he?

He wanted to do nothing more than go through that gate and hug his parents again. Be back in a place where he could be himself, leave all this behind. In the distance he heard sounds. Was his mother busy in the hallway? Where was his father? He so badly wanted to go through that gate, have it all be over, pretend nothing had happened—and yet, he couldn't. He almost believed it was all over, that he couldn't change anything here anyway. But he'd thought it earlier too. If he went through that gate, he knew for a fact he'd never come back.

Revan's bedroom door opened. Whoever came through that door, once they saw the gate, Revan would be away from here. He didn't have a lot of time to think, so he made the gate disappear.

He *couldn't* leave. Not now, when there was still a solution. Yes, he was a coward for bowing to Havelna, but he'd done that with a reason. Leaving now would squander all that. Revan was the only one who could do this.

"Just go." The voice startled Revan. In front of his cell was Havelna, still wearing a calm expression. "Through the gate."

"Sir?" Revan asked, confused.

"I wanted to grant you that. Go through the gate. You've been loyal to me. Erchina manipulated you, and I don't know if I can ignore that, but I don't need to. Go home and we'll both have what we want."

So Havelna had given him this. Whether earlier gates had come from him or the Flow wasn't clear, but this one was clearly Havelna. Revan wanted nothing more than to run through that gate, because there wasn't a solution to this problem anyway. Havelna didn't know he was Othercrystalled, so Revan would be safe.

He *had* been listening in, because the timing just after Javik leaving was too convenient. Revan didn't know how much Havelna had been hearing of that conversation. It didn't matter much, thankfully.

Now Revan looked at the principal and saw all the anger beneath that calm expression. He could use that by saying the right things. Havelna thought he loved authority? Revan would use that. If Revan could do *anything* to ease the lives of his fellow Othercrystalled, he'd have to. He *owed* it to them. *Even if* another solution wasn't possible, he *had* to try. If the best possible thing was waiting for a miracle, Revan would be excellent at waiting.

"I can't go, too much is happening here," Revan said, and it was all true.

"Excuse me?" Havelna asked.

Revan looked at Havelna and bowed his head in humility. "I thought about it in jail, about what you did and why." He swallowed. "You're right. The college is being purged of Othercrystalled and afterwards from people with different crystals. People who don't belong here." Putting all the disgust he could muster, Revan added, "At home they see it differently. There they work with those people. I want to help you. I'm sorry Erchina manipulated me. There's nowhere in the world I'd rather be than here by your side." Revan kept the disgust in his voice. Havelna wouldn't know he was disgusted at himself, rather than at those "disgusting" Else.

Havelna kept quiet for a couple seconds and then said, "Do you swear you'll never try to fool me like you did before?"

Revan had to suppress a grin. *This is working.* "I do."

"Don't just swear," Havelna said. "Swear it on your home, your parents and your sister."

Havelna was probably expecting Revan to still have some honor left. Revan's family briefly went through his head—he apologized to them. *If the Flow punishes me because I'm an oathbreaker, I'll deserve it. And it'll be worth it.* "I do swear that."

The cell door opened, and Revan sighed in relief. He was free.

Chapter Twenty-Four

Revan was almost deliriously relieved to take the elevator upstairs, out of the cells. He was free, it had worked. And of course, the first thing he did was to go back to his bedroom, where he found Gaveh, who was relieved and surprised to see him. Revan closed the door behind them, and Gaveh embraced Revan firmly.

For a couple seconds, Revan enjoyed the touch. Then Gaveh wanted to break the hug, but Revan held on. "We can talk this way," he whispered. "Havelna can make gates everywhere, as long as he knows the room. But now we hear each other and we can be quiet."

"Ah, I see," Gaveh said. "I don't hate this."

"We have to find a spot Havelna doesn't know," Revan whispered. "A place where we can talk quietly." They were very close together. Revan only realized now that he had a hand in Gaveh's hair. He felt a little guilty about that. Of course, Gaveh was his Koden, but he was sort of seeing Arana now, right? They hadn't made anything official, and yet, this wasn't fair to her.

"The hatch?" Gaveh asked softly.

"No," Revan replied. "Havelna's been there, and we need a spot where he's never been, a place that's confidential to both of us. What kind of spot comes to mind?"

"Arana's house," Gaveh whispered back, and Revan could have slapped himself. He'd been thinking of Arana all the time, but he'd forgotten *that*. "Assuming Havelna's never been there."

"I'll go and get Arana," Revan replied, and he let go of Gaveh. He was almost at the door when Gaveh said his name, so he stopped and looked back. "Gaveh?"

"I'm happy you're here," Gaveh said and he smiled. Except it wasn't quite a smile, but more half a grin, that half grin that Revan had always found so sexy.

Despite everything, Revan wanted to jump his bones right then and there. But he also wanted to do so much more. Hold his hand, ruffle through his hair, kiss him on the mouth. Just because of that grin. Revan hated and loved how strong an effect Gaveh had on him.

But there was no time for any of that. Revan turned away. "I need to go to Arana," he said. If there had been a moment in the first place, it was gone now.

* * *

Arana's father welcomed them. It was unorthodox that on a school day they were suddenly standing there, but if he'd found that strange, he didn't show it for long. "Come in," he said. "My wife's at work. What can I do for you?"

"Could we go to my room, Dad?" Arana asked.

The man looked at both Revan and Gaveh, and then at Arana. "What are you guys going to do, then?"

"Discuss things we can't do at the college. Please, Dad. It's important."

Arana's father sighed and let them in. "You all have school, right?"

"Correct," Revan and Gaveh both said. Revan added, "Our next class is in an hour, as we don't have magic lessons. You know, we want to use our time as best we can."

"You can't do that in the college?"

"No," Arana replied, and she opened the door to her bedroom, and both Revan and Gaveh went in quickly.

* * *

"Havelna still trusts me. We're alone without Mrs. Erchina and we need a new plan." It was Revan's opener. "I don't know if there's still a way out, but we have to try, and it's just the three of us. But whatever happens, I want to thwart Havelna every step of the way."

"There has to be a way out," Gaveh said. "Somewhere."

"Where?" Revan said.

"Havelna realizes he's a terrible person and suddenly makes everything right again?" Arana asked, then laughed hard and sarcastically.

Revan laughed along with her, but then said, "No, but the solution involves him making another gate to the Flow, as he cut me off."

"And then? We need to manipulate it," Arana said.

"Which we can only do with a strong will," Revan said.

"That's according to Havelna," Gaveh interjected. "We don't know that for certain."

Arana sighed. "We basically do. I did my research in the library."

"Hm?" Revan asked.

"Thanks to the plans we made on the committee, I had to spend a lot of time in the library, and I found a couple more books from Samillan. As soon as it became clear what you guys were doing, I tracked those books down again and read every single one from him. Obviously, there's the *Right Roads*, and the *Dance of Balance*, but there's also a small booklet he wrote about the Flow itself. What he writes there is very vague, and he almost speaks in riddles, but if I remember the quote correctly, it's something like, 'Only those strong of will can change the flow of history.' I asked about it, and it's a line that's usually interpreted metaphorically. With what Havelna told us, it's clear to me Samillan was being literal."

"So we basically know for certain," Gaveh said. "Flow, that's not good."

"What are you talking about," Arana said sarcastically, "We'll just find someone whose will is just as strong as Samillan's and Havelna's, we manipulate Havelna again so that he makes a new gate to the Flow, we somehow manage to get this other person through that gate, and they'll fix it all. Simple as that."

"Not just a strong will," Revan said. "A strong will times a thousand, because that's what you need when the Flow goes through your mind. That's what Havelna told me. If he wasn't lying, and we don't think he was."

"Mrs. Garedna?" Arana suggested. "Her will might be stronger than we think?"

"Mrs. Garedna stepped out of the principal's role as soon as Havelna took over," Gaveh said.

"Maybe she doesn't want to become principal," Revan said, "and that's not her will. To me, she comes across as someone who knows what she wants."

"Mr. Khandar," Gaveh said. "He's very religious and devoted to the Flow."

"As far as we know, that doesn't make you survive the Flow," Revan replied. "A strong will does. Does Mr. Khandar have that?"

"I mean, he's a teacher and yet he doesn't have a lit-up skill or central crystal..." Gaveh said, but it was clear he felt it sounded weak as well.

"Mostly because he's a priest and also a teacher," Revan countered, "and we are obligated to have Religion teachers."

"Yeah, I know..." Gaveh said.

"We don't know how many chances we're going to get," Revan said, "and we don't have the opportunity to try all the teachers. We're only going to get one shot at this."

"Maybe there's a student with a strong will..." Arana began.

"Yeah, that'll be even easier," Revan said. "Just trust a random student, hoping they're not on Havelna's side, and hope they'll fix everything. I mean, the chance is fairly slim it's one of us three."

Arana frowned and paused a bit before saying, "Are you sure?"

Revan looked at Arana, one eyebrow raised. "Is your will so strong, then?"

"Well, no..." Arana said. "I was actually thinking of you."

Dumbfounded, Revan could only stare at Arana. "Excuse me?"

Arana pointed at Revan's calm crystal. "You didn't tell anyone about your second crystal, no matter how often Havelna said he had to know all Othercrystalled."

Revan shook his head. "But..."

"You heard stories about Othercrystalled who were kicked out of school, but you pressed on and became one of the best in our year. From the start, you've been dead set on correcting the Flow, whatever Havelna tells you—even if you have the option to go home. And now, you started this talk by saying you want to thwart Havelna at every turn still, even though Mrs. Erchina's dead and it all seems lost, but you keep saying we'll fix it. That will sounds pretty strong to me."

Revan blinked. "But..." he started. Desperately, he looked at Gaveh, trying to find support, but Gaveh just shrugged. It was clear—Gaveh thought he was a little *too* awesome. So Revan just started with, "But as soon as someone with authority appears I'll immediately follow him. Havelna had authority, so I immediately listened to him."

"You go against it too," Gaveh said. "You went with me to the highest floor of the skyscraper to..."

"Yeah," Revan interrupted him mostly because he didn't need Arana to hear what they'd been up to there at that time. "Except that I just did that to do you a favor. You already had that plan."

"I didn't have much of a plan," Gaveh said. "You know I don't plan those things well ahead of time. You could've said no, and no harm would've been done."

"Okay, so maybe I was feeling a little bold. That doesn't mean that I..."

"You also went against Havelna," Gaveh continued. "When the two of you went to Mrs. Erchina together."

"And that went wrong," Revan said, "because I was so eager to fix the problem."

"So your will is stronger than your urge to follow people," Arana replied.

Revan stuttered. "But...but...I've been slavishly following Havelna."

"When you thought he was helping people," Gaveh countered again. "The moment you found out he wasn't, you dropped him as fast as you could."

"But I'm still...sort of helping him."

"You're lying to his face while plotting against him, behind his back, with us," Arana said. "You're terrified of him, and yet you're determined to stop him. And again, Revan, you're Othercrystalled but you didn't tell anyone. We only found out through circumstances. And you kept it to yourself, stubbornly, despite both of us trying to convince you otherwise. That's not just a strong will, that sounds like a strong will times a thousand to me." She smiled. "And in the end, your decision turned out to be the right one. After all, we asked you to tell Mr. Havelna. You did not."

"But I'm not Samillan..." Revan began.

"I think you might be," Gaveh said. "You're our best shot."

"And we're not the only ones who think this," Arana said.

"Who else?" Revan asked, frowning. Gaveh seemed confused too. "Mrs. Erchina didn't exactly..."

"Not her," Arana said. "The Flow itself. Didn't it *ask* you to manipulate it, pretty much?"

"But Havelna said..." Revan wanted to add that the Flow didn't have a will of its own and just reflected what he wanted, but instead said, "Never mind," because he realized it was just another one of Havelna's lies. He sighed. "It's not that I don't want it. I'm willing to die to solve this problem. Which, I guess, is another hint that my will might be pretty strong. But Erchina died too, she put her hand in the Flow, and..." He gestured around himself. "For a moment something seemed to change, then it was all back to normal. We only get one more shot at this, probably. I want to be very sure." He looked at Gaveh. "Do you have a stronger will? You're not as eager to follow as I am, and you're always optimistic. You're incredibly stubborn towards your parents regarding the Kodenship, and you trusted Mrs. Erchina even though Havelna said something else." He looked at Arana. "Or you? You also have a..." He stopped himself. Gaveh didn't know yet.

"Different crystal," Gaveh said indifferently. "I was aware. She told me when you were incarcerated."

"Oh," Revan said. "Okay, you have a different crystal, Arana. You didn't tell anyone except for Havelt either and you dressed differently. You wanted to practice magic; nobody could stop you there. You had the brilliant idea to have the students look in the library for answers. Why can't it be either of you?"

"I'm happy to die for this too," Gaveh said. "And you're right about the whole Koden thing. Yes, to my parents I can be very stubborn. But I want to become a magician just like you, and yet I'm not nearly as devoted as you are. I'm eager to solve this too, but usually I'm not the one with the solutions, you are. And...there's one person I'm very eager to follow."

"Oh, who?" Revan asked. Gaveh looked at him for a couple seconds. "Oh," Revan said. "*That* eager?"

Gaveh nodded. "You've always been right in the end. It's hard sometimes, but I don't mind following you."

Revan watched his Koden, and the silence that followed was somehow both comfortable and awkward. *Not in front of Arana,* Revan thought to himself.

Gaveh broke the silence. "But if need be, I'll die. My spirit will come haunt you if you miss me." He smiled.

Revan looked at Arana. "What about you?"

Arana shook her head. "I told Havelt about my different crystal," she said. "Yes, I work hard, but that's because I don't want to disappoint my parents. Don't get me wrong, they're great, but they have high demands. What you tell me of your parents is very different—you study hard for *you*, because you want to get good grades, and that's a thing *you* want." She swallowed. "But I'd go too. In your place, if I could." She smiled, and Revan got lost in her smile. He stared back at her until he didn't know what he wanted anymore. Yes, he loved Gaveh, couldn't live without him, but also Arana had changed so much that Revan felt comfortable with her. He really liked being with her.

Revan didn't know what he felt for Gaveh anymore. He seemed to have a better future with Arana, and yet...maybe he was in love with both, as if it wasn't complicated enough. But it didn't matter. The moment his thoughts went back to the Flow, everything was difficult again, and his dilemma was forgotten. "I'll do it if I have to," Revan sighed. "I just don't think I'll survive. And the idea of me being Samillan is...weird. It's just too much of a coincidence."

"But I think you're the best option we have," Arana said. Gaveh agreed, and Revan loved and hated them intensely.

"Okay, fine. I'll do it," Revan said, more out of frustration than agreement. "Next step. How do I get to the Flow? I can make three gates, but none of them are to the Flow. Havelna took that away from me. How do we deceive Havelna again, if the first time failed?"

The silence in the room was deafening, even if it lasted just a couple seconds. It was clear they hadn't thought of the next step. "Ah," Gaveh said.

"You lost some of his trust," Arana said. "You need to get that back, then. Somehow. He's not going to fall in any kind of trap unless he trusts you again."

"And then I can ask him," Revan said. He felt icky. "Which means pretending to bow down to him again. As long as we need to." He hated that thought.

"I guess you're going to have to go back to Havelna," Arana said. "And ask him how you can help. Somehow. Try and get his trust back."

"And wait, while more Othercrystalled die..." Revan sighed.

"Do you have a better idea?"

"No," Revan said. "I hate it, but I will comply. As long as you two use that time to try and find someone better matched than me. Because we only get one shot at this."

Gaveh and Arana reluctantly agreed.

* * *

They went back to the college, and Revan tried to find Havelna to try and get his trust back. He'd prepared a whole spiel about how much he regretted falling into Erchina's trap. He'd been ready to say he'd do whatever the principal wanted to get his trust back. But all of it was impossible, because Havelna was nowhere to be found. Not even at the principal's room, and Revan had knocked multiple times.

That night, Revan went to bed annoyed; at Havelna for disappearing, and at Gaveh because he said he hadn't found anyone else yet. Despite everything, Revan still managed to fall asleep relatively quickly.

It was in the middle of the night when someone knocked on the door, waking Revan up abruptly. Gaveh moaned—he was probably half awake and would slip back into sleep easily.

"I'll open it," Revan said, and he got out of bed. Thankfully he slept in his pajamas. What idiot would knock on the door at this hour? Revan had just caught himself some sleep, nights where he slept well had been rare as of late. He'd tell whoever it was the angry truth. He looked around briefly, trying to find the roll of tape he always put on his crystal since he slept without it since Gaveh found out he was Othercrystalled. Unfortunately, Revan couldn't find it that quickly. Didn't matter—it was probably just a quick visit.

But when Revan opened the door, Havelna was on the other side. Revan gasped for breath. "Revan, come with me," Havelna commanded. Revan looked over his shoulder to Gaveh, but as expected, he was back dreaming again. "He'll stay here. Follow me!"

Whatever Havelna had been planning, Revan couldn't go against it if he wanted to get his trust back. Revan wanted to ask if he had to put on regular clothes, but Havelna's expression told him now was no time for questions. Havelna turned around and Revan closed the door to run after him.

As soon as they were at the end of the hallway, Havelna picked a wall and made a gate against it. Revan immediately recognized the location, seeing the walls made of that same brown gem. Havelna was taking him to the Flow. *Now?* he thought. *This evening already?* He suppressed the panic and walked through the gate. Havelna went after him and closed the gate. "What do you want to do?" Revan asked. "I'm at your service."

"Follow me," the principal said, pacing ahead. Revan ran after him, having trouble keeping up, the man walked quickly. While following Havelna, Revan quickly tucked his pajama shirt in his pants, hoping Havelna wouldn't see the light of his second crystal. But when they had arrived on the other side of the hallway, Revan's courage vanished.

In a corner of the room, far away from the Flow, was Javik. He had crawled away in a corner, his eyes big with fear, clothed in nothing but pajamas. "You can win my trust back. Javik is Othercrystalled, I believe. He goes against the Flow in multiple ways. I heard you two were friends. Kill him."

Havelna *had* been listening in to Javik and him.

Revan, Arana and Gaveh had no time to think up a better plan.

Chapter Twenty-Five

"What…" Revan started, gobsmacked, a million questions swirling around for both Javik and Havelna. Javik looked back, his eyes wide in fear. Javik was Othercrystalled too, just like him. In a flash, Revan realized that Gaveh had been the only person from their group back then that *wasn't* Othercrystalled. He'd never been a minority with his three friends around, but he'd never known. How had Havelna found out? Javik didn't say anything, just stared into nothingness—which he usually did, but now it seemed far more desperate than usual.

"You violated my trust," Havelna said. He interpreted Revan's "what" as meant for him, clearly. "Erchina manipulated you, you claim. This is your opportunity to win my trust back. Kill him." Javik was trembling with fear and Havelna clearly didn't care. "I got him out of bed. I heard from several sources the two of you got along. After one of my speeches, he'd reported in as Othercrystalled. He doesn't deserve to live, Revan."

Javik swallowed. It was the only thing he showed in response to Havelna. It was clear he was terrified, and Revan could only feel along with him, as he felt the same fear—but Revan couldn't show it. And yet…

Revan looked at the Flow and back to Havelna. This was clearly the center of his power, the place from where he had commanded the Flow to kill all those Othercrystalled. Havelna was showing off.

"Don't try that," Havelna said calmly. "Erchina showed you what happens. Nothing, and you die. Your will isn't strong enough for that." Revan wished he didn't believe that. But he was, despite everything, still so certain he was nowhere near as strong-willed as Samillan. "Do you need proof? Javik, take off your shirt." Javik shook his head, his eyes still wide. "I can make you feel pain through the Flow, Javik. It's best if you listen."

"I'll die anyway," Javik said, his voice trembling with fear.

Havelna rolled his eyes. "Talking back to your principal. All right, the hard way it is." He put his hand in the Flow, looking as uncaring as when he fought Erchina.

Immediately Javik's arms started to move to his shirt and Javik's eyes widened. "What..." he said. "No!" Havelna didn't respond. Javik's arms took his shirt off by themselves. A single tear rolled down Javik's cheek. Revan couldn't look away, even if he wanted to. Havelna would suspect him. So Revan watched Javik's crystals, awaiting the light from multiple crystals—but there was no light. As soon as Javik took off his shirt, it was clear—he had *no* lit-up crystals. That also made him Othercrystalled.

"Is this proof enough?" Havelna asked casually. Revan decided not to look away, kept looking at Javik's face.

"Please..." Javik groaned.

Havelna ignored him. "Revan, here's a knife for you."

Revan forced himself to look away from Javik. Havelna indeed handed him a knife. "Take it. Stab him in the neck, that's a good weak spot. It's not hard, if he resists, I'll manipulate him through the Flow." Revan looked at the knife, then at Havelna, immediately getting another idea. "Stabbing me won't help," Havelna said. "I'll be ahead of you, and I'll have disappeared through a gate before you raised the knife. But you're not going to stab me, right? You'll attack Javik, because I can trust you."

Revan looked back at Javik, his hand trembling. "Why here?" he asked with a voice that was more stable than how he felt.

"Because," Havelna explained calmly, "I can make Javik do what I want through the Flow. But also, so that I can give you access to the Flow then."

"But...strong will..."

"Yes, but my will is stronger," Havelna said. "As soon as you kill him, I can command the Flow to calm for you. You can make certain adjustments. Nothing against my direct will, but I'll need someone to help me every now and then. You can finally manipulate the Flow in the way you were so eager to do at first. Revan, what are you waiting for?"

Part of Revan thought, *If I kill Javik now, Havelna will allow me access to the Flow. I might use that.* Yes, someone else would die—but what good was honor if the world was on fire? His knees trembled as he walked towards Javik. Havelna almost trusted him. If Revan could do this, he would have won Havelna's full trust. Gaveh, Arana and he would have time to find someone whose will was strong enough, and if they wouldn't be able to, they could perfect their plan.

Flow, I'm actually considering killing a person. Worse, I'm considering killing a friend, Revan thought. His hand trembled and for a moment he was terrified of himself. He wouldn't kill Javik, not in a million years. He'd rather just stick his hand in the Flow and die himself.

...Right? Revan wasn't so sure anymore. Gaveh and Arana wouldn't consider killing Javik, not even for a second. And yet, Revan was genuinely considering it. Not because he hated Javik, but to further his plans. To save all the Othercrystalled, to restore all magic.

Revan stood right in front of Javik—Javik still sat in that corner. "Stand up," Havelna commanded him. "Or I'll make you."

Javik's whole body trembled as he forced himself up. Revan tried to make eye contact with him, but Javik looked away, probably already having accepted the situation. Of course, Javik didn't know, as far as Javik knew he was taken prisoner, and Revan was Havelna's right hand. Perhaps reluctantly, but he still was.

I have to kill Javik. It was a thought he couldn't get rid of. He would do it, he realized. To save all the Othercrystalled. To win Havelna's trust. Javik's death would hurt Revan dearly—but he would do it. He hated that.

But Revan knew that might also mean he was strong enough to resist the Flow. Arana's words went through his mind again, saying he had such a strong will. Gaveh's words went through his mind too, agreeing with her. And Revan knew there was only one way out, even if he wouldn't survive it.

Revan turned around.

Havelna shouted, "See, all this time, despite all I've done for you!" Havelna would kill him. This was their last chance, and Revan had to be there first. So he ran, desperately.

He threw his knife to Havelna, distracting him for a critical few seconds while he ran to the Flow. Havelna cursed, avoided the knife and sprinted after him, but Revan was there just a little quicker—ready to die, ready to be absorbed into the Flow like Mrs. Erchina, but it was the best thing he had. He put his hand in the Flow.

A flood of images went through his head. On one island a baby was crying. On another two lovers were embracing each other. On yet another island someone shouted angrily at the elevator because it didn't come. Two fathers mourned the disappearance of their daughter, who they hadn't seen since the magic had disappeared. An older man had his ninetieth birthday party, a teacher at another college got a promotion. He'd felt all of it, and through it he'd forgotten who he was. He was the baby, the lovers, the fathers, the older man, the teacher, all of them and none of them.

Until he felt something else, in the distance, a vague distinct will. Something about...red and green? Crystals? Something about a boy, and another boy, and a girl, and a lieutenant...He knew he had to hold on to that, because that vague boy also saw something else, someone who had also put his hand in the Flow. A balding, at-first-glance-friendly seeming man. Hav...Havelna? Yes, Havelna.

I don't have a strong will. That was the young man's thought, but he simultaneously thought, *but I'm still alive.* What did the young man want, again? It was something with...disappearing. No, appearing. Undoing. *The Flow's holding back,* the young man thought to himself. *That's the only reason why I'm still alive.* But that made no sense.

The young man felt another will from a grown-up, of Havelna's, close to his. Keeping all of it the same. Or rather, making it all even worse. Kill everyone who wouldn't listen. Ultimate power. Everything the way he wanted it. Only then would society be right. And, of course, there was hatred for Othercrystalled people, but not as much as Revan would expect. Oh, Havelna hated them, but he hated them just a little bit more than he hated everyone else. Because he did, and everyone who wasn't him was just a stepping stone to power. That is what Havelna wanted. Power. And he'd kill all Othercrystalled in the world to do it, because they were the most vulnerable. The most killable. Havelna wanted everything in the world to be the way it was supposed to be, and to him, the only natural order of things was for him to have ultimate power.

And there was the young man's will. He didn't want all of that. He wanted to go back to the way things used to be. Back to the lessons, where everything was normal. He wanted...

So many things, he had an immense future ahead of him, and lots of desires. He wanted a place where he could just be himself, where no one would judge him, where he would be safe—and he had a dilemma. Two people circled around in his head—a tanned boy, a pale girl, and he had so much love for the both of them. They both understood different parts of him.

And he wanted something else, so desperately that it hurt.

To go home. Not just that, though—he wanted to go home with all the problems, caused by the other, solved. That young man thought he was going to die, but he was still alive. A thought went through his mind. *The Flow's being calm, but I'll feel the real deal soon enough.* It still didn't make any sense—the Flow hadn't been calm to Mrs. Erchina either. *Havelna's holding back,* the boy then thought, *he thinks I'm no match for him so he's not giving me his all.* But that made no sense either. Why would Havelna hold back? Could you really hold back a will?

There was only one solution, one answer. The young man's friends had been right. His will was just as strong as Havelna's, and that will was strong enough to manipulate the Flow. His thoughts were filled with not one, but two people he cared for so much it hurt. Both in different ways. The image of those two people brought him back into the world. Helped him realize that *he*, Revan, was that young man.

How is this possible? Revan heard in his mind, and he knew it was Havelna's thought.

"Let go," Havelna growled at the same time. "You can't deal with this, and you know it. You're keeping a strong front, but you'll lose this. You just follow. All you do is nod and say yes as soon as someone with authority comes to you. You *have no strong will.* It won't take long until the Flow swallows you whole. Let go, and we'll see what we can do. Or you'll turn into Erchina."

Revan didn't let go. He knew what Havelna wanted, he didn't need to be in touch with the Flow for that. Intimidate Revan. Make him doubt himself. Revan refused to let that happen again, because Arana and Gaveh were going through his mind—they had faith in him, they understood him. Gaveh understood him as a person, as intimately as he understood Gaveh—and Arana was full of mystery, but matched with him in one way that was so, so important. Thinking of them, *both of them*, kept him grounded among all those wills.

It made him fight on.

Because on the other side of the world a girl told her parents her crystals changed on a daily basis, and they didn't like the news. Another boy just wanted his girlfriend to accept him for who he was, because while his skill crystal lit up, he just wanted a lit-up art crystal instead. A girl was about to tell her parents her central crystal had stopped shining, scared for their response—but her parents already knew and wanted nothing else than for their daughter to be happy.

Revan didn't understand how his will was so strong, but he also thought of when he'd convinced Havelna to go to Mrs. Erchina. When he threw away his honor to save the Othercrystalled. That time he so strongly felt the urge to make a gate but managed to hold back until he was in his own bedroom. The fact that he had even been willing to contemplate murder to fix the world.

And all those times he'd thought he would tell Havelna of his second crystal, but he hadn't.

Slowly, as Revan's will turned out to match Havelna's, Revan *did* start to understand. Havelna kept staring at him furiously and kept talking to him, but Revan didn't hear the words anymore. Suddenly the man was just pathetic, and Revan knew what the only right choice was.

Revan made eye contact with Havelna.

With his spare hand, he took off his shirt.

Havelna saw it. His jaw dropped.

Revan's skill crystal—and calm crystal—were both shining brightly.

Revan knew he didn't have to say anything anymore. He just had to think it, and that was enough—because his own will was stronger than Havelna's. He was winning.

My will is strong because it has to be.

From one instant to another, Havelna's will disappeared. Revan saw what used to be Havelna rapidly turn into energy, in the same way as Erchina, then he was gone. Revan heard the echoes of a shout in his mind, but it landed with all the force of a whisper. All that was left was Revan and the Flow, and Revan knew exactly what to do, which changes to apply. It was clear as day to him—in a millisecond Revan the magic was in him, and he knew what to do to make everything right again, to undo Havelna's corruption, even though he couldn't explain it. He knew how to stop the command Havelna had given, how he'd given the Flow a whole list of people to kill off. Revan made sure not to look at the list and erased it immediately. Havelna had destroyed a part in the Flow that made magic accessible for everyone, Revan restored that and suddenly, everyone could make gates again, the way they were supposed to. Havelna couldn't protest anymore. He was completely gone.

Once he'd done that, he thought, *But I can do so much more.* He had the Flow in his hands, ready to manipulate it any way he wanted—he could solve it further, make the lava disappear, let everyone walk from place to place again, like before Samillan. He had the will for it.

But how would he do that? The Flow had no idea how to pull that off. It had been in this state for so long that it didn't know how to get back to any other state. Not to mention the other changes Revan wanted, like forcing society to accept Othercrystalled for who they are. Revan didn't know how to do it, the Flow didn't know either. Havelna knew exactly what to do. So had Samillan. Revan felt so much in his mind, so many people, so many desires and opinions...his will was strong enough to survive the Flow, but it was so hard to find the right things among all of it.

So Revan let go. All that wanting was immediately out of his mind and he was back in his own head. Javik was behind him. Revan panted.

Nobody else was in the room. Havelna was gone. Absorbed into the Flow, like Erchina. Havelna was dead, and the magic had returned.

"Flow," Javik cursed with a voice that was filled with fear and confusion.

Revan felt the ground's cold stones as he passed out, his dilemma solved.

Chapter Twenty-Six

When Revan woke up, Javik's face floated above him. "Everything okay?" Javik asked.

"Javik..." Revan groaned. "I..." *Barely know who I am anymore*, he tried to think.

Javik took Revan's hand. "You saved me, Revan."

Revan nodded, exhausted. "Help..." he said.

"You saved everything. Everyone. How long have you been working on this? Were you on Havelna's side this whole time? Or the side of..." Without any sense of shame he looked at Revan's lit-up crystals, then looked back at Revan. He swallowed. "Were you responsible for Wilan's death?"

That was a very difficult question for someone who had almost forgotten who he was. Revan wanted to say yes and no simultaneously, but didn't quite recall why both answers were right. Or even who Wilan really was. So he could only barely groan a word that could be a yes as well as a no.

Javik sighed. "I have questions, and you'll answer them, Revan. But not now, because I can tell you're not okay." He took Revan's shirt, which was right next to the Flow, and put it back on Revan—and then tucked it properly in Revan's pajama pants. "I don't understand," Javik continued, "but I think I should be grateful to you. So I'll be that. Your secret is safe with me. And mine with you too, I assume?"

Revan nodded dully. He barely recalled what the secret was again, but he felt he shouldn't even tell Gaveh and Arana. Gaveh and Arana. Two people that meant a lot to him. How could he ever...

The thought disappeared again. Javik picked him up, one arm draped over his shoulders. "Can you make a gate?" he asked. Revan groaned. What was a gate? "Oh," Javik said, and a gate appeared that Revan hadn't summoned. Javik flinched, and Revan knew that was because he'd thought he'd die, because Wilan had died in the same way. He didn't know that because he suspected it, but because he was in Javik's head for the briefest of seconds, and didn't know how he'd ended up there. Then Revan was back in his own mind and Javik's thought disappeared from his mind.

Then all thoughts disappeared from Revan's mind.

* * *

Revan barely remembered what happened next. Javik brought him to his bedroom, where he woke up Gaveh, and they talked. Revan had tried desperately to listen, but he couldn't grab the words the two others were saying. It was as if he'd heard the sounds, but his mind refused to turn them into a form Revan could understand. All he knew was that Gaveh had taken over carrying Revan and put him in his own bed.

Arana had appeared a little later. She'd talked to Gaveh, but once again, Revan didn't understand the words they were saying. It was as if they were speaking a completely different language. Revan floated in and out of sleep while he slowly found his way back to being one person, instead of the millions of people that were in the Flow. In between sleeping, his thoughts and worries slowly returned, including the dilemma that had been bothering him. He also tried to access the Flow one time, but he found he still couldn't reach it, and he realized that made him happy.

When morning came, Revan felt like one person again. He opened his eyes. Gaveh was lying next to him in bed, and Arana sat on the chair in the room. They were both asleep, though Arana didn't seem very comfortable. Revan recognized both of them and only felt his own thoughts, which no longer flowed out of his attention. That was nice. He rubbed his temples, massaging away a headache. No matter how strong his will had been, his head hadn't been big enough for all those wills. They'd left their damage on Revan. How Havelna had lasted, Revan didn't know.

Arana opened an eye and saw him awake, because she jolted out of sleep. "Revan!" she said. "Are you alive?"

"Arana," he groaned and smiled. "Yeah. You?"

"Yes," Arana laughed, relieved. "I didn't stick my hand into the Flow, you idiot!" She ran to him and wrapped her arms around him, but then apparently felt she'd gone too far, and let him go again, breaking the embrace. "You're alive," she said. "I'm so happy. I was so worried."

"Can you guys make gates again?" Revan asked.

Arana nodded. "Only recently. Not a lot of people have caught on. I think a couple people will wake up soon, and then lots of people will be celebrating."

Suddenly Revan felt a great pressure against himself, he could barely turn around. Gaveh had wrapped his arms around him and had pushed him very close. "You're alive," Gaveh said softly in his neck. "I'm so relieved, you're okay, you're alive."

Revan laughed and clumsily embraced Gaveh back, with one arm. And there was that thought again. Only now could he really grab it with both hands, because both people were present.

This is the way things should be. This is the only way it feels right.

"I love you guys," Revan said. Arana smiled. Gaveh laughed softly. And Revan was briefly frustrated, because they didn't get it. "No," he said. "I love you. Both." He looked at Arana, and he looked at Gaveh, determined to make them get it. They both got serious. "I can't choose. *Won't* choose." There was a better place and time to say this, but Revan had to say it at that moment.

"What..." Arana said.

"I like you, Arana," Revan said. "I love being with you. I know you a little bit, and as I get to know you better and better I keep liking you more and more, and I feel more and more that we'd be a great match. I want to have you with me. Hopefully for a long time. You understand me in a way few others can." Revan didn't say it in a way that would be rude to Gaveh—but he knew she understood. Arana smiled, uncertain. "But then I'll have to give up my Koden. And..." Revan looked at Gaveh. "I know you through and through, Gaveh. I know your body, your mind, your soul, like I've never known anyone. The sex is a part of that. But to keep that up, I have to give up Arana and start something with you. And…I can't choose between our Kodenship and Arana's presence. Won't." He swallowed. Only then did he realize where he was and what had just happened. Then he groaned. "I mean…Havelna's dead, hurray?" He sighed. The headache came back.

"You okay, Revan?" Gaveh said.

"Yeah," Revan said. "My head just hurts. But you're both here, and that's a good thing." For a couple seconds, it was awkwardly quiet. Gaveh slowly let go of Revan, and Revan sat on the edge of his bed. He didn't know where the conversation should go, as the timing was horrible, but their talk had started flowing and had to finish now. So after a while, Revan said, "I don't want to force you into anything. If you complain now that this isn't the way things should go and don't want anything to do with me, that's okay. I'll find something if you both leave me. But I love you both, and I refuse to choose."

After some contemplation Gaveh said softly, "Are we still Kodens to each other, Revan?"

Revan looked at Gaveh and frowned, briefly not understanding the question. Then he looked at Arana and did understand it after all. Kodens were only there for sex, and maybe some friendship on top of that. What Arana had with Havelt, that was a pure Kodenship. What Revan had with Gaveh… "I don't know if we've ever been," he admitted.

"We drew the same conclusion last night," Arana said. "We were watching you, got worried, and started talking. We concluded the two of you mean a lot to each other. I had proposed to take a step back, but then Gaveh said he didn't mind having me around. He likes me, though he doesn't love me. Not the way you do."

"I don't mind if you and Arana…do something," Gaveh said. "I can share what I feel for you."

"And I don't mind if you stay with Gaveh," Arana said. "There's enough Revan for both of us. So…as far as we're concerned, it's possible too." She smiled at him.

Dizziness took over again, so Revan crashed back down on the bed. They both immediately reached for him, worried. "I'm all right," Revan said quickly. This dizziness was *not* induced by the Flow. They were both agreeing to share Revan, and Revan realized this was the only outcome he hadn't seen coming. For a brief moment, he was terrified. "But relationships don't work that way," Revan said, arguing his own proposal. "You're not supposed to want to share me. That's not the way things are supposed to go." But before either Gaveh or Arana could answer, Revan quickly followed it up by the easiest counter he could think up. "Like two lit-up crystals."

It wasn't funny. But Gaveh chuckled, Arana along with him, then it flowed to Revan as well. Laughter filled the room.

Revan didn't know how things would go outside of his bedroom, but here he was safe, with the two people he loved the most. This was how it worked for him. It was different from everyone else, but Revan wasn't ashamed this time. In fact, with those two people with him, Revan couldn't find that big sense of shame that had troubled him for such a long time.

* * *

Once they'd left Revan's room, the air between the three of them felt different, and it was so much better. Without having planned it, they walked past Javik's room, exactly as Javik was leaving. Javik looked at Revan and said with his eyes, *We haven't yet had our last conversation.* He had more questions, and Revan would answer them. But being down there had rekindled their friendship in a weird way, as they now both knew the truth about how everything had unfolded. Though Javik would never know about the thoughts that had crossed Revan's mind in those moments.

In the eating hall, Mrs. Garedna held a big speech. Havelna hadn't come back, she said, and the logical conclusion was that he'd done something to fix the Flow as everyone could make gates again. A couple more experienced gatemakers had disappeared already, but Revan didn't yet have the guts. He felt he should stay for a while to hear Mrs. Garedna's speech. And because he didn't want to lose this feeling among him, Gaveh and Arana. They all sat together during that speech, and that meant Revan could suppress the urge to puke once Mrs. Garedna spoke with pride about Havelna's supposed deeds. He also didn't want to go home before he was all better. He felt he would be a bad big brother if Fenna saw him this way.

But he still felt good enough, even when the speech was done and everyone applauded. Mrs. Garedna had said something about her being the new principal now. Her speech was neutral, as if everything was back to normal, and she didn't want to remind anyone how Othercrystalled had died left and right.

But Revan knew the damage had been done. Hdar was grinning openly, still not wearing a shirt, her crystals shining, and she wasn't the only one in the eating hall. Lots of people had revealed themselves as crystallists, bigots, and they would never go back. Revan had no idea what would happen next.

And more damage had been done. Revan looked at Javik, who was also sitting at the eating table a bit farther away from them, and thought to himself, *I seriously contemplated murdering you, even though I called you my friend.* He would've done it, right then and there, if he hadn't realized he would survive the Flow. Revan would've hated every second of killing Javik, but he would've done it, not even considering how many people would grieve. Did that make Revan a murderer? Revan had a strong will, and perhaps this was the downside of it. It meant being fine with sacrificing everything and everyone to get what you wanted. That was why Havelna had gone so far. It might've been possible Samillan had been the same way.

Then there was the question of how Havelna had gotten access to the Flow in the first place. It had just appeared to him, he had said, and he'd sounded so genuine it was one of the few things Revan wasn't doubting. Perhaps because the Flow had come to him in the same way. Revan might never find an answer to that question.

He would come back to all of that later. For now, they were celebrating, with Javik still very much alive.

Once they were back in Revan's and Gaveh's room, Revan said, "We have a lot to figure out, and a lot to arrange. Before we've done that, it might be best to not make this public. But I love you both. We'll find a way. I think right now, we all just want to go home."

Arana nodded. "I'll talk to Havelt. I'll see what he wants. And what I want." She shrugged.

"There's enough Arana for both of us," Revan said and he genuinely meant it.

But Arana shook her head. "I don't know if I agree with that. But I'll figure that out with him." She kissed him on the mouth, right in front of Gaveh. Revan briefly flinched, then realized it was okay, so he kissed her back. "We'll talk about this," Arana said afterwards, "after the weekend. I want to see my big sister." She made a gate and waved, and Revan waved back.

Then Gaveh pressed his lips on Revan's, and once they were done kissing he said, "If my parents already thought I was weird, this isn't going to help." He smiled. "But I'll keep it to myself for now." He sighed. "I hadn't expected to be missing my parents, but I do."

Revan squeezed Gaveh's hand. "I guess you should go to them."

Gaveh nodded, and a gate appeared in their room. Gaveh briefly pressed his lips back on Revan's again. "Maybe my parents have turned around because they missed me so much. Or not. I don't think so, actually. But it doesn't matter—they're still my parents."

"I'll see you," Revan said, still smiling.

Then Gaveh stood up and walked through the gate, leaving Revan behind, on his own. Briefly, Revan looked at the spot where Gaveh had been. He missed both of them already. He already missed everything. But that was okay, because he missed three more people very badly, and now he could go back to them.

Revan made a gate appear to his bedroom at his parents' place. Once he was through that gate he felt the warm arms of his mother around him.

ACKNOWLEDGEMENTS

Getting Corruption to the state you're holding it in took a lot of effort and many different people. No book is a singular project, and a book like this with a world that needs so much fleshing out, one person isn't enough. Every author needs, at the very least, a "rubber duck"; a person they can talk to, who just needs to listen so that the author can talk themselves through a problem with their story. I've had the fortune of having many different rubber ducks in my life, and plenty of them thankfully talked back too, helping me further the story even more. Unfortunately, when a story's in the works for this long (I started brainstorming this story in 2018, and the earliest elements of it borrow from a story I wrote all the way back in 2015!) it's hard to trace back all the people who have been those rubber ducks; I have tried to include as many people as I could, but if I have forgotten you, my sincerest apologies.

First of all, a big thank you to my best friend Osanne, who heard the worldbuilding for this story in its earliest stages and helped me out a lot by pointing out the flaws in my world, as well as providing information on how best to further the story. I hope they'll be proud of the finished product.

Another big thank you to Ellen, who read one of the very first drafts of the novel and gave me a lot of pointers on how to proceed. Your feedback is invaluable to me; there's a reason why I keep coming back to you with my stories, because your honesty is incredibly useful. I hope you enjoy reading the stories as much as I enjoy your feedback.

Speaking of honesty, I also owe a big thank you to Arla, another test reader who also read an earlier draft of the story and was brutally honest in where its flaws were. You helped me beat the story into the shape it needed to be, and for that, you get a big thank you.

These three people have been instrumental in the brainstorming process and the edits, but there were more useful people who have helped me brainstorm. They are, in no particular order: Ori, Maes, Devin, Chris, Lex, Lyndsey and Sara. I am very grateful for the contributions you provided, however small or big they were.

There have also been a couple people who Beta read the story and provided me with some necessary feedback, and I am also very grateful to them for their feedback and contributions. These people are, also in no particular order: Ine, Esmée, Kari, Anna, Sean and Will.

Of course, a story like this would have gotten nowhere without a good publisher, and for that I have Bill and Heather Tracy to thank. Our conversation in the hot tub is a conversation I will cherish for a very long time, and I am grateful to both of you for taking a leap of faith in me, and being patient enough to allow me to translate the story in a good-enough form. I am also very grateful to Bill again for all the edits he suggested and the changes that made the book a better book; you helped me make my story more my story, and that is the sign of a great editor.

I am also grateful to the Writing Excuses gang for organizing multiple writing retreats, three of which I attended, and through which I gained a big network of friends, of which Heather and Bill are two. On top of that I want to thank Brandon Sanderson once more for talking to me in 2014 and telling me that no world was too weird to build and put in a story. If you, reader, have read the whole novel, I hope we can agree that I tried to listen.

I'm also grateful to my parents for always having been supportive of my writing and helping out whenever necessary. My love for fantasy is there because of them and their support, and I can never thank them enough.

And finally, the biggest thank you for Derk Anne, my husband, to whom this book is dedicated. When I told him I wanted to dedicate the book to him, he said he wasn't aware he'd contributed so much to it and thought it unnecessary—and that very evening he offered to make dinner so I could spend more time on this story. He understood then, after I pointed it out to him. I love you so much, honey, and this book was one of hopefully still many adventures for the both of us, and I'm glad you tolerate your husband being in many different other worlds sometimes. Here's to our next adventure!

ABOUT THE AUTHOR

Alexander Verbeek-van den Toren is a Dutch child psychologist who lives together with his husband and their dog Wiske in Spijkenisse, The Netherlands. He writes in both English and Dutch, and is fascinated by different cultures, both real and imaginary.

Please take a moment to review this book at your favorite retailer's website, Goodreads, or simply tell your friends!